DESTINY MINE

Anna Zaires

♠ Mozaika Publications ♠

Published by Mozaika Publications, an imprint of Mozaika LLC.
www.mozaikallc.com

Cover by Najla Qamber Designs
www.najlaqamberdesigns.com

e-ISBN: 978-1-63142-298-0
ISBN: 978-1-63142-299-7

PART 1

CHAPTER 1
SARA

Warm lips press against my cheek, the kiss soft and tender even as day-old stubble rasps across my jaw.

"Wake up, ptichka," a familiar accented voice murmurs in my ear as I mutter a sleepy protest and snuggle deeper into the pillow. "It's time to go."

"Hmm-mm." I keep my eyes closed, reluctant to let go of my dream. It was a pleasant one for once, involving a sunny lake, a pair of romping dogs, and Peter playing chess with my dad. The specifics are already fading from my mind, but the light, euphoric feeling remains, even as reality, along with bitter awareness of the impossibility of the dream, is creeping in.

"Come on, my love." He presses a gentle kiss to the sensitive underside of my ear, sending pleasurable shivers through me. "The plane is waiting. You can sleep on the way home."

The last of the dream fades, and I roll over onto my back, suppressing a wince at the lingering soreness in my left shoulder as I open my eyes to meet my captor's warm, silver gaze. He's leaning over me, a tender smile curving his sculpted lips, and for a moment, the euphoric lightness intensifies.

We're alive, and he's here with me. I can touch him, kiss him, feel him. His face is leaner than before, hollowed out by stress and sleep deprivation, but the weight loss just enhances his stark male beauty, sharpening the slant of those exotically angled cheekbones and highlighting the strong line of his jaw.

He's gorgeous, this assassin who loves me.

My husband's killer, who'll never set me free.

My chest tightens, my joy tainted by the familiar squeeze of self-loathing and guilt. Maybe there will come a day when I won't feel so conflicted, so torn about needing the man looking at me like I'm his heart, but for now, I can't forget what he is and what he's done.

I can't let go of the shame of knowing I'm falling for my tormentor.

Peter's smile fades, and I know he senses my thoughts, reads the guilt and tension on my face. For the past two weeks, ever since I woke up here at the clinic, I've been avoiding thinking about the future and dwelling on what led to the crash. I needed Peter too much to push him away, and he needed me. This morning, though, we're returning to his safe house in Japan, and I can't hide my head in the sand any longer.

I can't pretend the man I've been clinging to like he's my lifeline doesn't intend to keep me captive for the rest of my life.

"Don't, Sara." His voice is deep and soft, even as the warm silver of his gaze cools to icy steel. "Don't go there."

I blink and smooth out my expression. He's right: now is not the time. Pushing up onto my right elbow, I say evenly, "I should get dressed. If you'll excuse me…"

He straightens, giving me space to sit up. Grateful for my hospital gown, I slither out of bed and hurry to the bathroom before he changes his mind and decides to have the discussion after all. We do need to talk about what happened—the confrontation is long overdue, in fact—but I'm not ready for it. Over these past two weeks, we've been closer than ever, and I don't want to give that up.

I don't want to go back to seeing Peter as my adversary.

As I brush my teeth, I study the diagonal scar on my forehead, where a shard of glass left a long gash. The plastic surgeons at the clinic did a good job fixing what could've been a disfiguring mark, and with the stitches out, the scar is already looking less angry. In another few weeks, it'll be a thin white line, and in a couple more years, it might be completely undetectable, like the faint bruises that still decorate my face.

By the time the child Peter wants to force on me is old enough to notice and ask questions, there should be no traces left of my disastrous escape attempt.

My breath seizes at the thought, and I press my hand against my stomach, counting the days with growing dread. It's been two and a half weeks since we had unprotected sex during a potentially fertile window, which means my period should've started a few days ago. Between the surgeries and the drugs, I wasn't paying much attention to the calendar, but now that I'm doing the math, I realize I'm late. Not so late that I have to go into complete panic mode, but late enough to seriously worry.

I could already be pregnant.

My first impulse is to rush out, find the nearest nurse, and demand a blood test. I'm sure they tested me for pregnancy two weeks ago, when I was brought to the clinic after the crash, but the first traces of hCG in my bloodstream wouldn't appear until seven to twelve days after conception. I undoubtedly tested negative, and they would've had no reason to test me again.

No reason except that my period is now late.

I'm already reaching for the doorknob when I stop myself. The minute I take that blood test, Peter will know. He'll have access to the results before I do, and something in me recoils at the thought. I've had no choice, no control over anything in our relationship thus far, and I need to feel like I do, even if it's only in this one instance.

If there's a child, it's growing in *my* body, and I want to decide when to share the news.

It's not a rational decision, I know. Peter isn't stupid. He can also count the days. If he hasn't realized my period is late yet, he will soon, and then he'll know he's won, that for better or worse, we're bound together by the bundle of cells that might already be growing inside me.

By the child who'll be born to a killer hunted by authorities worldwide and the captive object of his obsession.

A painful throbbing begins behind my left eye, the headache sudden and relentless. I can't avoid thinking about the future any longer, can't afford to take each day as it comes and hope for the best.

I have to protect this baby, but I don't know how.

I can't escape, and Peter will never set me free.

CHAPTER 2
PETER

Sara is unusually quiet as we leave the clinic, her slender fingers cold in my grip, and I know she's again entertaining doubts about us, her overactive mind going over all the reasons why what we have is wrong and cannot work.

I wish I could reassure her, explain my new idea and tell her she just needs to be patient, but I don't want to make promises I might not be able to keep. There are so many layers to my plan, so many moving parts, that the odds of failure are much greater than those of success.

If I accept Danilo Novak's hundred-million-euro offer to eliminate Julian Esguerra, my team and I will be tangling with the most dangerous man I know.

Under different circumstances, I wouldn't even entertain the idea. Esguerra has sworn to kill me for endangering his wife in order to rescue him, but before that, I spent a year working for him as a security consultant in order to get the list of people involved in my family's massacre. I know the Colombian arms dealer; I've seen how violent and merciless he is. His organization singlehandedly wiped out one of the deadliest terrorist groups in history, and he's done unspeakably cruel things to other enemies. With his enormous wealth and contacts in governments all over the globe, Esguerra is next to untouchable, his compound in the Amazon jungle the equivalent of a military fortress. And that's why Novak is offering that kind of money: because no one in their right mind would go up against someone so powerful and ruthless.

The only reason I'm even thinking about embarking on my plan is Sara.

I have to make up for the crash that nearly killed her.

I have to do whatever it takes to give her the life she deserves.

―――――――――

Anton is already on the plane when the twins and I drive up with Sara, and as soon as I get her safely seated, we take off. It's a fourteen-hour flight to Japan, so once we're airborne, I remove Sara's sneakers and tuck a blanket around her feet, hoping she'll be comfortable enough to take a nap.

I myself haven't slept much since the crash, but I want her to rest and heal.

She regards me with somber hazel eyes as I reach for my laptop, and I ask, "Hungry, my love?"

We had breakfast before leaving the clinic, but she barely ate, so I brought extra sandwiches for the flight.

She shakes her head. "I'm okay, thanks." Her voice is melodious and a little husky—a singer's voice, I've always thought. I want to listen to it forever, whether she's speaking or belting out one of the pop songs she loves. Most of all, though, I want to hear it croon a lullaby to our baby, so the child knows he or she's safe and loved.

With effort, I push that alluring image away. I can't think about starting a family with Sara now... not when I have such a dangerous task ahead.

It's for the best that Sara is not pregnant, and until we're past this hurdle, I'll make sure she stays that way.

CHAPTER 3
PETER

"You did what?"

Anton stares at me like I've lost my mind, his bearded jaw slack with shock. Like me, the guys are up early despite our late arrival last night, so I figured I'd fill them in on our next mission before Sara wakes up.

"I scheduled a meeting with Novak," I repeat, cracking an egg into a mixing bowl before stirring in a little milk. "We'll be going to Belgrade mid-December. The Serbian bastard's too paranoid, said he'll only communicate the specifics of whatever asset he's got in Esguerra's organization in person, not over email or phone."

Yan leans against a nearby counter, his green eyes coolly amused as he crosses his trouser-clad legs at the ankles. "Why mid-December? It's only early November."

I shrug. "We're not in a rush, and neither is he." The latter is not true, actually. Novak wanted to meet next week, but I put him off until next month. Once we start the ball rolling, there'll be no stopping it, and I'm not ready.

I want—no, I *need*—to spend time with Sara before I embark on this mission. Also, our hackers are hot on Wally Henderson's trail and may uncover another lead soon. He's the last name on my list, and by far the most elusive. He's also the general who was in charge of the Daryevo operation—which makes him the person most directly responsible for the massacre of my wife and son. If not for Sara's accident, we might've caught him in New Zealand when his wife's picture appeared on Instagram, posted there by a clueless winery owner proud of his clientele. As it was, however, by the time we detoured to the Swiss clinic and I pulled myself together enough to send my men to capture Henderson, he'd performed his disappearing act again. Only this time, his trail is fresh, and our hackers have a better idea of where to look.

We're going to find Walter Henderson III, and when we do, I'll tear the *sookin syn* limb from limb.

Ilya frowns, his skull tattoos gleaming in the morning light as he sits down on a barstool. "Are you sure about this, man? A hundred million *is* juicy, but this is Esguerra we're talking about. Kent's going to get involved and—"

"Fuck Kent." I break the next egg so viciously it splatters on the side of the mixing bowl. "That bastard deserves it after the way he fucked up with Sara."

"But Esguerra?" Anton says, getting over his shock. "The guy's got a small army on his payroll, and that jungle compound of his—you said yourself it's impenetrable. How the fuck are we supposed to—"

"That's why we're meeting with Novak, to find out what he's got up his sleeve." I'm starting to lose patience. "I'm not fucking suicidal; we'll only do this if we can make it out alive."

"Really?" Yan crosses the kitchen and sits down on a barstool next to his brother. "Are you sure about that? Because Sara did get hurt on Kent's watch."

His voice is silky soft, but I know a challenge when I hear one.

Keeping my expression calm, I walk over to the sink and wash all traces of raw egg off my hands. Anton, who knows me best, prudently steps away, but the Ivanov twins don't budge from their seats, regarding me with identical green stares as I casually round the bar and approach Yan.

"So you think I'm reasoning with my dick?" The softness of my voice matches his. "You think I'm willing to get us all killed to punish Kent for letting Sara crash?"

Yan swivels his barstool to fully face me. "I don't know." His expression is mildly amused, but his eyes are cold and sharp. "Are you?"

My lips stretch in a grim smile as my right hand closes around the switchblade in my pocket. "And if I were?"

Yan holds my gaze for a few tense seconds as the air in the room thickens with challenge. I like Yan, but I can't let this insubordination stand. He knew what he was signing up for when he joined this team, was fully aware that to participate in the lucrative business I was building, he'd have to help me with my personal agenda. That was our deal, and I intend to hold him to it, even if it's now Sara who motivates my actions instead of my dead wife and son.

"Yan." Ilya's voice is quiet as he rises to his feet and places a massive hand on his brother's shoulder. "Peter knows what he's doing."

Yan remains silent for a moment longer, then inclines his head with a hard-edged smile. "Yes, I'm sure. He *is* the team leader, after all."

His words are conciliatory, but I'm not fooled. I'll have to be extra alert on this mission.

Yan could easily become a complication.

CHAPTER 4
SARA

As the five of us eat breakfast, I can't help but notice the tension at the table. I don't know if something happened before I came down, or if everyone is as jet-lagged as I am, but the easy camaraderie I've observed between Peter and his men doesn't seem to be there this morning.

Instead of bantering with each other and entertaining me with anecdotes about Russia, Peter's teammates wolf down their omelets in silence and swiftly disperse, with Anton taking the chopper on a supply run and the twins heading out for a training session in the woods.

"What's going on?" I ask Peter when we're the only ones left in the kitchen. "Did you guys have a fight or something?"

"Or something." He gets up to clear away the empty plates. "Let's just say that not everyone agrees with my chosen course of action."

"What course of action?"

"I'm contemplating accepting another job offer—a particularly lucrative one."

I frown and get up to help him stack the dishes in the dishwasher. "Is it dangerous?"

His smile lacks any hint of humor. "Our life is dangerous, ptichka. The work we do is just part of it."

"So why are the guys objecting?" I put down the plate I was rinsing and face Peter, wiping my hands on a dish towel. "Is it somehow worse than your usual *Mission Impossible* gigs?"

His steely gaze warms at my worried tone. "It's nothing you need to stress about, my love—at least not for a while. We won't even meet with the potential client until mid-December, and that meeting will decide if we take this job or not."

"Oh." My worry abates slightly, edged out by growing curiosity. "Are you meeting this client in person?" At Peter's nod, I ask, "Why? You don't normally do that, do you?"

"No, but we're going to make an exception this time." He doesn't seem inclined to elaborate, and I decide to leave it alone for now. Mid-December is weeks away, and he'll tell me when he's ready—probably when he hasn't just argued with his teammates.

We finish the cleanup in companionable silence, and I marvel at how natural all this feels: having breakfast with Peter and his men, doing dishes, talking about his work. Never mind that we're on an inaccessible mountain peak in Japan with a foot of snow already blanketing the ground, or that the work in question is gory assassinations. My time away from here—the days I spent in Cyprus with the Kents, followed by the two-week stay at the Swiss clinic—is already beginning to seem like a bad memory, a scary interlude in this new life of mine.

A life that's becoming more comfortable and real with each day that passes here, in this foreign place that's starting to feel like home.

I wait for the painful bite of self-hate and guilt, but all I feel is a kind of weary resignation. I'm tired of fighting myself and these confusing feelings, tired of resisting and pretending that the man watching me with those metallic eyes is nothing more than my captor—that I didn't cling to him at the clinic like a baby koala to its mother. When I woke up this morning, alone in an empty bed, I wanted to cry—and it had nothing to do with the fact that I still haven't gotten my period.

I shut the door on that thought before I can start freaking out again. Yes, I'm now several days late, but there are other potential explanations for the delay. Stress, for instance, both of the physical and emotional variety. Without a pregnancy test and in the absence of other symptoms, there's no way to know at this early stage if I'm dealing with the effects of the accident or the consequences of unprotected sex. So for now, since I'm not ready to bring up this topic with Peter, I need to put it out of my mind and hope for the best.

If I'm pregnant, we'll both know soon enough.

"Are you okay?" Peter asks, his dark eyebrows pulling into a concerned frown, and I realize I must've inadvertently grimaced, as if in pain.

"I'm just jet-lagged," I say, and to further allay his worry, I paste on a bright smile. "You know, long flight and all."

"Ah." He lifts his big hand, gently touching the healing scar on my forehead. "You should take it easy for the next few days. You're not yet fully recovered." His frown deepens. "Maybe we should've stayed at the clinic longer."

I laugh and shake my head. "Oh, no. We stayed about a week too long as is. I'm fine—just a little tired, that's all."

"Right." He doesn't look convinced, and impulsively, I rise on tiptoes and kiss the hard line of that sensuous mouth.

It's just a brief, playful kiss, but we both reel from it as though from a blow. I don't know why I did this, why it felt like the most natural thing in the world to soothe him like that. It wasn't because I want sex, though I do—he hasn't taken me since Cyprus and my body's aching for his touch. No, it was just something I wanted to do, something that felt right.

He recovers first, a slow, seductive smile curving those sculpted lips as he reaches for me, one arm sliding around my waist to draw me closer while the other hand curves gently around my jaw, his callused thumb stroking my cheek. "Sara…" His voice is low and husky, as warm as the glow in his gaze. "My beautiful ptichka… I love you so, so much."

My chest squeezes, compressing the air in my lungs. He's said he loves me before, but never like this… never with this depth of feeling. It shakes me to the bone, because for the first time, I believe him.

I believe him, and I want to say it back.

The realization is like a hammer to my skull. I fought so hard against this, did everything I could to avoid falling for this man, to escape him. Yet even as I ran from him, I knew I was escaping from myself as well, from the dark part of me that wants to embrace my husband's killer, to give in to the fantasy of a happy life with the assassin who stole me from everyone I love. I fought, I ran, and somewhere along the way, it happened anyway.

I fell for him.

I fell for the man I should hate, a monster whose child I may be carrying.

He holds my gaze, and in his eyes, I see the same fierce longing that I've been working so hard to squash. He needs me, this lethal captor of mine, needs me so much he's willing to do anything to have me. And for some reason, that knowledge no longer terrifies me as much as it once did.

I don't know if I somehow telegraph my thoughts, or if the abstinence of the past two and a half weeks has been as hard for Peter as it has for me, but the banked fire in his gaze burns brighter and the powerful arm around my waist tightens, drawing me flush against his body.

His hard, fully aroused body.

My own body tightens, clenching on a sudden empty ache as my hands come up to press against his broad chest. I want him, just as I wanted him all those nights at the clinic when I slept cuddled platonically in his embrace. He refused to touch me then, out of concern for my injuries, but I'm no longer hurting—not from injuries, at least.

His head dips, and I welcome his hard, devouring kiss. This is exactly what I want: to be possessed by him, to know the violence of his passion. He's not gentle any longer, and I don't want him to be. I want him just like this: rough and nearly out of control, consuming me with his need, making me burn with his overwhelming hunger.

My hands somehow end up in his dark hair, clutching at the thick, silky strands as I kiss him back with matching savagery, our tongues dueling as our bodies strain against each other through the barrier of clothes. I'm breathing hard now, and so is he as he backs me up against the edge of the counter, then lifts me onto it, pulling off my yoga pants and thong in one rough jerk. Then his zipper is down and his thick cock spears into me, making me cry out at the brutal stretch. If I weren't so wet, he would've ripped me, but I'm slick with need, and as he starts thrusting into me, I wrap my legs around his hips, taking him in, embracing everything he has to give.

It's not long before my body tightens, spiraling toward climax at a dizzying pace, and his thrusts pick up speed, the savage rhythm driving us both to the edge of sanity. "Oh, fuck," he groans, throwing his head back as the orgasm overtakes him, and I scream, shuddering in agonizing pleasure as my inner muscles clench around his pulsing cock. The hot jets of his seed bathe my insides, and my body spasms again and again, the release lasting an eternity.

Eventually, though, it does end, and I become aware of the unyielding stone of the sleek quartz counter under my back and Peter's heavy weight pressing me down. We're both breathing raggedly, and even through the layer of his shirt, I feel the sweat covering his back.

We just fucked on the kitchen counter, where anyone could've walked in on us.

We went at it like animals, as if it had been years since we'd had sex instead of weeks.

A manic giggle escapes my throat at the same time as Peter swears furiously under his breath and pushes off me. The thunder-dark expression on his face as he zips up his jeans makes me crack up even more. Gasping with hysterical laughter, I slide off the counter on wobbly legs, and spot my pants and thong wedged under the dishwasher.

I'm naked from the waist down.

My bare ass was on the kitchen counter, like a turkey waiting to be stuffed.

My hysterics reach a new height, and I bend over, laughing so hard tears stream out of my eyes. Peter is staring at me like I've gone insane, and that just makes it worse, because I know how I must look, bare-assed and hooting like a madwoman.

After a couple of minutes, I calm down enough to think about retrieving my clothes, but Peter catches my shoulders before I can get on all fours. The worried frown on his face propels me into renewed hysterics. "You... you're going to have to disinfect it," I gasp out between bouts of uncontrolled laughter. "Since you c-cook here and all..."

I'm laughing too hard to talk now, but he must catch my gist, because reluctant amusement glimmers in his eyes and curves his lips. And then he's laughing too, because there are still dirty dishes everywhere, and we just fucked where anyone could see us, and his semen is dripping down my thighs onto the clean tile floor.

Eventually, we calm down and retrieve my pants and underwear from under the dishwasher. My throat is sore and my abdomen aches from laughing so hard, but I feel cleansed somehow, emptied of all the bitterness and resentment. Peter's expression, however, is darkening again, and as he leads me upstairs to shower, I ask, "What's wrong?"

He doesn't reply at first, just busies himself with turning on the shower and undressing both of us when we reach the bathroom. I wait patiently, and when we step under the water spray and he starts washing my back, he finally murmurs, "Did I hurt you?"

I blink and turn around to look at him. Is that what worries him? That he was rough? My left shoulder is still sore from being dislocated in the car crash, but I'm pretty sure our vigorous sex didn't hurt it. "No, of course not. I told you, I'm perfectly fine."

He looks at me, unconvinced, then sighs and gathers me against him in a hug. I close my eyes to keep out the streaming water and wrap my arms around his hard-muscled torso. We stand like that, holding each other without words, and it feels so right, in all its wrongness.

It feels like we belong like this, like we were meant to be.

CHAPTER 5
PETER

The next morning, I wake up before Sara, and as has been my habit lately, I watch her sleep for a few minutes before forcing myself to get out of bed.

I don't know if it's just wishful thinking, but it felt different yesterday. It felt like the tentative truce we established at the clinic was still there. Usually, after sex, I could sense Sara scrambling to rebuild her walls amidst bitter self-recriminations, but not yesterday. Yesterday, I couldn't feel her inner conflict, and after I assured myself that I didn't hurt her, I stopped kicking myself for losing control—and for leaving off the condom yet again despite my earlier resolution not to do so.

At this point, filling Sara with my seed is instinctual, and those instincts refuse to heed the reasons for waiting until the Esguerra situation is resolved.

In any case, I doubt we were in any danger yesterday. Sara must be toward the end of her cycle, given when her period was last. Which was when exactly? Three weeks ago or four? I frown into the bathroom mirror as I wipe off the last of the shaving foam and put down the razor. No, that doesn't seem right. We were away for almost three weeks, and before that, she didn't bleed for at least—

A knock on the bathroom door interrupts my calculations. "Peter?" Sara's sleep-roughened voice is strangely tense. "Yan wants to talk to you."

Fuck. I rub a towel over my face to get rid of whatever foam might still be clinging to my skin and stride out of the bathroom. Sara is standing by the bed, swaddled in a thick robe that she must've pulled on to open the door for Yan.

"He said to come down as soon as you can," she says, a worried frown bisecting her forehead. "It's urgent."

I nod, already pulling on a pair of jeans. I figured as much, because my men are not in the habit of knocking on our bedroom door. Something must've happened, but for the life of me, I can't think what. There's no way the authorities, or any of our enemies, could've tracked us here, and that's the only emergency I can think of that would merit such urgency.

"Get dressed," I tell Sara as I head for the door. "In case we need to leave quickly."

Her eyes widen with understanding, and she rushes to put on her clothes as I hurry downstairs.

All three of my teammates are already there, clustered around Yan, who's peering at his laptop screen. Anton is typing something on his phone.

"What's wrong?" I ask sharply, and the twins turn to look at me, their faces grim.

"Sara is still upstairs, right?" Yan asks, casting an unreadable look at the stairs, and I nod, closing the distance between us in a few long strides.

"What's going on?"

"Take a look," he says and turns the screen toward me.

At first, all I see is the familiar shabby coziness of Sara's parents' kitchen, with its well-worn appliances and a windowsill full of potted herbs. Sara's elderly father, dressed in a robe, is shuffling around the kitchen with his walker, pouring himself coffee and getting a yogurt from the fridge. He's almost at the kitchen table with his breakfast when a ringing cell interrupts what must've been a serene morning.

Charles "Chuck" Weisman carefully places his coffee cup on the kitchen counter and reaches into his pocket to take out his phone. "Lorna?" His voice is strong and steady despite his age. "Did you forget to check—" He abruptly falls silent, and even on the grainy image, I can see him blanch, his mouth opening and closing in wordless shock.

His free hand gropes convulsively at his side but misses the rail of the walker, and I hold my breath as he stumbles. To my relief, he manages to catch himself on the edge of the counter. As frail as Sara's father is, the fall could've easily killed him.

"Where?" is all he asks after a minute of tense listening, and then he slips the phone back into his pocket and stands for a moment, chin trembling, before pulling himself together and walking laboriously to the bedroom to get dressed.

"This was recorded approximately ten hours ago," Yan says when I look up from the screen, ready to rip into him with furious questions. "We just finished listening to the complete audio of this call. It sounds like Sara's mother was in a car accident—a bad one. They weren't sure she'd make it. Our hackers are accessing the hospital records as we speak, but the ER doctors are notoriously slow at adding their notes into the system. The good news is that Sara's father is still at the hospital—or at least, he hasn't been home."

"I just got in touch with the American crew," Anton says, putting his phone away. "They're on their way to the hospital, so we'll get an update on her condition shortly. I told them to be extra careful; I'm sure the Feds will be watching the place, on the off chance Sara turns up."

Fuck. I close my eyes and rub my temples to offset a burgeoning headache. This is Sara's worst nightmare come true: one of her parents is hurt and she's not there. She always feared it would be her father, because of his heart troubles, but this is her relatively young and healthy (for seventy-eight years of age) mother. Sara will be beyond devastated, and all the progress we've made in our relationship over the past couple of weeks will be lost.

She'll never forgive me for keeping her away from her mother's deathbed. It'll create another rift between us, one that may be even harder to surmount than the one left by her husband's death.

I open my eyes, a twisting, sucking pain settling low in my gut. My men are watching me with a mixture of curiosity and pity, and I know they understand. They've come to know Sara over the last few months, and to like her. They've seen how devoted she is to her elderly parents, how she asks about them every day and diligently watches the videos we provide her.

They know this will destroy her.

She'll blame herself as much as she'll blame me.

"Keep me posted on any updates from the Americans," I order hoarsely and head upstairs.

I have to catch Sara before she comes down.

She can't find out about this until we know all the facts.

CHAPTER 6
SARA

I rush through my morning routine, showering and brushing teeth in under five minutes. It takes me another three minutes to get dressed, and then I debate what to do. Should I run downstairs to find out what's going on? Or pack in case we do have to leave in a hurry?

Pragmatism wins out over curiosity, so I find a backpack in a closet and begin stuffing it with necessities: three pairs of clean underwear, both for myself and for Peter, then socks, jeans, shirts, sweaters, all for the both of us. I'm sure Peter and his men will be able to get new clothes if we have to abandon everything and evacuate to a different safe house, but it will be helpful if we have a few days' worth of things to wear, so it's less of an emergency. I haven't forgotten the flight here, when my only dress options were the blanket Peter stole me in and hugely oversized men's clothing.

If I can avoid schlepping around in Peter's sweatpants, I'll gladly do so.

Clothing dealt with, I move on to toiletries, packing our toothbrushes and toothpaste in a plastic Ziploc bag I find under the sink. As I zip them up, along with Peter's razor and a small tube of moisturizer, it strikes me that I'm being oddly calm about this. My palms are sweaty and my heartbeat is elevated, but I'm no more stressed than I'd be if we were running late for a flight. I suppose it's because deep inside, I expected something like this to happen. As skilled as Peter and his men are at evading the authorities, sooner or later, they're bound to be found. If not by the FBI or Interpol, then by some criminal out to avenge one of their targets.

Even drug lords and corrupt bankers may have someone who loves them.

I'm running back into the bedroom to get a belt for Peter's jeans when he walks in, his expression pitch black.

"What happened?" Dropping the backpack on the bed, I rush toward him. "Do we have to—"

He catches my face between his callused palms and slants his lips across mine in a hard, violently hungry kiss. We didn't make love after the encounter in the kitchen—I passed out early from jet lag and Peter considerately let me sleep—and I can taste the pent-up lust in this kiss, the dark fire that always burns between us.

Backing me up against the bed, Peter tears off my clothes, then his own, and then, with no preliminaries, he thrusts into me, stretching me with his thickness, battering me with his hard heat. I cry out at the shock of it, but he doesn't stop, doesn't slow down. His eyes glitter fiercely as he stretches my arms above my head, his hands shackling my wrists, and I realize it's something more than lust driving him today, something savage and desperate.

My body's response is swift and sudden, like oil catching fire. One minute, I'm gritting my teeth at the merciless force of his thrusts, and the next, I'm hurtling over the edge and screaming as I splinter in brutal ecstasy. There's no relief in this orgasm, only a lessening of impossible tension, but even that doesn't last. The second peak, as violent as the first, comes right on its heels, and I cry out at the agonizing spasms, the pleasure ripping me apart as he drives into me, over and over again, riding me through the climax and beyond.

I don't know how long Peter fucks me like that, but by the time he comes, spurting burning-hot seed inside me, my throat is raw from screaming and I've lost count of how many orgasms he's wrung from my battered body. The hard muscles of his chest gleam with sweat as he withdraws from me, and I lie there panting, too dazed and exhausted to move.

He leaves, then returns a few moments later with a wet towel, which he uses to pat at the wetness between my legs. "Sara…" His voice is rough, thick with emotion as he leans over me to brush a lock of hair off my sweat-dampened forehead. "Ptichka, I—"

A hard knock on the door jolts us both.

"Peter." It's Yan, his voice as sharp as earlier this morning. "You need to hear this. Now."

Swearing under his breath, Peter jumps off the bed, finds his discarded jeans in the pile of clothes on the floor, and pulls them on without bothering with underwear. The look he gives me over his shoulder is fierce, almost angry, but he doesn't say anything as he strides out of the room.

I sit up, wincing at the soreness between my thighs, and force myself to get up and take another quick rinse before getting dressed again.

I have no idea what's going on, but I'm getting an awful premonition.

CHAPTER 7
PETER

It's a testament to the seriousness of the situation that there isn't a suggestive smirk in sight as I stalk into the kitchen barefoot and shirtless, the smell of sex clinging to me like some primal cologne.

"It's bad," Yan says with no preamble as I approach. "A drunk driver T-boned her at an intersection, and the car rolled three times before landing on its roof. She has over a dozen broken bones and is hemorrhaging internally. They just took her in for a second surgery, but it's not looking good. Given her age and the extent of her injuries, they don't think she's going to make it."

Every word he speaks stabs deep into my gut. "What about Sara's father?" I ask, my mind spinning. "Is he—"

"He's holding himself together so far, but his blood pressure is dangerously high." Anton's dark gaze is grave. "They tried to send him home to get some rest, but he refuses to go. Some of their friends are there with him, but there's only so much help they can provide."

"Right." I stare at my teammates, and in their eyes, I see the bleak knowledge of what I'm going to have to do.

The patter of light footsteps on the stairs captures my attention, and I turn to see Sara hurrying down the steps, her heart-shaped face pale with worry.

"What's going on?" Her sock-clad feet slide on the kitchen tiles as she skids to a stop in front of us. Her hazel gaze jumps from me to my teammates and back. "Did something happen?"

"Give us a minute," I tell the guys, and they immediately disperse, the twins going upstairs while Anton heads toward the closet by the door.

"Do you want me to prep the chopper?" he asks in Russian as he passes me, and I nod, keeping my gaze on Sara, who's looking more anxious by the second.

"What happened?" she asks again, coming up to me, and I know I can't delay it any longer. Reaching over, I clasp her delicate hand between my palms and, as gently as I can, convey what I just learned.

Her face lacks all semblance of color by the time I'm done, and her fingers are ice cold in my grip. Her eyes are still dry, but I know it's the shock that's keeping her from falling apart. My songbird was just dealt a devastating blow, and if I don't act now, she'll never recover from it.

I will lose her.

I know it.

I feel it.

It's the hardest thing I've ever had to do, but I say evenly, "I saw you packing earlier. Are you ready to go?"

She blinks uncomprehendingly. "What?" Her voice is dazed, even as her gaze focuses on me with a sudden desperate hope. "Where?"

"Home," I say, and the sucking pain in my gut intensifies, the hollowness spreading to engulf my heart. "I'm taking you back, my love, before it's too late."

CHAPTER 8
SARA

I stare out the plane window at the clouds below, my thoughts scattered and my chest agonizingly tight. Maybe it's because I'm still in shock, but everything happened with such speed that I simply can't comprehend it, can't make sense of this development and the tangle of emotions choking me up inside.

Mom was in a car accident. She might die.

Peter is taking me home.

My breaths are shallow, yet each time I inhale, it hurts, like the air inside the cabin is too thick. It feels like it took only minutes for us to leave, to get on the chopper and fly out, as though this was the plan all along, as if we talked it over and decided it was time.

Time for me to go home.

Time for Mom to die.

My breath hitches on a particularly thick inhale, and I have to fight to get my lungs to expand, to drag in oxygen through a windpipe that feels no wider than a pinprick.

The thing is, we didn't talk it over. Not at all. Peter informed me, and that was it. Then there was just the hustle to get going, to grab whatever we need and get on the chopper. And once we were there, he was on the phone, arranging something, speaking lots of Russian and some English. I caught bits and pieces of his conversations, but I was too out of it to make sense of them. To make sense of anything, really. How can he take me back when they're looking for him? When he knows that the moment I show up, I could be whisked away somewhere he may never find me?

How can he let me go when he swore he never would?

I want to ask Peter all this and more, but he's not next to me. He's on the couch, huddled over a laptop with the twins. I hear a barrage of rapid-fire Russian as they point at something on the screen, and I know they must be planning the logistics of this unforeseen operation, figuring out how to swoop in and drop me off right under the nose of the authorities.

I could get up and demand answers from them, but that could throw them off, make them miss some crucial detail that might mean the difference between life and death, or at least capture and freedom. So I just sit and look out the window, focusing on the exhausting task of breathing.

One inhale, one exhale. Slow and steady. I fight to use the unnaturally thick air as I keep my gaze on the fluffy clouds outside. Concentrating on them helps me cope with the knowledge that out there, thousands of miles away, Mom is under a surgeon's knife, her frail body cut open and bleeding. I've seen hundreds of surgeries, have performed dozens of C-sections myself, and I know how it looks and feels, how human flesh is just meat at that point, something the doctor cuts and slices and stitches in order to save the person who's not a person to the doctor at that moment but an assignment, a challenge to complete.

My stomach coils into a knot, my chest squeezing ever tighter, and I swipe at an annoying tickle on my cheek, only to lower my hand when it feels wet.

I didn't realize I was crying, but now that I do, I try to pull myself together and focus on something besides the mental image of Mom's body on a gurney, her stomach sliced open to repair the damage. And of Dad in the hospital waiting room, exhausted and sleep-deprived, his bad heart overwhelmed and overworked.

Why is Peter doing this? I try to think about that, because it's better than the images in my head. Is he letting me go for good, or is he planning to return for me? If it's the latter, he has to realize that stealing me the second time won't be as easy. He's taking an enormous risk by bringing me back, and yet he's doing it. Why?

Could he be bored with me?

No. I slam the door on that pathetic, insecure idea. Whatever else he might be, Peter is the polar opposite of fickle. Once he sets a course of action, he doesn't deviate from it, whether it be avenging his family or inserting himself into my life. Yesterday, he told me that he loves me, and I believed him. I still do.

He's not taking me back because he wants to get rid of me.

He's doing it for me. Because he loves me.

He loves me enough to risk losing me.

We land at a private airstrip near Chicago just as the sun is setting. I have no idea how many favors Peter had to call in to clear this with air control, but the plane touches down on the runway with no interference. A nondescript sedan is waiting for us when we exit the plane, and Peter leads me to it, his strong fingers gently restraining my elbow.

His face is like a block of granite, as hard and remote as I've ever seen it. We didn't have a chance to talk during the flight, and I have no idea what he's thinking. For the majority of the trip, he was on the phone and planning with his men, and I alternated between restless naps and silent crying. A few hours ago, we learned that Mom made it through the surgery, but her vitals continue to be unstable.

It's not a good sign.

We stop in front of the car, and I see a man in the driver's seat.

I look up at Peter's shuttered face. "Are you going to—"

"He's going to drop you off at the hospital," he says in a hard, flat tone. "I won't be coming with you."

I expected as much, yet the words still slice across my heart. "When—" I swallow the growing lump in my throat. "When will you come back for me?"

He stares at me, his emotionless mask briefly cracking. "As soon as I can, ptichka," he says thickly. "As soon as I fucking can."

The lump in my throat expands, and tears sting my eyes anew. "So I'll be here until Mom recovers?"

"Yes, and until I finish with—" He breaks off and takes a deep breath. "Never mind. You have enough on your plate. All you need to know is that I *will* be back for you." His eyes sear into me as he cups my face between his big, rough palms. "You hear me, Sara? No matter what happens, as long as there's breath in my body, I will come back for you. You are mine, ptichka. For as long as we're both alive."

I wrap my hands around his solid wrists, burning tears streaking down my cheeks as I hold his gaze. Once, his statement would've terrified me, but now it lessens the squeezing ache in my chest, gives me something to hold on to as he leaves and my new world—the one that's centered around him—falls to pieces.

Coming home is what I've fought for all these months, but I feel no joy today, only a terrible void in my heart where Peter has so ruthlessly carved a space for himself.

He leans in and kisses the tears off my cheeks. "Go, my love." Releasing me, he steps back. "There's no time to waste."

And before I can say anything—before I can tell him how I feel—he turns and walks to the plane, leaving me standing by the car.

Leaving me to return home alone.

CHAPTER 9

PETER

I should be pleased that we outwitted the US authorities and this mini-operation went off without a hitch, but the pain in my chest is too crushing, too raw. I know this is only temporary, but I feel like someone ripped me open and tore out my beating heart.

My ptichka was crying when I left. And maybe it's wishful thinking, but I got the sense she wasn't overjoyed to be home—and not just because of the circumstances. The way she asked me when I'll return for her—*when*, not *if*—and the look in her hazel eyes…

It was everything I've ever wanted, and I had no choice but to walk away. To set her free when every selfish instinct screamed for me to hold her tight, to chain her to me and never let her go. And above it all is the irrational fear for her safety, the terrible paranoia that something could happen to her while I'm not there. It stems from her accident, I know, but that doesn't lessen it one bit.

I'm going to have her watched, but I won't be nearby and that kills me.

"Are you sure about this?" Ilya asks, buckling himself into a seat next to me as our jet lifts off, the wheels folding in with a screech. "It's not too late. We could still turn around and—"

"No." I close my eyes and force my breathing to even out. "It's done."

I would give anything to keep Sara with me, but I can't—not without destroying her and whatever chance we have at a future together.

In any case, it might be for the best that she's nowhere near me when I do what it takes to ensure that future.

I will be back for her, but first, I must deal with Novak and Esguerra.

CHAPTER 10

SARA

The drive to the hospital takes nearly two hours—we hit traffic on the way—and my nerves are stretched thin by the time the driver drops me off by the hospital entrance and disappears. He didn't reply to any of my questions, so I have no idea who he is or what his relationship is to Peter and his team. And maybe it's for the best. I have no doubt I'll be questioned as soon as the FBI learn I'm here.

My hope is to see Mom and Dad before that happens.

Fighting to contain my anxiety, I hurry through the familiar hallways. I need no signs to point me to the ICU. This hospital is where I did my residency and where I worked all those years; it's more home to me than the house I lived in.

"Lorna Weisman?" I ask, rushing up to the ICU check-in desk, and then I wait, silently screaming with impatience as a middle-aged receptionist with a garish red perm leisurely looks up the name.

I see the exact moment she finds whatever special notes the FBI left in the system. Her eyes fly up to my face, wide and startled behind her green-rimmed glasses, and she stutters out, "J-Just a moment."

I grip the edge of the counter. "Where is she?" I lean in, imitating Peter's scariest tone. "Tell me *now*."

"Sh-she's in surgery." The woman shrinks back as much as her sizable frame allows. Her ring-laden fingers scramble for the phone on the table. "They t-took her in an hour ago."

"Again?"

Frantically bobbing her head, she finds the emergency button on the phone. "There was more internal bleeding and—"

I don't stay to hear the details. In a few minutes, security—and possibly the FBI—will be here, and I have to find Dad before that. The last Peter heard, Dad still hadn't gone home, and given what I just learned, I have no doubt he's here, waiting to see if Mom pulls through.

There is a big waiting room by the ICU, but I don't see him there. It's possible he went down to the cafeteria to get a bite to eat, or he might be in the bathroom. Either way, I don't have time to hang around, so I run to one of the smaller waiting rooms that are off to the side. Some families prefer those for greater privacy, so there's a small chance that Dad might—

"Sara?"

I pivot to the right, my heartbeat jumping at the familiar voice.

It's my friend Marsha. She's dressed in her nurse's scrubs and staring at me like I just jumped out from under her bed. Behind her is another shocked—and familiar—face: Isaac Levinson, one of my dad's closest friends. He and his wife, Agnes, are sitting in the corner of the small waiting room I poked my head into, and next to them is—

"Dad!" I rush over, nearly tripping over a chair as tears blur my vision and choke off my breath.

"Sara!" Dad's arms fold around me, so much thinner and weaker than I remember, and I realize he's crying too, his frail frame shaking with sobs. Pulling away, he stares at me in disbelief mixed with dawning joy, his mouth trembling as he grips my hands. "You're here. You're really here."

"I'm here, Dad." I squeeze his shaking hands and step back, wiping my tears as I steady my voice. "I'm here now. Tell me... How's Mom?"

His face crumples. "She's still hemorrhaging. They thought they had it under control, but they must've missed something or the stitches tore after they sewed her up. Her blood pressure dropped again, so they're going back in and—"

"Dr. Cobakis."

My muscles lock up as I turn to face the unfamiliar male voice.

It's a security guard, accompanied by a baby-faced policeman. Their expressions are wary but determined, and the policeman's right hand is hovering over his gun, as though he expects me to get into a shootout with him.

43

"Dr. Cobakis, you need to come with us," the security guard says, and I realize his blond goatee looks vaguely familiar. I must've seen him around the hospital. Not that it matters. Judging by the resolute look on his freckled face, I can expect no help or sympathy from him—or from the young policeman, who's staring at me like I'm wearing a suicide vest instead of jeans and a sweater.

"Now wait a minute—" my dad begins indignantly.

"He's not here," I interrupt, raising my hands above my head to show my lack of weapons. I understand where their wariness is coming from, and I intend to do what I can to diffuse it. "I'm all alone, I promise."

Marsha, apparently recovering from shock, steps forward, frowning at the guard. "What are you doing, Bob? This is my friend Sara. She's—"

"We know who she is." The young policeman's voice quivers slightly, his fingers closing over the hilt of his weapon as he cautiously edges closer. "We don't want any trouble, but—"

"Oh, for heaven's sake, the girl's mother is in surgery!" Agnes Levinson elbows her way past her husband and my dad to glare at the guard and the policeman from her full four-foot-eleven height. Her salt-and-pepper hair poofs out like a halo around her small face as she steps in front of me, hands on hips in a wrathful pose as she states, "My husband and son are both lawyers, and I can assure you, we *will* file harassment charges. Let the girl talk to her father, and then you can have your turn." She turns toward me, her brown gaze softening. "Sara, dear, are you all right?"

I blink and slowly lower my hands when neither Bob the guard nor the policeman make a move toward me. "I'm... I'm fine. Thank you." The Levinsons' friendship with my parents goes back almost two decades, and my parents have always said that Agnes and Isaac consider me to be the daughter they never had. Until this moment, I was convinced it was an exaggeration; I certainly never thought of them as anything more than a nice older couple who happened to be my parents' friends. Agnes's defense of me, though, is more like something family would do, and I find myself absurdly touched, especially when Isaac comes forward and starts haranguing my would-be arresters with all the legalese at his disposal, giving my dad a chance to grab my arm and pull me aside.

"Quickly, darling, talk to me." Dad's voice is low and urgent as his gaze roams over my face before lingering worriedly on the half-healed scar on my forehead. "What happened? What did he do to you? How did you get away?" Before I can answer, he leans in and whispers in my ear, "We need to get you to a lawyer right away. I know you had to say those things on the phone, but they refuse to believe me. I overheard them talking about it, and they're going to invoke the Homeland Security Act on account of his links to terrorism. We need to get you a good attorney or—"

"Sara! Holy shit, girl, where have you been?" Marsha joins us, grabbing my arm like I'm about to evaporate into thin air. Her Marilyn Monroe curls sway wildly as she spins me to face her. "What happened to you? Where did you go?" Her blue gaze hones in on my scar, and she gasps. "What happened to your face?"

Overwhelmed, I take a step back. "Marsha, please—"

"Sara Cobakis." The baby-faced cop somehow got past the Levinsons and is shoving Marsha aside, his hand once again on the hilt of his weapon. "You need to come with me *right now.*"

I raise my hands again. "No problem. Please, I'm cooperating, I promise."

Now it's my dad who belligerently steps forward. "She's not going anywhere until she gets a lawyer and—"

"Everybody freeze!"

And as we all gape in shock, SWAT commandos swarm the room, face shields lowered and weapons drawn.

CHAPTER 11
SARA

"I told you, I don't know where he is," I repeat for the fourth time. "I don't know how he got in and out of the country undetected, and I don't know the man who drove me from the airport—I've never seen him before. I'm sorry, but I really can't help you."

Agent Ryson stares at me, his eyes cold in his weathered face. "You might want to rethink that, Dr. Cobakis. You're facing some very serious charges, and the less you cooperate, the worse it will go for you."

"I'm cooperating fully." My nails cut into my palms under the table, but I maintain a calm tone. "I've told you everything I know. I was kidnapped and taken to a remote mountain in Japan, where I stayed for the past five months except for a brief sojourn to Cyprus, where my failed escape attempt resulted in a two-week stay at a clinic in Switzerland."

Ryson leans in, and I catch a whiff of stale coffee breath. He must've had to chug quite a bit to stay alert at this late hour. "How idiotic do you think we are, Dr. Cobakis? Nobody's buying into your act again. One of Sokolov's shell corporations owns your house and has for months. We have eyewitness reports of your meetings with him at Starbucks and in a club downtown several weeks before your so-called abduction—not to mention, the recordings of all your phone calls to your parents."

"I already explained all of that." I'm holding on to my calm by a thread. "What I told my parents on the phone was an attempt to allay their worry about me—nothing more. As to my meetings with him, yes, they happened. After breaking into my house—when he drugged and waterboarded me, remember?—he disappeared for a few months, and then he returned and began stalking me. I reached out to you at that point and told you I felt like I was being watched. I asked you if he could possibly be back, and you assured me I was safe. But I wasn't. He was there, watching my every move, and you had no clue. You failed to protect me from him, just like you failed to protect George, so don't pretend like I had no basis to think that turning to you might be worse than useless."

The agent's mouth thins as he leans back. "So you what? Decided to handle this psychopath on your own when he did show up? Do you really expect us to believe that?"

My face burns at the derision in his voice. "In hindsight, it wasn't the best decision, but at the time, I didn't see a lot of options. He said he'd come after me no matter where you hid me, implying that more people could get hurt that way—and I believed him. I didn't know what to do, so I went along with what he wanted, taking it one day at a time until I could figure out a better solution."

"Oh, really? And what was it that he wanted?"

I meet Ryson's accusing stare with one of my own. "What do you think?"

He's the first to blink and look away. Sighing heavily, he rubs his forehead in a weary gesture, and for a moment, I almost feel bad for him. If he accepts that I'm innocent, he'll also have to accept that he failed at his job—that he allowed a monster to invade my life and snatch me away right under their noses. It would be so much easier if I were the villain in this story, if they could somehow prove that I plotted against them all along. Except the facts don't really support it, and they know it.

I've been here for over an hour, and for all their threats and posturing, they still haven't charged me.

A knock on the door is followed by a female agent poking her blond head in. "Agent Ryson? We need you for a sec."

He follows her out, leaving me alone in the small interrogation room, and I slump in my uncomfortable metal chair, exhausted. Then I recall that I'm likely being watched and sit up straight, trying to avoid looking at my pinched, pale face in the big mirror on the wall. I'm so stressed I'm on the verge of breaking, but I don't want them to know that. The interrogation, combined with the inevitable effects of jet lag and my worry about Mom, has taken everything out of me, and if I could, I'd collapse and sleep for the next eighteen hours. Unfortunately, I have to stay sharp and alert.

I have to convince them of my innocence, so I can be there for my parents.

After the SWAT team stormed the hospital and dragged me out, I decided my best bet is to answer the agents' questions as truthfully as I can, omitting only what I'm certain I can get away with. Peter didn't give me any instructions in this regard, so he must expect me to reveal everything and is already taking steps to mitigate the fallout—moving the team to a different safe house and so on. As for the Kents, I'm pretty sure they're untouchable with all their wealth and connections, but I'm still playing it safe by not mentioning their names—there is no reason for the Feds to assume such details would be shared with me, a prisoner.

The main thing I intend to conceal, though, is the current state of my relationship with Peter—and that he'll come back for me soon.

"Any news about my mom?" I ask Agent Ryson when he returns to the room a few minutes later, and he nods, taking a seat across from me again.

"The surgery went well," he says, and a giant knot of tension unravels between my shoulder blades. "They found the source of the hemorrhage and fixed it," he continues. "It's still too soon to pronounce her stable, but it's looking more encouraging."

Despite my determination to remain stoic, I have to blink rapidly to contain an influx of tears. "Thank you." My voice is thick with barely contained emotion. "I appreciate this."

He shifts uncomfortably in his chair. "Of course," he says gruffly. "We're not monsters here, you know. Which brings us to my next question, Dr. Cobakis." He folds his arms across his chest and fixes a hard stare on me again. "If what you're saying is true—if Sokolov stalked, threatened, and kidnapped you; if he kept you captive all these months—why would he bring you back now?"

I push all thoughts of Mom aside and focus on getting through this interrogation. The sooner I answer Ryson's questions, the sooner I can see her.

"Sokolov got bored with me," I say without blinking, having mentally practiced the lie on the drive over. "He tried to get me to warm up to him, allowing phone calls with my family and treating me fairly well in general, but I kept rebuffing his advances, and he finally got fed up. I suspect he might've found another unfortunate woman to fixate on, but that's purely speculation on my part."

"Right." The agent's tone drips with sarcasm. "He got 'bored' with you just when your parents needed you most."

"No, he'd already begun cooling on me when this"—I touch the scar on my forehead—"happened. Afterward, he couldn't even bring himself to touch me. Still, he kept me around until Mom's accident gave him an excuse to get rid of me."

Ryson's bushy eyebrows lift mockingly. "He needed an excuse?"

"Don't all monsters fancy themselves angels?" I keep my gaze steady on his face. "Even the worst criminals like to think they're good people and just happen to be misunderstood—you, of all people, should know that. And Sokolov is no different, I can assure you. He convinced himself that he cared about me, and when he got bored with his new toy, he needed an excuse to throw it out. Mom's accident provided it, and here I am, only a little worse for the wear." I touch the scar again, as if bitter about the disfigurement.

"Uh-huh." Ryson stares at me without saying anything else, and I realize he's waiting for me to say something to fill the increasingly uncomfortable silence.

When I just keep looking at him calmly, he rises to his feet and gives me a stiff smile. "All right, Dr. Cobakis. My colleague informed me earlier that the lawyer your family engaged is already here, barking at our door. Since we have not yet formally charged you, you are free to go… for now. We'll be checking out your story, and if it turns out you lied—and I do mean about *anything*—no fancy lawyer will save you."

"I understand." I hide my relief as I follow him out of the room. As I hoped, my cooperation gambit paid off. On the way here, I considered lawyering up, but I decided it would be best to act like someone who has nothing to hide, even at the risk of accidentally incriminating myself by answering questions without a lawyer. This strategy might still come back to bite me, but for now, I'm free to do what I came here for: spend time with my parents.

A tall, sandy-haired man meets us once we exit the interrogation area hallway. To my shock, I recognize him.

It's Joe Levinson, Agnes and Isaac's son—and apparently, my attorney.

Keeping a poker face, I shake Joe's hand and thank him for coming. He smiles politely at Ryson, promises that I will not leave town without notifying them, and calmly leads me to the elevator. It's not until we walk out of the building together and get into a cab that I let my astonishment show.

"I thought you practiced corporate law," I say, staring at the man who is, if not exactly a childhood friend, at least a very close acquaintance. "How did you—"

"I was having drinks with clients downtown when my father called me," Joe explains, grinning. "Naturally, I rushed over as soon as I could. You probably don't remember this, but right after law school, I did a two-year stint at a human rights nonprofit, defending alleged terrorists' right to trial and such. The pay was shit and, frankly, many of the clients terrified me, so I switched to corporate law. But the old skills and lingo are still there, so if you ever get accused of aiding and abetting a suspected terrorist and need a lawyer on an hour's notice, I'm your man."

Peter is an assassin, not a terrorist, but I don't bother arguing that point. "You're right," I say, smiling. "I remember that now. Your parents worried about you the entire time you worked at that place."

"Yep." His grin widens for a second. Then his expression turns serious, and he says quietly, "I'm sorry about your mom. She's an amazing lady, and I hope she pulls through."

"Thanks, me too." My throat tightens, and I have to blink again.

Joe considerately lets me look out the window at the night-dark streets until I regain control. Then he says gently, "Sara... Obviously, I'm not really your lawyer—your father will find someone much more qualified to handle your case—but I want you to know that you can still talk to me if you want. I don't know what happened to you, and it's totally fine if you don't want to discuss it, but I just want you to know that I'm here for you, okay?"

I look at him, at the earnestness in his blue eyes, and for the first time, I wish I'd made a different choice back in college. That instead of jumping into a committed relationship with George when I was barely eighteen, I'd taken things slower and paid more attention to the son of my parents' friends... the nice, quiet one who'd always been on the periphery of my life. It's true, he had never excited me, but maybe attraction would've grown with time—if I'd given it a chance.

I grew up hearing stories about Joe, about his successes in school and how proud his parents were of him, but I never paid much attention. He's seven years older, and that age difference seemed insurmountable when I was a teen. By the time I was in my twenties, it was nothing—but by then, I was married.

We never had a chance to explore what might've been, and we're certainly not going to get that chance now—not with a Russian assassin dominating my life and my heart.

"Thank you, Joe. I appreciate it." I keep my tone light, pretending like the offer meant nothing, like he didn't just indicate a willingness to involve himself in the terrifying mess that is my life. I don't know what my parents have told the Levinsons about my situation, but between the "suspected terrorist" comment and having to get me from the

FBI building downtown, Joe must have some idea of what he'd be facing.

He understands my dismissal for what it is and falls silent. For the rest of the ride to the hospital, we don't speak, and it's just as well.

There is no room in my life for Joe, and it's not safe for him to think otherwise.

CHAPTER 12
PETER

We don't return to Japan—with Sara in the FBI's clutches, it's too risky. Instead, we fly to Prague, where our safe house is in a small village some twenty kilometers from the city. It snowed overnight, and the place looks remarkably picturesque, with a pristine white layer covering all the roofs and bare tree branches.

"Why couldn't we have gone someplace warm?" Anton grumbles as he exits the car into a pile of snow. "Seriously, that safe house in India sounds fucking good right about now."

If I hadn't just let go of the woman who is my life, I'd have laughed at the disgusted look on his face. But I'm not in the mood for Anton's bullshit, so I just say tersely, "Because Eastern Europe is where we need to be." Not that I need to say it—he knows as well as I do why we're here.

During the flight, I rescheduled the meeting with Novak, moving it up to next week.

Henderson is still AWOL, and if I can't spend time with Sara, there's no point in putting the meeting off.

"I like it here," Ilya says, looking around the snowy landscape. We don't have as much privacy here as we did at Japan, but the house is sufficiently far from the neighbors to give us at least the illusion of having a private winter retreat. "It's pretty."

"I'm with Anton on this one. I'm sick and tired of the cold," Yan says, heading toward the house. "At least we'll be warm soon; I hear Esguerra's compound in the jungle is nice and toasty." He glances at me as he says this, but I don't rise to the bait.

At this point, no one needs to know what I'm really planning.

It's safer for everyone that way.

It's not until we're unpacked and settled into the new house that I allow myself to think of Sara and feel the agonizing emptiness that is her absence in my life. It's only been a day, but I already ache for her, want her so much it tears me up inside. The Americans are keeping tabs on her, so I'll be getting daily reports, but it's not enough. I want her here, at my side. I want to hold her, to see her smile and hear her laugh. To fuck her until she's too hoarse to scream my name and the raw burn in my veins subsides.

Soon, I promise myself as I head out to explore the area and set perimeter alarms. I will have my ptichka again soon.

For now, she can enjoy her former life.

CHAPTER 13
SARA

"*M*om!" I bend over her bed, smiling through the tears. Her eyes are cloudy with painkillers, but they're open, and as I gently fold my fingers around her uninjured right hand, her cracked lips move.

"S-Sara?"

"It's me, Mom." The tears pour down my face unchecked, and I don't bother wiping them away. I'm too relieved, too overjoyed.

After an entire night of touch-and-go, Mom has woken up.

"Here, drink." I lift a cup with a straw to her lips, and she manages one sip before closing her eyes again.

I squeeze her hand and turn to Dad, who got to his feet behind me. His cheeks are wet as he stares at his wife.

"She's going to be okay now, right?" His eyes are red-rimmed but hopeful as he glances at me, and I nod, not hiding my elation.

"Her vitals are stable and have been for the past three hours. Barring an infection, she'll pull through."

Mom's fingers twitch in my hand, and I look back to find her eyes open again.

"Sara, are you really...?" She blinks and tries to focus through the lingering haze of anesthesia. "Darling, is that really you, or am I dreaming?"

"I'm really here, Mom." My voice cracks. "I'm home."

"She came back, Lorna." Dad wraps an arm around my waist, his smile both tremulous and triumphant. "Our little Sara came back."

"What..." She starts to cough, and I quickly give her another sip of water. "What happened?" Her confused gaze wanders from me to the pulleys holding up the casts on her legs and her left arm, and then back to me again.

Dad sinks into a chair next to the bed as I wipe the tears off my face and say as steadily as I can, "You were T-boned by a drunk driver on your way to the grocery store. You have cracked ribs, your legs are broken in several places, and your left arm is basically crushed. You also had internal injuries, which necessitated three surgeries back to back." I could've sugarcoated it, but Mom hates being babied when it comes to important medical stuff. She always wants to know the full extent of the problem in as much detail as possible. I'll never forget how she hounded Dad's doctors when he had his heart attack a few years back.

By the time Dad left the hospital, she knew more about his condition and treatment options than most cardiologists.

Her dry lips move again. "No, I meant…" She struggles to form the words. "You're here. How did you…?"

"Peter brought me home, Mom," I say softly, squeezing her hand again. "As soon as we heard about the accident, he brought me home."

It's a dangerous game I'm playing—maintaining the lie (which is now the truth) of being Peter's lover for my parents, while denying it to the FBI. But I don't see any other way to handle it. Peter will be back for me, and I can't have my parents thinking he's a monster when he takes me away again. As risky as it is, they need to believe we're in love. And at the same time, the FBI need to believe I'm Peter's victim. I have no idea how I'm going to manage this tightrope act, but I'm going to try my best.

Not that Dad actually believes me. While we were waiting for Mom to wake up, he put me through an interrogation that made the FBI's pale in comparison. His goal was to poke holes in the fairy tale I've been telling them all these months, and despite my best efforts, he wasn't entirely unsuccessful.

No, I didn't know Peter was a wanted man when we met and started dating, I told Dad, repeating what I said before about believing my new boyfriend was a contractor working for various firms in the US and abroad. No, I didn't know he was in trouble with the law when I left the country with him, though I was beginning to have some suspicions. No, he's not as dangerous as they say; it's all a big misunderstanding. He does, in fact, work as an independent contractor doing security consulting; it's just that some clients of his are not entirely law-abiding, and that's what got him in trouble with the FBI. Yes, we first met in a nightclub in Chicago and dated in secret for several weeks. Yes, he bought my house through a shell corporation, like the FBI said. Why? Because he thought I'd regret selling it so impulsively.

Some questions were more difficult to answer. I know what the FBI have told my parents about Peter's alleged crimes: next to nothing, invoking the classified status of his case. However, my parents aren't stupid, and they did some investigating on their own. The "suspected terrorist" and "killed people" bits came from a conversation Dad overheard between the agents, but he also somehow linked my abduction to a high-speed chase on I-294, during which a police helicopter blew up, causing a massive pile-up and a renewed outcry about gang-related violence in Chicago.

"It happened the night you disappeared and was all over the news for weeks," Dad told me. "The FBI wouldn't admit it to us, but I know it was him. It had to be. Why else would they send an entire SWAT unit to retrieve you? The man is dangerous, and the Feds know it. I don't know if he's involved in drugs, terrorism, or what have you, but he's bad news."

And no matter how much I tried to convince Dad that Peter's alleged crimes are white-collar in nature and that I don't know anything about that interstate incident (which I don't, because I was drugged during my abduction), he refused to believe me.

"Tell me about Marsha and the Levinsons," I finally said, desperate to change the topic. "How did they come to be there with you?"

Thankfully, that worked, and for the next couple of hours, we talked about my parents' life in my absence and how the Levinsons really stepped up, helping my parents through the crisis in a variety of ways. And Marsha too—apparently, she'd taken to calling my parents every week, checking on them and inquiring about me.

"As soon as she heard that Lorna was brought into the ER, she showed up, getting the best doctors on her case and helping us cut through the red tape," Dad said, his eyes gleaming with tears. "If it weren't for her, I don't know if your mom would've—" He broke off, dragging in a shuddering breath, and I hugged him, feeling the familiar burn of guilt and shame, of self-disgust mixed with rekindled anger at Peter.

Yes, my tormentor brought me back, but first, he stole me. For months, he kept me from my family. I can't forget that. *I* should've been there for my parents, not Marsha and their friends. *I* should've been the one to make sure Mom got the best care. Instead, I was in Japan, falling for my husband's murderer… letting him burrow into my heart and mind as I lied to my parents, over and over again.

I want to hate Peter for that—for everything, really—but instead, I just hate myself. I hate that I already miss him, that being home hasn't lessened my desperate longing one bit. I crave him so intensely it's like a physical ache; my skin literally hurts when I think of how badly I want his touch.

Soon, I tell myself as I bend down to kiss Mom, who closed her eyes again. I know Peter—he won't stay away from me for long. I should enjoy this time with my family instead of pining for the man who'll take me from them.

I'm a terrible daughter, but they don't need to know that yet.

They'll find out soon enough.

CHAPTER 14
SARA

By noon, I finally convince Dad to go home and get some rest, and I stay at the hospital with Mom, alternating between keeping her company and napping on a cot the nurses brought to her room. Whenever I come out to grab a coffee or a bite to eat, several suspicious-looking men follow me. FBI agents, most likely, though they could also be plain-clothes police—I have no idea how their jurisdictions work. I'm obviously not off the hook, but for now, they're letting me get on with my life, and I'm grateful for that.

I don't want to spend what little time I have here in jail.

Marsha comes by Mom's room after getting off her shift, and after verifying that Mom is sleeping deeply, I let Marsha talk me into going to Patty's to catch up.

"So," she says as we take a seat at the corner table. "You're back."

"I'm back," I confirm, then wave for the waiter to come over. I'm running on almost no sleep, and I'm craving something really greasy and unhealthy. In general, I feel like I'm falling apart, my whole body aching with exhaustion and my lower back killing me from spending the night curled up on the hospital cot.

"Burger and fries, with extra cheese and pickles," I tell the waiter when he comes over. "And make it fast, please. I'm starving."

Marsha raises her eyebrows, but doesn't comment on my upcoming greasefest. Instead, she orders a Greek salad and two beers, one for each of us.

"So we can celebrate the prodigal daughter's return," she says, and I attempt to match her grin as guilt floods my chest again.

"Thank you for keeping an eye on my parents while I was away," I say when the waiter leaves. "Dad told me how helpful you were with Mom, and I'm hugely grateful. If there's ever anything I can do for you…"

She waves away my thanks with a perfectly manicured hand. "Oh, please. It was my pleasure. I like your folks, and I'm really sorry that happened to your mom. I hope she recovers soon."

"Me too." I attempt another smile. "So tell me… how have you been? And Andy and Tonya? Is Andy still with—"

"Oh, no, you don't." Marsha folds her forearms on the table and leans forward, skewering me with her gaze. "We're not going to talk about any of that until you tell me where the hell you've been, who this man that you ran off with is, and why the fuck I didn't hear a peep about him until you disappeared off the face of the Earth."

"I didn't disappear. I called my parents all the time and—"

She cuts me off with another wave. "Semantics. You were *gone*. Not a word to anyone beforehand, no notice to your practice, left all your patients hanging—including that one girl who needed a C-section the next day, mind you. Oh, and the FBI hounded us all about you for weeks. If that's not a disappearance, I don't—"

"Okay, okay, fine. You win." I grab my beer from the waiter as he approaches the table, but I don't drink it beyond wetting my lips. Not only am I jet-lagged and sleep-deprived, but there is a chance I might be pregnant.

Putting down the glass, I stare at the brown liquid, forcing all thoughts of a potential pregnancy away so I can focus. I don't know which version of the story to give Marsha: the one for the FBI, in which I'm Peter's victim all the way, or the one I've been feeding my parents, in which I'm in love with a man who's embroiled in something shady but is, for the most part, wrongly persecuted by the authorities.

"You're stalling," Marsha says, and I sigh, looking up from the beer.

"You're right: I did disappear," I begin slowly, still trying to decide what the best story for Marsha would be. "You talked to my parents, though, right? They must've told you what happened."

"What they knew, which wasn't much." Marsha picks up her beer. "Nor did it make any sense, what with the FBI sniffing around us like bomb-detecting dogs."

"Uh-huh." I instinctively glance around and see two of the men who've been following me around the hospital at a table on the opposite side of the bar. Three tables over are two more of my stalkers, and I'm pretty sure I've seen the guy at the bar before as well.

Well, that decides it. The "bomb-detecting dogs" are out in full force, and I have no doubt Marsha will be questioned shortly after our conversation.

In fact, there's no guarantee she's not working with them right now.

As soon as the thought occurs to me, I feel like a horrible friend, but that doesn't make the suspicion go away. It makes too much sense. We've known each other for a number of years—I met Marsha when I started my residency at the hospital—but we've always been more work friends than anything else. For one thing, Marsha's always been single and on the hunt, whereas I was married and working eighty-hour weeks. I could never accompany her on the girls' night outings she loves, and she found sedate activities like family dinners boring, so our friendship tended to revolve around the hospital and our conversations rarely ventured beyond the superficial. She was kind and supportive after George's accident, always ready to lend a sympathetic ear on a coffee break, but she never went out of her way to involve herself in the messier aspects of my life.

Marsha is a good friend, a fun friend, but not the kind of friend who'd take to calling my parents every week—not without a nudge, at least.

A nudge that could've easily come from the FBI.

Of course, it's just as possible that I'm way too tired to think straight—either that or being with Peter has made me far too paranoid. Still, on the off chance that my suspicions are right—or on the far more reasonable assumption that I can't expect Marsha to lie to the FBI for me—I decide to go with the victim version of the story.

Unfortunately, that means I have to go back to the beginning and explain about George. And since I'm pretty sure that the FBI would not want me to reveal any classified information, I need to get creative here as well.

My head hurts just thinking of all the half-truths and lies I'll have to keep straight.

By the time I'm done spinning the beginning of the tale, Marsha's eyes are wider than the burger I'm devouring. "George was on this Russian assassin's hit list? Why? What did he—"

"I never learned all the details, but it had something to do with a mafia story George ran." I decide to use the FBI's original lie to me as justification for Peter's actions. "In any case, he broke into my house, waterboarded and drugged me to find out George's location—and then he killed him."

I let Marsha digest that while I stuff two fries into my mouth. I really am starving. When I see that she's about to launch into more questions, I say, "So yeah, that's how we really met. You see why I couldn't tell this to my parents, right?"

She nods, her face sickly pale underneath her foundation and her salad forgotten in front of her.

"Right," I continue. "So it took me a while to start getting over that, and then you invited me for a night out with

Andy and Tonya. We went to that club downtown, remember? The one with the cute bartender who later asked about me?"

Marsha nods again, still mute.

"That's when he approached me again," I tell her. "Right there at that club. That's why Andy thought I was acting weird when I bailed: I'd just been approached by my husband's murderer and ordered to meet him the next day at Starbucks. And things just went downhill from there. He had cameras installed all over my house, he followed me everywhere I went, and when I tried to escape to a hotel, he showed up in my room and… Well, never mind that." I let Marsha draw her own conclusions—which, judging by the horror on her face, are far worse than what actually happened.

I feel awful about that—my instinct is to shield my friend from the dangerous mess in my life, as I've been shielding my parents—but this is what I told the FBI and I have to stick with it. Besides, it's all true, or at least factual. The only part I'm withholding is my own confusion about all of this—my unwilling attraction to the man I should've only hated and despised.

An attraction that has grown into so much more.

"Oh God, Sara…" Marsha looks like she's on the verge of throwing up whatever little salad she consumed. "I'm so, so sorry, hon. I had no idea. And this… this *monster*—he then kidnapped you?"

"After a few weeks, when the FBI discovered he was in the area, yes. Before that, he let me go on with my life, and he was just… in it." I motion the waiter for water, since I can't drink my beer. I'm thirsty and strangely lightheaded, as though I've already had alcohol.

In general, I feel terrible, the ache in my lower back intensifying unbearably and my stomach roiling from all the greasy food. I'm also uncomfortably hot and feel like I want to cry—must be all the stress catching up to me.

"I don't understand," Marsha says as I take a deep breath in an effort to clear my head. "Why did he do this? Why you? Is this something he does, kidnapping women? Did he have a whole harem of victims at—where was it that he took you?"

"Japan, and no. To the best of my knowledge, I'm the only one he's ever done this to. As to why, well, why do some men do anything?" I manage a wobbly smile. "He got obsessed with me, I guess. In any case, eventually he got bored, and here I am."

Marsha is staring at the scar on my forehead. "Did he do that to you?" She touches her own forehead, her voice strained. "Did he hurt you?"

"No, that scar is from a car accident, when I tried to escape and crashed instead," I say. "In general, he didn't really hurt me. The whole kidnapping and murdering of George aside, he treated me fairly well."

"Right. That's… that's good, I guess." Marsha's voice shakes as she reaches for her beer. I notice that her hand is unsteady as well, and fresh guilt scours my insides. I wish I could tell her everything, make her understand how complicated Peter is, how he can be cruel and kind at the same time. How being with him was both wonderful and terrifying, like riding on a roller coaster with no brakes.

I wish I could tell her the whole messy truth, but I can't, so I paste a plastic smile on my face and excuse myself to use the restroom. My stomach is churning so hard it's starting to cramp, and I'm sweating despite the cold draft sweeping into the bar from the open door.

As I enter the small, dingy bathroom, the cramping sensation intensifies, and a sudden suspicion occurs to me, making my breath stall in my lungs.

Could it be? Is it finally here?

Sure enough, when I check, I find a smear of blood on my underwear. My period—now over a week overdue—has finally started. That's why I'm feeling so shitty: it's the first day, and all the symptoms are there, from the lower back pain and the hot flashes to the moodiness and the cramps.

It's official.

I'm not pregnant.

Peter and I are not having a baby.

It should've been a relief, but as I stare at that reddish-brown smear, it grows in my vision, coloring my world the same bloody shade. Shaking, I press my fist to my mouth, but I can't contain the sob that rises in my throat, nor the one that follows. As insane as it is, I feel like I lost something, like some perverse part of me had not only reconciled to the possibility of a child, but had also been looking forward to it.

This baby—the one I was so sure I didn't want—never existed outside of my fears, yet I feel its loss as keenly as if I'd miscarried.

"Are you okay?" Marsha asks when I emerge from the bathroom some twenty minutes later, and I nod, not bothering to hide my swollen eyes and blotchy face as I gulp down my now-warm beer. I know what she's thinking: that telling the story of my abduction took an emotional toll on me, reminding me of the trauma of what I went through. And I let her think that, because it's better than the truth.

It's better than her knowing that despite what Peter has done—despite the awful crimes he's committed, both against me and others—I'm as obsessed with him as he is with me.

That as wrong as it is, I now belong to him, mind, body, and heart.

CHAPTER 15
PETER

The week leading up to the meeting with Novak is among the longest of my life. We replenish our supplies, procure more weapons, and step up daily training, pushing ourselves to the point of complete exhaustion, but it's not enough to make the hours pass any faster. Each day feels like a month, each night a never-ending struggle to sleep without Sara by my side. If it weren't for the daily reports from the men I hired to watch her, I'd already be on the plane to the US, her parents' need for her and my plan be damned.

Not that the reports are all that thorough. The FBI are all over Sara, following her around everywhere she goes, and my men have to hang back, being careful not to attract attention. Aside from the obvious danger to them, it wouldn't be good for Sara if the FBI knew I'm still interested in her. Thanks to our hackers getting into Ryson's files, I know what Sara told them, and I don't want to undermine any aspect of her story. The agents have to believe I got bored with her and let her go for good; otherwise, they'll hide her away, and likely charge her with aiding and abetting. The only reason they haven't already done the latter is Sara's family's connections. Between her dead husband's media contacts and her parents' lawyer friends with Washington ties, this case has the potential to make national headlines—something a lot of highly placed individuals, Henderson included, are desperate to avoid.

For now, Sara is safe, but she won't be if she gets caught lying.

In any case, while she was away, the FBI found all the cameras and listening devices I placed in her house, and after she appeared so fortuitously following her mother's accident, it occurred to them to do a thorough sweep of her parents' house as well. So all I have to go on now are the FBI notes our hackers send me, and the generic reports about her movements from the men I hired to follow her. It's not nearly enough, and it eats at me, the need to know what she's doing, how she's feeling, what she's thinking.

If I was obsessed with her before, now that I've had her with me all these months, it's more like a physical addiction.

"Just fucking go get her already," Anton mutters, wiping the blood off his lip after I punch him far too savagely for a training session. "Or at least take a chill pill. Seriously, man, can't you go a few days without getting your fucking rocks off?"

For that, I land a hit directly to his solar plexus, and when he's bent over, gasping like a landed fish, I grab a weighted pack and go for a run to avoid killing him on the spot. I know my friend is right—my temper's been at the boiling point, and I've been taking it out on the guys—but that doesn't lessen my rage and frustration. I haven't slept a full night since... well, since Sara's accident, come to think of it. The nightmares about my family's deaths—the ones that had all but disappeared thanks to Sara—are back, only now they're accompanied by an even more terrifying dream in which I lose her.

It's my nightly reality, and every time I wake up, covered with cold sweat, I reach for the most recent report on her, reading it over and over again to reassure myself that it was just a dream, that my ptichka is alive and well without me.

That given what I'm about to do, she's far safer at home than she would be by my side.

It's this last thought that enables me to keep going, to resist the urge to do exactly what Anton said and steal her from under the Feds' noses again. I can do it—their agents are no match for me and my team—but Sara's mother is still far from well and Sara would hate me if I took her away from her family so soon. Besides, I have an entirely different goal in mind, and to achieve it, I have to stay on this path, no matter how difficult it might be.

I have to believe that ultimately, it will all be worth it.

CHAPTER 16
SARA

*O*ne week without Peter.

It feels unreal, like a dream from which I'm waiting to wake up. Or maybe it's the fact that I don't sleep properly that gives my days this strange, dream-like quality. In some ways, it's like I entered a time machine—I'm in a hospital, waiting for a loved one to recover from a debilitating car accident. Only that time, it was George who was the patient, and he never made it out of his coma.

Mom's prognosis is much better. The doctors did a good job patching her up, and her wounds didn't get infected. She's still immobilized with all the casts, and she may never regain full use of her left arm—too many nerves and tendons were damaged there—but once her broken legs heal, with sufficient physical therapy, she should be able to walk again.

Dad is over the moon, both about Mom's prognosis and the fact that I'm home. Every time he enters her room and finds me sitting by her bedside, his mouth quivers, like he's about to cry, but instead, he breaks out in a joyous smile.

"I keep thinking you're going to disappear," he confesses when we sit down to eat dinner in the hospital cafeteria. "That if I turn away for a second, you'll go poof." He uncurls his hands in a magician-like move. "There one moment, gone the next."

"Oh, Dad..." I grimace and look down, poking my pasta with a plastic fork. The guilt is eating me alive, because that's precisely what's going to happen in the near future—as soon as Peter deems my mom well enough. With effort, I manage to look up and smile at my dad. "Please, don't worry. Everything is fine, okay? I'm here, and all is well."

I know I sound evasive—Dad has been accusing me of that all week—but it's hard to be convincing while juggling all the lies, half-truths, and facts I've been feeding to different people. The story for my parents and their friends is that Peter is my lover, and that he brought me home despite his ongoing "misunderstanding" with the FBI because he loves me and wants me to be there for Mom. The implication here is that one day, Peter's legal troubles will be over, and at that point, we'll have a shot at happiness together.

In contrast, the picture I'm painting for the FBI and everyone else is that of a monster who kidnapped me on a whim and eventually got bored enough to let me go. The only reason I'm able to make the dual stories work is that the Feds don't want my parents—or anyone, really—to know about George's role in all of this. And that goes double for the events that set Peter on his path of vengeance. After I spoke to Marsha that day at the bar, Ryson brought me to their downtown office again, and not-so-subtly ordered me to keep my mouth shut, confirming my suspicion about Marsha's involvement with the FBI.

It was too noisy at the bar for the agents to overhear our conversation, so the only way he could've known exactly what I told her is if she'd reported it to him right away—or maybe even wore a wire.

Naturally, I acted contrite and promised to be more discreet. And in return, I extracted a promise that the Feds will keep their mouths shut around my parents, doing nothing to dispel the less worrisome paradigm I created for them.

"As you know, my dad's heart is weak, and he doesn't need the stress of knowing I was forced to lie to them all these months," I told Ryson, and the agent was only too happy to agree.

I'm guessing he extracted a vow of silence from Marsha too, because when I ran into Andy in the hallway, she didn't know anything more than what she must've heard earlier.

"What happened?" she asked, eyeing me with unabashed curiosity and confusion. "You just disappeared one day, and the FBI were all over the place, questioning everyone. People were saying you hooked up with some criminal?"

"It's a long story," I said, giving her an uncomfortable smile. "Maybe we can get together one of these days and catch up. For now, my mom is waiting…"

"Oh, of course." She attempted to rein in her obvious disappointment. "Marsha told me what happened with your mom. I'm so sorry. I hope she recovers soon."

"She will, thanks. I'll see you around." I waved at her and continued down the hall, trying not to think about how out of place I feel here, at this hospital that was once my second home.

How lost and alone I feel without Peter.

Soon, I tell myself. He'll come for me soon. All I have to do is wait.

And pushing away the guilt that comes with the thought, I put on a bright smile and enter Mom's room.

CHAPTER 17
PETER

We meet Danilo Novak at a café in Belgrade, a modern, stylish-looking place that has been entirely taken over by the Serbian arms dealer's men. Other than the two young baristas behind the glossy white counter, every person in the café is armed to the teeth—and for all I know, the pretty teenage baristas are too.

Anton is providing backup—a precaution in case things go to shit—but the twins are with me.

Walking in, we stop and take in the situation.

Novak is sitting at a small round table in the middle of the café. It's a location designed to make us uncomfortable—we'll be surrounded on all sides—but I just give the arms dealer a cool smile as we make our way over.

"Nice place," I say in Russian, going on the assumption that he's more likely to be fluent in my native language than in English. "Do you own it?"

Novak's thin lips curl up. "I do. Glad you like it." His Russian is accented, but as fluent as I suspected. Of course, I could speak to him in Serbian—I know most Eastern European languages, as well as Arabic and a few others—but I'd rather not reveal that I understand his native tongue.

When dealing with men like Novak, every little advantage counts.

He leans back, studying me with a peculiar lack of interest. A tall, thin man in his mid-forties, with a receding hairline and thick glasses, Novak looks like a cross between an accountant and a math professor. Only his eyes betray what he is—expressionless and pale, they look like they belong to a lizard... or a stone-cold killer.

There's surprisingly little our hackers have been able to learn about the man. He appeared ten years ago, seemingly out of nowhere, and has since built an illegal weapons empire in Eastern Europe, eliminating rivals with a speed and ruthlessness I've only seen once before—with Julian Esguerra, the man Novak wants us to kill.

The only arms dealer left whose criminal enterprise exceeds Novak's own.

"So," Novak says when I match his detached look with one of my own. "You're Sokolov."

I nod coolly, not allowing my expression to change, and I know the twins look just as calm. He's not going to disconcert us with these games, and he might as well learn that.

"Sit." He gestures at the two empty chairs remaining at his table.

I don't move, and neither do Yan and Ilya. This is yet another little test, a way to see who's the least important, least valuable on the team. Three of us, two chairs—the math doesn't work, and he knows it. Someone is going to have to stand, be the odd man out, and I'm not going to allow that.

He's not going to sow the seeds of discord among us. I won't let him.

His unblinking eyes study me for a few long moments; then he motions at one of the thugs at the other table. "Victor. Another chair for our guests, please."

I wait until Victor brings over the chair, and then I sit down. The twins follow my lead. Ilya's face is stony, but Yan looks amused. He understands the importance of these little dominance games, knows the necessity of setting the right tone early on.

The teenage baristas come over to take our orders for drinks, but I decline to get anything. Ilya and Yan do the same.

"We're not thirsty," I say calmly, and Novak's mouth curls again.

"I have no reason to poison you," he says, and I shrug, dismissing his reassurance like the bullshit it is. There are many substances one can use, from mind-altering drugs to poisons so slow-acting the symptoms don't manifest for weeks or months. He could easily slip something deadly into my drink, and I'd walk out of here not realizing that until after I do the job for him.

Until my usefulness to him is over.

"So," Novak says when he sees that I'm not about to change my mind. "Esguerra."

I cross my arms over my chest and look at him. Finally, we're getting to the point of this meeting.

"You worked for him," Novak continues as one of the baristas brings his drink—a high-end scotch, judging by the smell and color.

"I did," I confirm. I expected him to know this, and he does. He's clearly done his due diligence on me. "Is that a problem?"

"I don't know. Is it?" His pale eyes bore into me.

"We didn't part on the best of terms. In fact, he's vowed to kill me if I ever cross his path again. But you know that, don't you?" I give Novak a cold smile. "Isn't that why you reached out to me in the first place? Because I'm in the unique position of having once been in Esguerra's inner circle?"

Novak's gaze remains unblinking. "Yes. Is that a mistake on my part? Is your team capable of what I'm asking?"

"That depends." I uncross my arms and lean forward. "What are the assets in play that you mentioned? The ones that would help us get this job done?"

"Aside from you and your familiarity with Esguerra's compound?" Novak's eyes glint as he glances at the twins, who have stayed stoically silent so far. "I assume your men can be trusted?"

I look at him, not bothering to dignify that with a reply.

A smile stretches his thin lips again. "All right. I might have someone on the inside. You don't need to know who that is yet. Suffice it to say, certain things could be arranged to happen at certain moments, enabling you to carry out your part."

Irritation stabs at me. He's not telling me anything I didn't already suspect. Keeping my expression unchanged, I rise to my feet. "In that case, you are welcome to find another team," I say as Yan and Ilya follow my lead.

I turn to head to the exit, only to be confronted by a wall of Novak's goons, their weapons drawn and faces feral.

"Not so fast," Novak says softly. "We still have much to discuss."

I turn back to face him, ignoring the artillery at my back. "We have nothing to discuss," I say evenly. "I don't entrust my team's safety to vague assurances of aid from unknown sources. If we are to take this job, we need to know everything, down to the smallest logistics. That's how we operate; that's why we're as successful as we are. If you want our services, you tell us everything—or we walk and you get someone else to do this."

His bland features tighten. "You're making a mistake, Sokolov. I'm not someone you want to fuck with."

I bare my teeth in a humorless smile. "Neither is Esguerra, yet here we are."

He stares at me, then jerks his head to one side. "Let them pass," he orders, and I turn to see the wall of goons parting, their weapons lowered but postures tense. He doesn't want it to get ugly, and I'm glad. Anton's sniper's rifle would've probably taken out a good three or four of Novak's men, and the three of us could've gotten another seven or eight, easy, but bullets flying is never a good thing. The ultrathin bulletproof vests we're wearing under our clothes wouldn't protect us from a head shot, and as skilled as we are, we're not immune to lead.

"You're making a mistake." Novak raises his voice as we head to the exit. "Mark my words, Sokolov. You're making a big mistake."

I don't respond, and we walk out onto the busy street, blending in with the pedestrians as we head back to our meeting place.

———————

"He's not going to come through," Anton says as we fill him in on what happened over dinner at a local restaurant. "We wasted our time. Whatever asset he's got at Esguerra's compound must be the real deal, if he's guarding it so carefully. He's not going to tell us what it is, so we might as well forget it. You saw some of the other offers we got recently, right? They're not bad either. We do a few of those gigs, and there's our hundred million. We don't need Novak and his secretive shit."

I nod, cutting into my steak. "I agree. Let's focus on other jobs."

Yan raises his eyebrows. "Really? Just like that?"

I meet his gaze. "We're not going to go into this blind, and Novak isn't going to come through, so we're done here. Is that a problem? Because I got the impression you weren't pleased when I wanted to take this job."

Yan stares at me, and I stare back at him, my expression calm. I can feel the growing tension between us, but I can't afford not to play this game.

As far as I can see, there's only one way forward for me and Sara, and this is my best shot at it.

"I think Peter and Anton are right," Ilya says, breaking into the uncomfortable silence. "We don't need this job. It's too risky. Let's just do a few extra gigs instead."

I fork a piece of steak into my mouth, chew it, and swallow. "It's decided, then," I say and pick up my water. "We're done here. Tomorrow morning, we fly home."

———

I lie awake, listening and waiting, and at four in the morning, I hear it.

The quiet *snick* of the hotel room lock opening and the squeak of hinges as the door starts to move.

I react instantaneously, my body moving like a coiled spring. In a blink of an eye, I have the intruder on his knees, immobilized in a chokehold as I crouch behind him, holding a gun to his temple.

He's choking and writhing, trying to escape, but he doesn't have the leverage to either hit me or throw me off, and each bucking movement only depletes his air supply.

"Who sent you?" I ask when his frantic struggles start to weaken. "Why are you here?"

I loosen my hold just enough to let him have some air. He resumes fighting, so I tighten my arm again, cutting off his air supply completely. This time, he only lasts a few seconds, and I loosen my grip just before he slips into unconsciousness.

"Who sent you?" I repeat, and he finally sees the wisdom in cooperating.

"N-Novak," he chokes out hoarsely.

"Why?" I press, not letting go. I already know what he's going to say, but I want to hear it from him anyway.

"He… wants to see you," the thug gasps out. "Just you, no one else."

I tighten my grip, as if upset, but then I let go and stand up, simultaneously shoving him forward to sprawl face down on the floor. While he's sucking in air and struggling to get up on all fours, I turn on the light and put on my winter jacket and boots. The rest of the clothes I'm already wearing, as I was expecting just such a visit.

"You win," I tell the thug when he glares at me, resentfully rubbing his throat as he clambers to his feet. "Lead the way."

My gambit of staying at a hotel in Belgrade has paid off. It's time to see what Novak has up his sleeve.

CHAPTER 18
PETER

A black limo is waiting for us by the hotel entrance, and when I climb inside, I see Novak there.

"That wasn't very welcoming of you," he says when the thug climbs in next to us, still rubbing his throat and glaring at me like he wants to incinerate me on the spot. "Victor was merely conveying my polite invitation."

"By breaking into my room in the middle of the night?"

The arms dealer shrugs. "He didn't want to knock and risk waking your colleagues in the neighboring rooms."

"I see." I give him an icy smile. "Very thoughtful of Victor."

Novak's answering smile matches mine. "I'm sure you weren't too discomfited, given your profession. Now, why don't we set aside the manner of my invitation and focus on the matter at hand?"

"By all means." I lean back, stretching out my legs to cross them at the ankles. "Go right ahead."

Novak studies me for a few long moments, then says bluntly, "I don't trust your men. I know *you* have a history with Esguerra, but they have no reason to cross him."

"Other than a hundred million euros, you mean?"

"It *is* a lot of money," he allows. "But your team is not hurting for cash, from what I hear. What was it that you said? A few extra gigs, and you'll have your hundred?" His lizard eyes gleam in the light of the street lamp.

I keep a poker face, showing neither surprise nor dismay. It's easy, because I feel neither. I knew there was a solid chance we'd be overheard at that restaurant, and I played the odds, my every word calculated to bring about this precise outcome.

"Why am I here then?" I ask when Novak just continues to stare at me. "If you don't trust us or our motivations, why come to us... and why drag me out here tonight?"

"I didn't say I don't trust *your* motivations." His thin lips curve. "I know the full story of your employment with Esguerra. You did your job well—saved his life, in fact—and for that, you ended up on his shit list. Can't feel good, I'm sure. And now you have a chance to balance out the scales and make a little money in the process."

I allow my shoulders to relax slightly, as if relieved. "That's very insightful of you."

Novak's expression doesn't change, but I feel his satisfaction. He undoubtedly prides himself on being a good judge of people, and right now, he's congratulating himself on doing his due diligence and reaching the right conclusions. He might even know about my break with Kent after the incident with Sara, possibly by bribing someone at the clinic to eavesdrop on my team while we stayed there. That would explain the auspicious timing of his offer.

He acted as soon as he found out my last remaining link to Esguerra's organization was severed.

Of course, if his due diligence is that thorough, he knows about Sara, too. That worries me, but I'm hoping he buys the story Sara is telling the FBI: that I got tired of her, that the scar on her forehead somehow made her less attractive to me. Certainly, what I did—letting her go and risking not being able to retrieve her—is not something a man in our world would do when he's still interested in the woman he abducted.

My forced relationship with Sara is not that unusual in Novak's circles, but letting her go when I still want her *is*. This is why it's safer for her back home.

If Novak knew how I truly felt about Sara, he'd use her as leverage, and I can't allow that.

"So," he says when the silence stretches into an uncomfortable minute. "I take it you do want the job."

I incline my head. "I do—but it doesn't matter what I want. I'm still not going in blind. That's not how I operate, and as much I want Esguerra dead, I'm not willing to commit suicide to make it happen."

Novak studies me for another long minute, then says, "All right. Here's what I'm willing to tell you at this point. The asset that I have in place can't be activated yet. It will take about eight months for me to make the appropriate arrangements. A few things have to fall into place first."

"Eight months?" Only my training enables me to keep my expression unchanged as my guts twist at the shock of his words.

Eight months until I can resolve this.

Eight agonizing months without Sara.

Novak nods. "It might be a little sooner, but there's no guarantee of that. In any case, that gives you and your team plenty of time to figure out your plan of action."

I swallow the rage bubbling up in my throat. "There's no plan if we don't know the specifics of what we're planning for," I say evenly. "Where is your asset? On Esguerra's compound or elsewhere? What is it exactly that you're expecting us to do that your asset can't do himself? If it's someone on the inside, why don't you have him carry out the job? I assume he has access to Esguerra."

"Not yet, but she will." Novak registers my involuntary blink of surprise with evident pleasure. "Yes, that's another thing I'm willing to tell you: that my asset is a woman. She will have access to Esguerra, but neither the skills nor the inclination to carry out the task. However, she can be at the right place at a specific time, providing a distraction, disabling certain security measures, et cetera. The particulars of the help will have to wait until she's in place and can assess the situation, but rest assured, you *will* have someone on the inside."

I stare at him, torn. This is still not enough information, but I have a strong feeling that if I walk away this time, Novak will not approach me again. Also, given what he's revealed thus far, it might be a bullet that finds me next, not one of Novak's goons. I'm not too worried about that possibility—I'm used to people gunning for me—but Sara is vulnerable, and I can't risk Novak coming after her in lieu of me.

It's unlikely, given the "he's bored with me" scenario she's painted for the FBI, but I can't chance it.

"So let me get this straight," I say, leaning forward. "You will have a woman on the inside, but not much sooner than eight months from now. She's not capable of getting her hands dirty herself, but she'll render some assistance, facilitating our task." At his nod, I ask, "Why can't you get her in place sooner? What's going to change over the next eight months?"

"You'll have to wait to learn that," Novak says. "As of this moment, there's still a chance I won't be able to place the asset as expected. If certain things don't unfold as they should, we might have to wait for another opportunity— that, or your team goes in unassisted." He looks at me expectantly, and I shake my head.

"No. That's not happening. Esguerra has layers upon layers of security at his compound. I know, because I helped him install them. And yes, though I know what they are, I still can't get past them. They're designed to be impenetrable. The only way in is with assistance from the inside, and if you can't provide that…" I shrug, showing my empty palms.

Novak nods. "Right. I figured as much. So you understand the value of my asset. Once she's in place, Esguerra *will* have a hole in his security. However, it will take time."

"There is no way to accelerate this process?" I figure I know the answer, but I still have to ask.

"No. I've tried to get to others on the inside, but they're all too loyal—or too afraid of Esguerra. This is the only one that shows promise. However, the timing is what it is."

I digest that for a moment, then ask, "So why approach me now? Why not wait until you have the asset in place?"

"Because if you're not on board, I need to make alternate arrangements—and it takes time to find a skilled team and vet them. And in this particular case, with Esguerra's reputation... Well, I'm sure you know how it is."

"Right." Even with the incentive of a hundred million euros, few people would be willing to cross someone as dangerous as Julian Esguerra. Almost everyone has something to lose, and Esguerra has no mercy when it comes to his enemies. I know, because I helped him decimate those who crossed him, wiping out entire communities in the process. The Colombian arms dealer doesn't distinguish between the innocent and the guilty; everyone connected to his enemies pays.

"So." Novak leans forward, his pale gaze intent on my face. "Can I count on you and your team when the time comes?"

I consider that for a moment and nod. "Yes, you can." My tone is steady, though inside, I'm still reeling. My separation from Sara was supposed to last a couple of weeks—a couple of months, at most. Not the better portion of a year. It's possible, of course, that what I need will come about meaningfully sooner than eight months, but right now, it doesn't sound likely.

Novak won't disclose the identity of his asset any sooner than he has to.

"Good." His thin-lipped smile oozes satisfaction. "I was hoping I had the right man, and it sounds like I do. Just one more thing…"

I lift an eyebrow. "Yes?"

"I hope you understand that the information I shared with you today is highly sensitive, and for your ears only. That means not sharing with anyone on your team."

I was expecting that much after his preamble, so I nod. "Understood. And on our end, we'll require a deposit. Usually it's half upfront, but given the extended timing, we can accept twenty-five mil now, and another twenty-five closer to the job itself."

Novak doesn't bat an eye. "You'll have the money in your account tomorrow."

We shake hands, and as we do, I try to ignore the agonizing void expanding in my chest at the thought of the months ahead. Now that I've embarked on this path, there's no choice, not really.

I have to do this. This is the only way forward.

If I want Sara for the long term, I have to give her the life she deserves.

PART II

CHAPTER 19
SARA

The rest of November passes in a blur of hospital visits, random FBI interrogations, and waiting. Endless waiting. I feel like I'm constantly on edge, waiting for Peter to show up. Each time I cross the hospital parking lot, walk down the street, or fall asleep in my old bedroom at my parents' house (my house, by virtue of belonging to a wanted criminal, has been seized by the government), I expect to be snatched up and carried away—if not by Peter, then by one of the men he hired to watch me.

And they are watching me. I know it. I feel it. It's the same itchy feeling as before, the same paranoia-inducing sensation of hidden eyes following me. Some of it is due to the FBI agents stalking my every move, but not all. I've gotten good at spotting the Feds. It's always the nondescript car across the street, the pedestrian who doesn't quite belong, the lone man or woman at the bar.

Peter's men are different. I never see them; I just feel their presence. They're the shadow around the corner, the echo of footsteps in the parking lot, the itch between my shoulder blades. They're there all the time, but never close enough for me—or the Feds—to spot them.

Of course, it's possible I really am paranoid this time, but I don't think so. I know Peter. He wouldn't leave me here without keeping tabs on me. Or so I keep telling myself as week after week passes by without a word from him… without so much as a hint that he's coming back for me.

I try to focus on the fact that I get to spend all this time with my parents, and I'm glad about that. I really am. Dad seems to have gotten a new lease on life since my return, swimming and doing his doctor-assigned exercises with renewed vigor and dedication. And Mom is getting better every day, her bones healing with the speed of a woman half her age. She's still bedbound for now—a fact that drives her insane—but the doctors promise that she'll start physical therapy as soon as her body can take it, possibly by the middle of January.

November rolls into December, and still, the interminable waiting continues. It's like I exist in a limbo between my old life and the one I'd started to settle into with Peter. I'm living in my childhood home, surrounded by my family and friends, yet I can't shake the sensation that I'm a guest, a visitor at a place I no longer belong.

I think my parents sense that, because as December advances, they start questioning why I'm not doing certain things, like looking for a new job or finding another place to live. I fend them off by saying that I want to focus on Mom for now, but as her health continues to improve, that excuse sounds increasingly hollow.

"Sara, honey… you don't have to be here all the time," Mom says when I come to visit her one chilly December morning. "Your dad can entertain me just as well, and I know you have things you've been putting off because of this." She waves her uninjured hand at the leg casts that keep her immobile.

Smiling, I shake my head. "There's nothing that can't wait, Mom. Thanks to the sale of the house, I have money in the bank, and I like living with Dad. Unless he's tired of having me underfoot?"

"Of course not," Mom says right away, as I knew she would. "He loves having you back home. You have no idea what a relief it is to have you back. If you want to live with us forever, you are more than welcome. I just know that you've always been independent, and I don't want you to feel obligated to take care of us instead of getting your life back on track."

Life back on track. I bite back the urge to tell her that I don't know what that means anymore. That there's no "track" for me, no straightforward path that I can see. My future, once so clear and linear, is now shrouded in darkness, full of twists I can only guess at.

"Don't worry, Mom," I say, shaking off the gloomy thought. "I'm happy to be here with you and Dad."

And smiling, I gently steer the conversation away from me.

Away from the future I can no longer envision.

We celebrate Hanukkah at the Levinsons', then Christmas and New Year's at the hospital with Mom. At the celebrations, I laugh and smile, exchange gifts and pretend I'm back for good. I tell my dad that, yes, I will look for a new job soon, and I discuss the purchase of a new house with Joe Levinson. He recommends a good real estate agent to me, and I write down the name, as though it matters.

As though any of it matters when, at any moment, I might disappear again.

By the time mid-January rolls around, the strain of waiting and pretending, of constantly juggling all the half-truths and lies, takes a toll on me. Peter's absence is a raw gash in my heart, and no matter how hard I try to focus on my family and friends, I miss him all the time, so much that he's all I can think about throughout the day. I know how wrong that is, and I kick myself for it, but at this point, I'm so used to the smothering guilt that it doesn't feel as awful as it once did.

Wanting my tormentor doesn't feel as heavy of a betrayal.

I still can't forget that Peter killed George and held me captive for months, or that he murders people for money, but when I think about him, it's the sweet, tender moments that come to mind, all the little ways he demonstrated daily how much he cares. I catch myself daydreaming about how he'd rub my feet and bring me breakfast in bed, how he'd take care of me when I wasn't feeling well.

How I'd fall asleep in his arms instead of in my cold, empty bed.

The nights are definitely the worst. That's when my longing for him is most acute, my need crossing over into the physical. Every evening, I toss and turn, struggling to fall asleep while my body burns for a man who's thousands of miles away. I try playing with toys, reading erotic stories, even watching porn, but nothing quenches that aching emptiness inside me. It's like that time when Peter was away on his Mexico gig, only a thousand times worse, because back then, at the very beginning of our strange relationship, he was still a terrifying stranger. Now, however, he's a part of me, having wedged himself into my heart and mind to the point that life without him feels as empty as my bed.

It's so bad that I consider giving in to my parents' urgings and actually looking for another job. Instead, however, I decide to go back to volunteering at the women's clinic.

To my relief, they are more than happy to have me back.

"We missed you so much," Lydia, the receptionist, tells me. "We didn't even realize how much we needed you until you were gone. Is everything okay now? The FBI showed up, questioning all of us, and—"

"Yes, everything is fine. It was just a misunderstanding about the guy I went on vacation with," I say, not wanting to do the whole song and dance here as well. "It's all resolved now, don't worry."

I can tell that Lydia is dying of curiosity, but she holds her tongue, sensing my reluctance to discuss things further.

I have no idea what rumors were going around here, but luckily for me, the clinic staff and volunteers deal with sensitive situations all the time, and they know when to pry and when to leave things alone. After one round of "what happened" and "where have you been," everyone leaves me to focus on the patients—which I do full time and then some.

Basically, whenever I'm not with my parents.

"How the hell are you managing to overwork yourself while unemployed?" Marsha complains a month later when I call to decline her invitation to go out yet again, claiming exhaustion from a night shift at the clinic. "Seriously, hon, I haven't seen you outside of the hospital hallways in weeks. First, it was your mom who needed you twenty-four-seven, now it's this. We haven't hung out at all after that one time at Patty's."

"I know, I know." I sigh into the phone, pinching the bridge of my nose. "I'm sorry, Marsha. Maybe next week will be easier."

It won't be—I'm on schedule at the clinic for over sixty hours next week, including two nightshifts—but I will make time for Marsha regardless. I've been avoiding her after learning about her involvement with the FBI, and I'm starting to feel bad about that. What she did felt like a betrayal, but that's not an entirely rational reaction. She was probably doing what she thought was best, maybe even imagined she was helping me. In any case, cooperating with the Feds is generally the right strategy for the average law-abiding citizen—which is something I can no longer consider myself to be.

Not when I'm concealing my true feelings about a wanted killer.

I think Agent Ryson senses that I'm not telling the full truth, because he keeps dragging me into the FBI office downtown. At this point, I've endured at least ten interrogations, and each time, I've stuck to my story, telling the agents only what I disclosed in the beginning and nothing more. It helps that whenever they start probing deeper, my heart rate jumps, and my body goes into a full-blown panic attack mode.

It's like my PTSD or whatever is on Peter's side.

"Are you seeing a therapist, Dr. Cobakis?" Ryson asks after they have to bring in Karen, their agent with medical training, to calm me down after a particularly thorough questioning session. "If not, I can recommend someone."

My breathing is still shallow and unsteady from the panic attack, but I manage to shake my head. "I have someone, thanks."

I haven't seen my therapist, Dr. Evans, since my return, but he's good. He helped me before, when I couldn't cope with the nightmares and anxiety resulting from Peter's attack in my kitchen. I should go see him again, but I can't bring myself to walk into his office and feed him the same confusing mix of truth and lies I've been regurgitating for the FBI.

I'd rather deal with my issues on my own while I wait for Peter.

He'll be back for me any day.

CHAPTER 20
PETER

I count the days on a calendar, marking them down like a man waiting to get out of prison. My liberation day—the day when I'll be reunited with Sara—can only be guess-timated, so I pick a date eight months from my meeting with Novak and count down to that, because finding out the specifics of Novak's asset is step one toward my plan of ensuring a real future with Sara.

With our Japan hideout presumed compromised, we go from safe house to safe house, never staying in one place for longer than a couple of weeks. Along the way, we do various jobs, some more challenging than others, but none as complicated or dangerous as the one we agreed to with Novak.

My teammates—even Yan—accepted my decision to take the Esguerra hit, as well as the fact that we will find out more about the asset when the time is right. As

I promised Novak, I didn't tell them any of the details we discussed. Partially, that's because there's really nothing to talk about yet, but mainly, it's because I need Novak to trust me. My guys can act as well as anyone in Hollywood, but when dealing with someone of Novak's vast resources, one never knows who's listening and when. Our safe houses are secure, but we do venture out, and a parabolic mic can be used from surprising distances.

That, more than anything, is why Sara is no longer a topic of conversation among us. As far as anyone on my team is concerned, she might as well not exist.

"I don't want to hear her name, or even the pronoun *she*," I told them. "Don't mention her to me, and don't ever discuss her among yourselves. She's gone, and that's that. Got it?"

They all nodded, understanding my concern, and I added more layers of security to my communication with the hackers and the men we hired to watch Sara in the US. I can't *not* watch my ptichka, but for her safety, nobody can know of my continued obsession with her.

And I *am* obsessed. It's a sickness made worse by her absence. I dream about Sara every night. Sometimes, it's about something as innocuous as holding her and brushing her silky hair, but often, the dreams are dark and violent. In some, I'm losing her; in others, I'm the cause of her pain. Our first meeting, where I drugged and waterboarded her, has been haunting me in recent weeks, the recollections invading my mind in exquisitely brutal detail. Worst of all, I wake up from the dreams of hurting her with my cock hard and aching, and I know that as much as I miss her—as much as I love her with all my heart—my feelings for Sara will never be simple and sweet, untainted by the darkness of our past.

By the things I've done to her... and may do again.

If the nights are bad, the days are even worse. The first thing I do every morning is go over the reports on Sara, both from the hackers and the Americans watching her. That's how I know that she's gone back to volunteering at the clinic and that her mother has started physical therapy. Occasionally, the Americans manage to get a long-distance video of Sara as well, and on those days, I watch the recordings several times before breakfast, and then a dozen more times in the evening right before I fall asleep. In between, I train with my team and run the business, but my mind is not on any of it.

It's on her.

My beautiful ptichka, whom I miss like a severed limb.

I think about retrieving her constantly. Thanks to Sara's story about me getting bored with her, the Feds haven't tried to hide her from me. They still watch her in case I return, but they haven't deemed it necessary to put her in the witness protection program or anything along those lines. I think it's because they're *hoping* I'll return for her.

She's bait, though they won't admit it.

And I'm tempted. Fuck, am I tempted. Now that her parents no longer need her as much, I fantasize about getting her back daily, to the point that the whole operation is mapped out in my mind. I know exactly how we'd bypass the air controls and where we'd land, how we'd create a distraction to lure the Feds away from Sara and how we'd plant a false trail to throw them off our scent while we escape.

We could do it tomorrow, if we were so inclined.

Some twenty hours from now, I could be holding Sara.

Most of the time, I can shake off the fantasy, reiterating to myself the reasons why I'm doing this, reminding myself that she's safer where she is. However, there are days when the fantasy is all I can think about, and I catch myself seconds from giving in and ordering Anton to prep the plane.

To maintain my sanity, I intensify the search for Henderson, the last and most elusive person on my list. The fact that we haven't already found him and his family substantiates the rumor about his CIA background. The fucker is good at this—as good as someone in my profession.

It may be time to turn up the heat.

"We're going to North Carolina," I announce at the breakfast table the following morning. "Going to shake things up in Asheville, see if we can flush the fucker out the hard way."

My teammates look up from their plates with identically unsurprised expressions. This has been the fallback plan all along. We'd rather not involve innocents—Henderson's friends and distant family members who had nothing to do with the Daryevo massacre—but given our target's elusiveness, it's the only option left.

"He'll be expecting us," Anton says, pushing his plate aside. "It's most likely a trap."

I smile grimly. "I know."

The difficulty of this operation is what I'm looking forward to the most. Not only will we have to get in and out of the country undetected, but Henderson will undoubtedly have the Feds keeping an eye on his connections. Logistically, this will be similar to stealing Sara back, only instead of kidnapping one woman, we'll be interrogating half a dozen people, all of whom are likely watched by Henderson's buddies from the FBI, and maybe even the CIA.

"Should be fun," Yan says, his green eyes gleaming. "Beats sticking around here." He waves his hand to indicate the rustic cabin where we've been staying for the past week—our safe house in eastern Poland.

Ilya shoots him a glare and resumes eating. He's been on the outs with his brother for the past week, ever since Yan fucked a Budapest waitress Ilya also wanted. It's not the first time the situation has arisen—the twins have a similar taste in women—but in the past, they would just amicably share, either by double-teaming the girl or taking turns. I have no idea what made this waitress different, but Ilya has been pissed with Yan ever since we got here.

I'm not about to get in the middle of that dispute, so I just pretend not to notice the tension at the table. "Get ready," I tell the guys. "I want to be in Asheville before the end of the week, so we need to have a viable plan by tomorrow."

And getting up, I go to email my US contacts.

CHAPTER 21
SARA

I meet Marsha at a club in the West Loop neighborhood of Chicago. It's new, trendy, and so loud my ears throb from the music blaring from the speakers. Marsha is already on the dance floor, grinding against two young banker types, so I make my way to the bar and order myself a gin and tonic. I'm hoping the alcohol will soothe the ever-present ball of tension in my stomach.

Any day now. Any day. I've been telling myself this for weeks, yet I'm still here, still in this unsettling limbo. Five days ago, Mom walked the entire distance from her bed to the bathroom with only her crutches for assistance, and yet I'm still here, living in my parents' house with no idea when—or if—Peter is coming back for me.

Could it be? Could the lies I've been telling the FBI have turned out to be the truth? Maybe my Russian assassin did get bored with me. Maybe my clinging to him at the clinic made him lose interest. I know he thrives on danger and challenges of all sorts, and maybe that's all I meant to him: a challenge. After all, what greater achievement is there than winning the affection of your enemy's widow, a woman who has every reason to hate your guts?

The thought keeps invading my mind, and I keep pushing it away, remembering the look on Peter's face when he vowed to return for me. "As long as there's breath in my body," he said, and I didn't doubt him for a moment—not after the lengths he went to in order to make me his.

I still don't doubt him—not really—and that means only one thing.

If Peter hasn't returned for me, it's because he can't.

It's because something happened.

I've been trying not to think about that, to force the terrifying possibility from my mind, but I can no longer ignore it. Peter's life is such that he might as well be a soldier in a war zone. Between the authorities hunting him worldwide and the powerful criminals he deals with all the time, he defies the odds just surviving from day to day. And when his "jobs" are added to the mix, the chances that he's hurt or worse are not insignificant.

In fact, they're so high my insides are in a permanent knot these days.

The only thing that gives me solace is that I'm still being watched, both by the FBI and by Peter's shadowy men. That itchy feeling between my shoulder blades never abates when I'm in public. In fact, at this very moment, I'm certain there are at least a couple of my stalkers in the club—the nondescript Fed who followed me in and is nursing a beer on the other side of the bar and someone else, someone I can't identify but whose presence I feel.

If Peter was dead or captured and the FBI knew it, they'd stop following me around. Same goes for whoever Peter hired.

It's not much of a relief—he could still be badly hurt somewhere—but it's something.

It's what lets me get up every morning and go about my day despite the gnawing pit in my stomach.

"There you are!" Marsha pops up next to me, beaming with that unique glow that only alcohol-enhanced dancing generates. "I was beginning to think you wouldn't show."

"I'm here," I assure her as the bartender hands me my drink. "Just got delayed at the clinic—you know how that goes."

She nods sympathetically and tells the bartender, "A Corona, please."

He hands her the bottle, and she clinks it against my glass. "To finally getting you out," she says, and I laugh as my friend takes a long sip.

"So," she says, "how have you been? I can't believe March is around the corner, and we haven't hung out since your first week back."

"Ugh, I know." I make a face. "Sorry about that. It's just that with my mom and everything—"

Marsha cuts me off with a wave of her beer. "Say no more. I get it, I do. Just tell me one thing…" She looks around, then leans closer, laying a hand on my forearm. "Are you okay, hon?" Her voice is soft despite the blaring music, her gaze lingering on the now-faded scar on my forehead. "We never really talked about… well, about what happened."

My throat tightens. "I told you what happened."

She nods gravely. "I know. I'm not talking about that. How are you handling it?"

"I'm"—*stressed to the max, unable to eat or sleep, having nightmares about Peter hurt or dead*—"fine."

"Uh-huh." Marsha glances down at my forearm, which looks particularly skinny and pale under her tan, sleekly manicured fingers. "That's why you're imitating an anatomy lab skeleton."

I pull my arm away. "I'm on a diet."

She sighs and leans back. "I see."

I sip my drink, wishing I could tell her the truth: that I'm not suffering from psychological trauma but missing the man who did this to me, that I'm waiting for him to return and reclaim me. Except if I say that, I might as well sign my own jail sentence.

"I'm fine," I repeat. Putting on a bright smile, I say, "How about we stop talking about depressing stuff and just go dance?"

Marsha hesitates, then grins. "All right. Dance it is."

I grab her hand, and we make our way to the crowded dance floor. They're just starting to play one of Nicki Minaj's latest hits, and I laugh as I remember belting out my own version of this song to the guys back in Japan.

Marsha laughs too, tilting her head back to gulp her beer, and we start dancing. I sing along, substituting some of my own lyrics at key spots, and before long, we're genuinely having fun. The beat vibrates through my bones, making my feet move of their own accord, and I giggle as some of my drink spills on my hand.

"Hold on," I tell Marsha and down the rest of my gin and tonic to avoid another accident. Setting the empty glass on a nearby table, I push my way through the crowd to the bar and order a bottle of beer—much more dance-floor friendly. By the time I return, Marsha is already dancing with a couple of new guys, and as I approach, she grabs my hand, pulling me toward them.

"This is Bill and Rob," she shouts over the loud music, and I smile uncomfortably. This is not what I had in mind when I agreed to this outing with Marsha.

"I'm going to go use the restroom," I say, leaning in so Marsha can hear. "I'll be back soon."

"Wait, I'll come with you." Marsha abandons her companions without a second look and follows me through the crowd.

It's still early in the night, so the line to the ladies' room isn't too bad. As we wait, Marsha tells me all about the club she went to with Tonya last weekend and the hot guy she met there. I listen, smile, and nod, marveling the entire time at how different my friend's life is, how straightforward and uncomplicated. When was the last time my biggest concern was whether a guy is likely to call me? College, maybe? When I met George, my dating life ground to a halt, and I didn't resume it after his death.

Peter claimed me before I got the chance.

We finally make it to the bathroom, take care of business, and then return to the dance floor. It's even more crowded now, so after a half hour of being shoved around and having drinks spilled on us, Marsha yells in my ear, "Let's get out of here."

I gratefully follow her out, and we go to a lounge a couple of blocks down the street, where we plop down at the bar and listen to a live band playing eighties rock songs interspersed with recent Top 100 hits. "You sing, right?" Marsha asks after we knock back a couple of shots, and I nod, my head spinning from the alcohol.

"All right, then." Marsha grins. "Let's do this." She hops off the barstool and grabs my wrist, raising my arm in the air. "Hey, everyone," she shouts over the music. "My friend here can belt out a mean one. You all want to hear?"

I want to sink through the floor, but a few people in the crowd—mostly tipsy dudes—respond with a chorus of "hell, yeahs."

"Come on." Marsha all but pushes me onto the stage, where the band members look less than pleased to be dealing with an amateur.

Normally, I would slink away and yell at Marsha later, but between the alcohol loosening my inhibitions and my little performances for Peter and his men in Japan, I somehow find the courage to remain on the stage.

"Do you guys know 'Karma' by Alicia Keys?" I ask the guitarist, hoping I'm not slurring my words.

The guitarist—a ruddy-cheeked guy with a receding hairline—gives me a wary look. "Maybe. You going to sing as we play?"

"Do you mind?" I give him my prettiest smile. "Just one song, and I'll be out of your hair."

He exchanges a look with the other musicians, then shoves a mic into my hands and says, "Oh, what the hell. Go for it, girl. Show us what you've got."

They play the first few notes, and I turn to face the crowd, my pulse quickening as I realize what I've gotten myself into. The last time I performed in front of so many people was back in middle school, when I got a lead role in a school musical. And just like then, I feel a swarm of butterflies in my stomach, a jittery kind of excitement.

Use it, I tell myself, and taking a deep breath, I begin to sing, letting my own lyrics mix with the familiar words of the song. Despite all the drinks, my voice comes out strong and pure, so powerful I can feel the vibration of the sound. All other noise in the lounge dies down, and I see both surprise and wonder on the faces looking up at me—including that of the undercover Fed who followed us from the club and is now nursing a drink in the corner.

Marsha looks amazed too, and I realize she's never actually heard me sing on my own. We've done the "Happy Birthday" song for a couple of nurses as a group, and she probably heard me sing along with the DJ's selection at that club outing a few months back, but never like this.

Never as a performance... especially with my own lyrics.

I almost choke up at that thought. I've never shared my lyrics with anyone but Peter and his team. However, I manage to keep going, and as I sing my version of the chorus, I notice people in the audience starting to sing along, slapping their palms on the tables and tapping their feet to the beat. The butterflies inside me expand, filling every crevice in my chest until I feel like I will float away on their beating wings, and I keep singing as my body starts to follow the music, my dancing training coming to the forefront.

I'm not conscious of feeling like I'm soaring until the song ends and thunderous applause erupts. Coming off the high, I see Marsha clapping and hooting madly at the front, and I beam as I turn around, wanting to thank the band. Except they're clapping too, and it feels like a fantasy, like something my adolescent self might've conjured in a daydream.

"That was incredible. Do you have more songs like that?" the guitarist asks, and I nod, though the butterflies are now more like hummingbirds in my chest. In Japan, I composed and recorded dozens of songs, some to existing music, others to my own mixes, and I performed them for my captors as part of our evening ritual. Peter always told me I'm good, but I chalked it up to flattery and a lack of other entertainment. These people, however, are complete strangers; there's no reason for them to flatter me.

If anything, the musicians should shoo me off the stage so they can get back to real music.

"I have this one other one," I tell the guitarist breathlessly when the fantasy shows no signs of dissolving. "Do you know the tune to Bruno Mars's 'Just the Way You Are?'"

He grins. "Sure do. All right, let's do it—what's your name?"

"Sara," I say and instantly regret it. My name is beyond ordinary, and this night deserves something else. Something like Madonna or Rihanna or SZA—

"Let's get a round of applause for Sara!" the guitarist shouts, and I forget all about my ordinary name as the people in the audience clap and hoot.

The band starts playing "Just the Way You Are," and I take a deep breath to prepare myself. As it gets to the words, I again use my own lyrics, and the soaring feeling returns as I see the reaction of the audience. They're loving it. They're genuinely loving it.

All too soon, the song is over and I crash back down to earth, only to soar again as the audience demands one more song, then another and another. I perform seven of my best numbers in a row, and then my voice starts to give out.

"That's it," I tell the band, handing the mic back to the guitarist. "Thank you so much for indulging me."

"Girl, you can sing with us any time," he says. "In fact…" He turns around, locks eyes with his bandmates, then turns back to face me. "We'll be performing here all weekend, and we'd love it if you joined us."

"Oh, I—"

"We'd obviously split the earnings with you," he says, as though I was about to refuse out of monetary consideration. "It's a pretty sweet gig here."

"You guys can't afford her," Marsha says, and I turn to see her coming up on the stage, hips swaying. "She's a doctor, you know."

"For real?" The guitarist gives me a onceover. "Talented, pretty, *and* smart, huh?"

I flush as Marsha says, "You bet. So if you want to book her, you got to talk to me first. Here." She grabs his wrist, pulls out a pen, and scribbles her number on his forearm, right next to a tattoo of a heart pierced with an arrow. Winking, she adds, "I'm available any time."

I laugh, realizing what Marsha is doing, and tug her off the stage before my friend starts making out with the musician right then and there. According to the rumors at the hospital, she's done crazier things when drunk.

We push our way through the still-clapping audience and burst outside, the frigid February air doing little to cool our excitement. I'm still buzzing from the alcohol and the performance high, and Marsha is excited as well, laughing and chattering about what just happened and how she can be my agent so we can both be rich if I make it big.

We're having so much fun I forget for a moment that none of this is real, that my life right now is just one big waiting game. However, when I get into a cab to go home, I remember, and my high fades without a trace.

While I was out singing and getting drunk, another evening passed.

Another day ended without Peter returning.

CHAPTER 22
PETER

I think about contacting Sara as we land at a small private airport in the foothills of the Great Smoky Mountains, some ninety kilometers from Asheville and only a few states away from her. It's beyond tempting to pick up the phone and call her, so I can hear her voice. But if I did that, the Feds—who are still watching her and listening to her calls—would be all over her, once again doubting her story and putting her through the wringer.

It's not the first time I've considered reaching out to her. I think about it all the time. As careful as the Feds are, I could still get one of the men I hired to watch her to surreptitiously pass her a letter. It would be risky, but I could do it.

What stops me are not the logistics, but that I'm not sure what I would say—and what Sara's reaction would be to getting such a letter. As much as I'd like to think that she misses me as much as I miss her, I know there's a very real possibility that the fragile accord we built toward the end of her captivity is gone, that being back home has made her hate and fear me again.

She might be hoping I'm gone for good, and getting my letter would upset her.

Besides, what can I tell her about why I'm staying away? I can't disclose anything about Novak and Esguerra—too dangerous if the letter got intercepted—so that leaves me with basic assurances that I'm still alive and coming for her.

Assurances that she could easily interpret as a threat if she's happy to be home without me.

I can tell that my guys are dying to say something about the situation, but the rule about No Sara Talk remains in place and they know better than to break it. So they keep quiet, and I focus on getting through the days without Sara, relying on the daily reports about her to feed my obsession.

A couple of days ago, she went out with her friend Marsha and ended up singing at a lounge, performing one of her songs in public. Just reading about that filled my chest with a warm glow, and I instructed the Americans to record her the next time, so I could listen to her and watch the reaction of the audience. I feel absurdly proud at the thought of my little songbird putting herself out there like this, shaking off her inhibitions and displaying the talent that I've always known was there.

Of course, pride wasn't my only reaction to that report. The idea of her going out to places where other men might hit on her is like a burning coal in my side. Sara is mine.

The physical distance between us doesn't change that fact. So far, the reports haven't indicated anyone seriously sniffing around her, but that doesn't mean it hasn't happened. With the FBI constantly tailing Sara, my men have to be extra careful, and there are times they simply can't get close enough to make sure some asshole isn't begging her for a phone number or offering to buy her coffee.

If I could have a listening device on Sara herself, I'd do it in a heartbeat.

I'd plant a chip inside her brain if I could.

"You ready?" Yan says, and I realize I've been mindlessly cleaning my gun for the past minute instead of grabbing my bag and getting off the plane.

"Yeah," I say, reassembling the gun and stuffing it into my waistband. "Let's do this."

Lyle Bolton, Wally Henderson's first cousin, owns a small organic grocery store in Asheville. As far as his friends and neighbors are concerned, he's a kind, peaceful man, with the requisite two-point-five kids—two preschoolers and a baby on the way. His pregnant wife is a stay-at-home mom, and to the outsiders, they seem like the perfect suburban couple.

Too bad none of them know what our hackers have uncovered.

We wait for him in the hooker's mountain cabin, our SUV parked out of sight behind the shed. Technically, the girl is an escort, but sex for money is all the same as far as I'm concerned. Bolton comes here every Tuesday and

Thursday on his way back from the local farms, where he gets produce for the store. His wife is completely clueless, and so is everyone else in the community.

Nobody would imagine that the quiet, churchgoing Mr. Bolton, who's passionate about animal welfare and the environment, would pay a barely legal "escort" to let him defecate on her twice a week—after he beats her up.

Henderson has his buddies keeping tabs on Bolton's home and work, which is why this cabin is a perfect place to question the fucker. His dirty little habit is a secret from everyone, his cousin included, and thanks to all the precautions he's taken to account for this stretch of time, nobody will come looking for him until he doesn't show up at the store some four hours later.

We can do a lot in four hours.

The cabin is empty except for us. Yan lured the hooker away this morning by pretending to be a high-paying client. Once he got her into a hotel room, he tied her up and left her there. If we have time, he'll untie her later today; if not, housekeeping will find her tomorrow morning. Either way, the girl is not going to go to the cops, especially once she finds the payment on the nightstand.

Lyle Bolton is prompt, as usual, showing up at a quarter to ten. His truck rumbles into the graveled driveway, and I motion to the guys to get ready.

Nabbing our prey is child's play. He has no idea what's in store for him. The fucker walks in with a big, shit-eating grin on his chubby face, and Ilya steps out from behind the door and punches him in the stomach. He does it lightly—as lightly as someone that massive can—but Bolton still flops over on all fours, gasping and wheezing and trying to scramble away.

Yan kicks him in the ribs, and then I step in, pulling up the fucker by the back of his shirt as he starts to blubber and plead for mercy.

"Your cousin," I say calmly, depositing him into a kitchen chair. "Where is he?"

He gapes at us, and I see a new kind of fear on his face. He realizes now this is not a mistake, that we're not burglars who just happened to be here.

"I d-don't know," he stutters out, and I sigh before pulling out my gun.

"One more chance," I say, putting the barrel to his forehead. "Where the fuck is Wally?"

He pisses himself. A dark stain spreads over the crotch of his corduroys, and I smell the acrid stench of urine. It annoys me nearly as much as the tears and snot running down his face.

"I swear to you, I don't know!" he wails, and I lower the gun, squeezing the trigger twice in rapid succession.

His screams are deafening as he falls off the chair and rolls into a little ball on the floor. I just planted two bullets—one in each foot—and I wait a minute for the screams to die down before repeating, "Where is your fucking cousin?"

"I don't know, don't know, don't know!" He's hysterical now, holding his bleeding feet with both hands. "Please, I swear, I don't know. He disappeared over two years ago, and I haven't heard anything since."

"Nothing? No calls, no emails, no letters?"

I already know the answer to that thanks to our hackers, so I'm not surprised when the blubbering idiot shakes his head like a wound-up toy. "No, no, I swear! Nothing! No one's heard from him since he left."

I turn to Yan. "What do you think?" I ask in Russian. "You believe this piece of shit?"

He studies him, then nods. "Yeah, I think so. Henderson's too careful to reach out to this one."

"Okay, then. Let's go."

Bending down, I take Bolton's phone from his pocket and leave him to blubber and bleed on the floor as we walk out of the cabin. Before we leave, I disable his vehicle to make sure he can't leave for a while.

We have five more assholes to interrogate before this one's fate is discovered.

CHAPTER 23
PETER

The next two people on our list pose about as much challenge as Bolton. The first, Ian Wyles, is a retired schoolteacher who's Henderson's uncle twice removed. The two of them used to exchange emails on a regular basis before Henderson's disappearance, and it's possible that Henderson might still keep in touch with him somehow.

However, the minute we nab the old man on his way home from the post office, it becomes obvious he doesn't know anything. He's so fucking clueless and stunned by our questions that we don't even bother roughing him up. We just tie him up and leave him with his disabled vehicle in the woods, where he'll be found in a few hours when his wife comes home and discovers him missing.

The second person, Jennifer Lows, is Henderson's wife's friend. A plump, middle-aged woman, she literally shits herself when we grab her outside her parents' nursing home. Within the first minute of our interrogation, it becomes clear that she's clueless as well, and we leave her tied behind a dumpster in an alley, gagged and terrified out of her wits but otherwise unharmed.

"Zero for three," Anton remarks as we peel out of the alley, but I just shrug. This is not unexpected. If Henderson kept in touch with these people, we would've likely uncovered it by now. Also, the security around them would've been tighter. The fact that they were relatively easy to get to tells me they're not in Henderson's inner circle.

The people who matter to him—his wife and children—are as well hidden as any treasure.

In any case, getting information about Henderson's whereabouts is not our primary goal. This is about sending a message, telling him that no one in his life—no matter how distant a connection—is safe.

We want to enrage and frighten him, because angry, scared men make mistakes.

The next person we go after is a local police officer who happens to be Henderson's childhood friend. Jimmy Gander, age fifty-five, is one of the oldest cops on the force, and when we grab him outside his favorite bar, he manages to slug Anton in the face before we knock him out.

"I'm going to fucking kill him," Anton mutters as we pull into the woods where we intend to interrogate our captive. "Bastard's going to get it."

"No killing unless necessary," I remind him. "We're just going to rough him up some if he doesn't cooperate."

Anton scowls. "Fuck that shit. I'm going to have a black eye."

"Shouldn't have let grandpa get the better of you," Yan says, smirking. "Maybe we should have him take your place on the team. He certainly seems more skilled."

"Shut it," I tell the two of them as our SUV stops in a forest clearing. "You can slug it out later."

We drag the cop out and wait until he comes to before starting to question him. Like the others, he seems genuinely bewildered by the situation. However, unlike our other targets today, he refuses to answer our questions at first. To Anton's joy, we end up having to hit him a few times before we hear the usual "don't know anything" and "haven't heard from him." Under other circumstances, I would admire Gander's loyalty to his friend, but given that we have less than two hours left to question the two remaining people on our list, the delay merely frustrates me.

"Put a fucking bullet in him," I tell Anton when the cop balks at telling us about the last time he saw Henderson, and Anton gladly obeys the order, shooting Gander in the right shoulder.

After that, there's no more withholding of answers, just verbal vomit and pleas for a hospital.

"Let's go," I tell the guys when I'm confident we got everything we can out of the cop. "Tie him up and leave him here."

As we drive away, I make a mental note to call 911 and tell them the man's location when we're safely in the air.

Henderson's friend or not, there's no reason for the cop to die.

We're on a time crunch now, so we expedite the process by nabbing our last two targets and interrogating them together. We left them for last because they're even more distant connections of Henderson, so if we hadn't gotten to them for some reason, it wouldn't have been a major loss.

The first guy is Henderson's daughter's ex-boyfriend, Bobby Carston. He's twenty, some three years older than the daughter, and according to our files, they broke up when he slept with her best friend at their high school prom. I can't abide cheaters, so we rough up the kid a little as we question him—a move that ensures our last captive, Henderson's son's favorite teacher, is cooperative from the start.

In fact, Sam Briars is so verbose in his answers about Jimmy Henderson that we get something we didn't expect.

A possible lead.

"—and then they vacationed in Thailand five years ago and Jimmy was saying how much they loved the local culture and all the fruit and how they wanted to live there. There was a local family that they really bonded with in Phuket. Not in one of the touristy areas, mind you, but deeper inland, away from all the crowds. Jimmy was telling all his friends in class about it. And then there was Singapore, which Jimmy's mother always loved because of how clean it is, and there's Iceland where Jimmy's parents were going to go for their anniversary, and there's Maryland where Jimmy's sister was going to go to school, and I can think of more if you just give me time…"

The teacher is speaking so fast he's practically babbling, so we let him talk, jotting down notes on the places he mentions so we can check them out later. We've looked at most of these locations before, including Thailand, but the Hendersons have been moving around to avoid detection, and we didn't know about that local family in Phuket.

It's certainly a lead worth exploring.

Ten minutes pass, and the teacher shows no sign of running out of steam, his verbosity undoubtedly fueled by the wails of the bruised ex-boyfriend. At this point, he's just repeating himself, going in circles with everything he knows about the Hendersons, so I nod to Ilya and he taps him lightly on the ribs.

"Enough," I say when Briars starts screaming like that gentle tap broke his ribs. "Tie them up and leave them here. We have to go."

As we drive to our plane, I watch for signs of pursuit, but we make it there without incident.

The operation is officially a success: we've sent Henderson a message and obtained a possible lead in the process.

I should feel good, but as the wheels of the plane lift off the ground, all I can think about is that I'm no closer to getting what I really want.

That I'm still months away from reclaiming Sara.

CHAPTER 24
SARA

"He did what?" I stare at Ryson, my palms damp with sweat and my heart hammering. My first reaction—joy that Peter is alive and well—is being quickly replaced by a painful knot in my stomach.

"He assaulted six people in North Carolina," the agent repeats. "Two are hospitalized with gunshot wounds, and the other four are bruised and traumatized by a violent interrogation. Innocent citizens, all. Anything you can tell us about the incident?"

"I... what?" I shake my head to clear it of the gruesome images. "Why would he do this?"

"According to the victims, he wanted to know the location of an acquaintance of theirs—one Walter Henderson III. He has the misfortune of being on the same list as your late husband." Ryson crosses his beefy arms. "It seems that Sokolov is resorting to more extreme measures to get to

129

this man. Anything you can tell us about that? About what he's after?"

I swallow the bile rising in my throat. Over the past couple of months, I'd somehow managed to forget the brutal reality of the man I've been missing, to gloss over the darker parts in my memories. "You don't know?"

"I told you, much of his file is redacted." Ryson uncrosses his arms and leans in. "Dr. Cobakis, you know as well as I do that this man is lethal. He needs to be stopped before more innocent people get hurt. It's important that you tell us everything you know about him, so we can have a better idea where he might strike next."

I stare at him, feeling alternately hot and cold. "He... didn't tell me much of anything." That's what I've been telling the agents, and I have to stick with the story, no matter how sick I feel at the knowledge that Peter is hurting innocents in his quest for vengeance.

In any case, even if Ryson knew about the massacre of Peter's wife and son, it wouldn't change anything. Peter won't stop until he finds Henderson and crosses him off his list, and as he vividly demonstrated in North Carolina, the Feds are still no match for him and his crew.

Peter and his men entered the US undetected, assaulted six citizens, and left.

He was in the same country as I, and if Ryson hadn't decided to question me, I would've never known.

My stomach tightens further, and to my horror, I realize I'm not just upset about the pain and suffering he put those people through.

I'm also hurt and mad that Peter didn't come for me.

We were just a few states apart, and he didn't come for me.

"Dr. Cobakis." Ryson peers at me intently. "Are you all right?"

"I… yes." I ball my hands under the table, letting my nails dig into my palms. The hint of pain steadies me, enabling me to say in a semi-normal tone, "I'm sorry. It's just a lot."

And it is. It's too much, in fact. Until this moment, I didn't fully comprehend how messed up I am, how those months with Peter have twisted me, skewing my sense of right and wrong. Here I am, having just learned that the killer I've been obsessing about hurt six innocent people, and I'm upset that he chose them over me? That he didn't abduct me when he clearly had the chance to do so?

I'm sick.

It's obvious to me now—as is the fact that Peter may never come for me. All along, vengeance has been his true love, his real obsession, and whatever he felt for me didn't last… if it was even there in the first place. I don't know why I'm still being watched, or if I even am—that itchy feeling may well be paranoia—but it's clear that I'm no longer his priority.

I somehow endure the rest of Ryson's interrogation, answering his questions on auto-pilot, and when I get home, I pick up the phone and call Dr. Evans, the therapist who helped me before.

It's time to rebuild my shattered life.

It's time to accept that whatever Peter and I had may be over.

PART III

CHAPTER 25
PETER

We spend the next two months following up on the Thai lead—it's not easy to figure out which local family the Hendersons befriended—and when that doesn't bring us any closer to our target, we take a job in Russia, where an oil oligarch wants us to eliminate one of his business rivals. It's not as lucrative of a gig as some of the others, but the location makes it worthwhile.

We haven't been in our home country in years.

"Does this feel as weird to you as it does to me?" Anton asks as we walk past Red Square, and I nod, knowing exactly what he means. Walking down these streets and hearing Russian speech all around us is a lot like going back in time. The last time I was in Moscow was when I killed my supervisor, Ivan Polonsky, for helping with the Daryevo massacre cover-up—seemingly a lifetime ago.

"Do you miss it?" I ask Anton, and he shrugs.

"Nah. I mean, it's not exactly fun to always be the for-eigner, but I've gotten used to it. And thanks to Sara, my English has improved, so..." He stops, his gaze turning wary as he realizes what he just said. "That is, while we were—"

"Enough." My neck muscles are painfully tight and my hands are clenched into fists, but my voice is soft and even as I repeat, "That's enough."

Anton wisely shuts up, and we walk the rest of the way in silence. He knows he's forbidden to talk about her, and it's no longer just about her safety. Sara is a trigger for me these days, so much so that the mere mention of her name is enough to make me homicidal. The gaping wound left by her absence isn't healing; it's festering.

I ache for her every second of every day, and I fucking hate it.

The daily reports only make it worse, because it seems as though she's forgotten me. Last month, she got another job, joining two older OB-GYNs in their practice, and she moved out of her parents' house into a new apartment. I'm glad about all of that—I want her to be happy—but for the past six weeks, she's also gone out every weekend, drinking and dancing with her friends. On top of that, she started singing with a band on Friday nights—a development that pleased me until I saw a recording of her performing in a sexy dress and realized every man in the audience is drool-ing over her.

They watch her like a pack of wolves slobbering over a hare.

If I were there with her, I could've stopped that—rear-ranged a few faces, if need be—but I'm half a world away, and it eats at me. More than that, it raises the possibility that Sara might've forgotten me so completely she might fall for another man… maybe even one of the idiots who come up to her after every performance to gush over her and beg for her phone number.

The only thing that keeps me from ordering a hit on those assholes is that so far, she hasn't gone out with any of them.

It's only a matter of time, though. I know that. The longer I'm gone, the more likely it is. And that is why, right before we took this job, I finally ordered a message delivered to her.

She should get it shortly.

In the meantime, we have a very rich—and very corrupt—man to kill.

CHAPTER 26
SARA

"Sara! Sara! Sara!"

The chanting of the audience combined with the deafening applause is like a shot of heroin into my veins. I'm so high I feel like I'm flying, and I bow, laughing, as the chanting intensifies.

My bandmates—Phil, Simon, and Rory—are bowing alongside me. The audience, though, seems focused on me. Probably because the guys changed the name of the band from *The Rocker Boys* to *Sara & the Rocker Boys* last month, completely ignoring my objections. For whatever reason, Phil decided that the band is much more marketable with me as the lead singer, and every poster now prominently features my face in addition to my name. Last week, I actually had a patient at the clinic recognize me as "that Sara" and request my autograph—a highly embarrassing incident that resulted in the clinic staff nicknaming me "The Celeb."

This is the first time we've done a larger outdoor venue, and I wasn't sure we'd be able to pull it off. Though it's almost May, the weather is still unpredictable, and up until two days ago, we didn't know if it was going to be fifty degrees and raining or seventy and sunny. It ended up being somewhere in the middle—sixty-seven and partly cloudy—and we got a great turnout. Our goal was to sell at least a hundred tickets to cover the venue costs, but judging by the number of enthusiastically clapping spectators, we sold close to four times that amount.

We finish bowing and do one more song as an encore before leaving the stage. As always happens after a successful performance, it's hard to come off the high, so we go to a nearby bar to celebrate and unwind.

Like me, my bandmates do this as a hobby. Phil, our guitarist, is a math teacher; Simon, the drummer, is a freelance writer; and Rory, our bassist, works in a call center. Unlike me, however, all three of them would like to do this as a career, and as often happens after a great performance, they immediately start talking about going on tour.

"We could start in Seattle, then make our way down the West Coast," Phil says, picking up his beer. His blue eyes glitter feverishly in his ruddy face. "From there, we could go all across the Southwest and—"

"Fuck Seattle." Rory knocks back a shot of tequila and slides the glass toward the harried bartender. "We go straight to California. San Francisco, then L.A. It's the best for artists like us, not to mention the weather and the culture and the food…"

He continues, gesticulating wildly as he talks, and I grin as I notice several women openly staring at him. With his freckled face, unruly red curls, and a bodybuilder's physique, Rory looks like a cross between Little Orphan Annie and an Abercrombie model on steroids. It's a combination that shouldn't have worked, but it does—and I suspect the success of the band owes as much to his looks as it does to our combined talent.

Not that Phil and Simon are bad-looking. Simon, in particular, reminds me of a young Denzel Washington, only with a punk-rock vibe. Phil is a bit more average, with a receding hairline and a hint of a beer belly, but his outgoing personality more than makes up for any physical shortcomings. All three of my bandmates are attractive in their own way—and each has hinted, at one point or another, that he'd like to take me out.

It's too bad all I can see when I look at a man these days is that he's not Peter.

The guys don't know that, of course. They're happily oblivious to the terrifying mess in my past and the FBI agents who still stubbornly follow me around. All my bandmates know is that I'm a widow, and they think grief for my dead husband is the reason I don't date.

"How long has it been?" Phil asked sympathetically when I joined the band back in February, and I told him my husband passed away about a year and a half earlier, having never awoken from a car accident that left him in a coma. Phil expressed his condolences and has tactfully avoided the topic since, as have Simon and Rory.

In fact, after carefully letting me know that they're interested and just as carefully being turned down, they've completely backed off and have taken to treating me as some kind of saintly figure, an untouchable Madonna encased in a bubble of grief.

They're not far off, only the loss I'm grieving has little to do with George, who's fading more from my memories each day. At this point, it's been over three years since his accident, and even longer since our love suffocated under the weight of his addiction. Each time I think about him now, all I remember is how I felt when I found out about his double life as a CIA agent... about the secrets and the lies that brought Peter to my door.

I wish I could forget *him* as well, but it's impossible. Though it's been nearly six months since my captor brought me home, I think about him every night as I drift off to sleep. Sometimes, I'm convinced I can feel him. Not next to me, but somewhere out there, reaching across the continents to torment me, his pull both magnetic and lethal, like the gravitational force of the sun.

I dream of him, too. Of the tender way he'd hold me when I cried and the brutal way he'd fuck me, of all the big and little things that make up the contradiction that is Peter. At times, I wake up from those dreams aroused and frustrated, but more often, I find my pillow soaked with tears and my arms wrapped around my blanket to stave off the agonizing loneliness that keeps me frozen inside.

I need to move on, I know. And I try. I go out with Marsha and the girls every weekend, and when a particularly attractive guy asks for my number, I give it out more often than not. But that's where it ends for me. I can't take the next step and actually agree to the date when they call or text me.

"Why even bother giving it out, then?" Marsha asked last week, when she learned that I did it yet again. "Why not just turn them down on the spot?"

I shrugged, not knowing what to say, and she let it drop, not wanting to stress me out. Like most of my acquaintances who've heard the FBI version of the Peter story, Marsha has been treating me like I'm made of crystal and might shatter at the slightest pressure. I think she— along with others at the hospital—thinks my ordeal was even worse than I disclosed. One time, when Mom was still in the hospital, I overheard two nurses talking about how I escaped a "sexual slavery ring" and am still dealing with the aftermath of being "forced into prostitution."

It's aggravating, but the only way to address those rumors would be to tell the truth, and I'm not about to do that.

Fortunately, my new coworkers don't know anything more than my bandmates. Drs. Wendy and Bill Otterman, the married couple who own the small OB-GYN practice, were so impressed by my resume and academic credentials that they barely asked any questions about the nine-month gap in my work history. I told them I took a hiatus to travel around the world, and they hired me on the spot, with the caveat that I start immediately so they could take a long-awaited cruise to Alaska for their fortieth wedding anniversary.

I could've looked for better-paying, more prestigious opportunities, but I accepted the offer right away and started the next day. With Mom barely out of the hospital, I wanted something fairly low key, so I could still keep an eye on her and Dad. But what really cinched the deal for me was the office's location—a fifteen-minute drive from my parents' house and a short walk from my new apartment.

"Earth to Rory." Simon waves his beer bottle in front of Rory's face, interrupting his oration on the wonders of California. "Let's just be real here. Sara, are you going to go on tour with us?"

I smile and shake my head. "No can do, sorry. Work won't let me take off for so long."

"See?" Simon triumphantly surveys his bandmates, as though he's won a bet. "She's not going. It's not happening."

"Oh, come on." Phil grabs the beer from Simon and finishes it off in two gulps before motioning to the bartender to bring more. Turning to face me, he gives me the full dose of the famous Phil Hudson charm. "Sara, sweetheart..." His voice turns cajoling. "We all have work and other responsibilities, but opportunities like this come once in a lifetime. We're catching fire, I can feel it, and we have to seize the day. *You* have to seize the day, because you know what happens tomorrow?"

I shake my head, grinning. I've heard versions of this lecture from him before, and he gets more creative each time. "No, what?"

"Exactly." He wags his index finger, teacher style. "You don't know, and neither does anyone else. Life is but a series of random events, one that seems to have a pattern but doesn't. You may think you know what tomorrow will bring, but all it takes is a change in a single variable, and boom! Off you go in a totally different direction."

"Like on a tour?" I say dryly, and both Rory and Simon laugh.

"A tour, yes—that would be a new variable," Phil says, undeterred. "But it's one that *you* would introduce. Most of the time, the new variable comes from where you least expect it, and then all your carefully laid plans go to shit."

"Shit—is that an official algebra term? Did I just learn math?" Rory asks, scratching his curls, and we all burst out laughing as Phil rolls his eyes, muttering under his breath about ignoramuses and drunk assholes.

"I have to run," I tell the guys apologetically as the laughter dies down. "Early day at work tomorrow."

"No worries, we know." Simon pats me on the shoulder. "You go do what you got to do and leave these idiots to dream of fame."

I laugh, shaking my head as I walk out of the bar and head to the parking lot in the back. I had my doubts about joining the band, but it turned out to be the best decision ever. Not only do I feel like I was born to do this every time I'm up on that stage, but my bandmates are a lot of fun. I actually prefer hanging out with them versus Marsha and the girls; it's less pressure, somehow.

I'm pulling open my car door when I notice it.

A piece of something thick—folded-up paper, maybe?—taped to the inside of the door handle.

My initial reaction is to pull it out and immediately take a look, but some sixth sense stops me. The itchy feeling between my shoulder blades—the one that's so omnipresent I barely notice it anymore—is far more intense all of a sudden, and instead of yanking out the object and staring at it, I unobtrusively pry it loose, hold it in my closed fist, and get in the car.

Slipping the object—now definitively identified as a piece of folded paper—into my jacket pocket, I pull out of the parking lot and head home. Behind me is the inevitable FBI tail, and as I drive, the paper feels like it's burning through my pocket.

It takes everything I have to park in front of my apartment building and walk through the lobby to the elevator calmly, without hurrying. It's possible that this is some kind of advertisement that's just weirdly placed, but somehow, I'm certain that it's not.

Stepping into my apartment, I lock the door and glance around. I don't think there are any cameras or listening devices in here; after all the high-tech equipment found in my old house and then months later in my parents' house, the Feds sweep my place on a semi-regular basis, and they themselves would need a warrant to do that kind of invasive surveillance. However, just to be on the safe side, I kick off my shoes and walk toward my bedroom closet, maintaining my calm demeanor the entire time.

If someone is watching me, I'm not going to give them reason for suspicion.

My one-bedroom apartment is fairly small, with a tiny kitchen and a cramped living room, but it does have one nice feature: a spacious walk-in closet in the bedroom. I go in there, as I normally would to undress, but instead, as soon as I'm out of sight of any potential cameras, I take out the paper from my pocket and unfold it, my hands shaking.

It's just a couple of lines, scrawled on the thick paper in sharp, masculine handwriting.

Remember, ptichka. For as long as we're both alive.

CHAPTER 27
PETER

The Moscow job goes smoothly—we eliminate our target in one short week—and then we're back to hunting Henderson while we await word from Novak. Last month, the Serbian arms dealer confirmed everything is on track for the original eight-month timeline, but he's still close-mouthed about his asset within Esguerra's organization—the key piece of information I need to implement my plan.

Unfortunately, Henderson remains as elusive as always, so as May progresses, we do another round of shaking down his acquaintances for any leads. This time, we focus on his wife's connections in her hometown of Charleston, just to switch things up.

"Nothing again," Ilya says with disgust as we board the plane, having interrogated our five targets. "The idiots didn't know a thing."

I shrug and take my seat. "It was to be expected."

I still consider the operation a success. We got away without so much as a car chase, and we again showed Henderson that nobody in his life, no matter how remote a connection, is safe. Sooner or later, it will sink in, and then he'll make a mistake. Maybe his wife will get worried about a friend of hers and reach out to check on her, or maybe the teenage daughter will freak out and call her ex.

No matter what happens, the moment they fuck up, we'll be ready, and my dead wife and son will be avenged.

It's the beginning of June when it finally happens.

I get an email from Novak that he wants to meet next Wednesday.

Just you, the email reads. *No one else.*

I suppress a surge of savage joy and begin making the arrangements.

For the past two weeks, we've been staying in our Polish safe house, waiting for Novak to reach out, so Wednesday morning, I have the guys drop me off in Belgrade and assume their positions.

They won't be with me, but they'll certainly be around.

I meet Novak in the same café as before. As I walk in, I notice that his goons are conspicuously absent—as are the pretty baristas. Novak himself is sitting at the small table in the middle of the café, with nothing but a brown leather folder in front of him.

"All alone?" I ask, trying not to let my surprise show, and Novak's thin lips curve as he stands up and comes around the table to greet me.

"I thought we could dispense with all the bullshit." His pale eyes gleam as he shakes my hand. "We need each other, and I think it's time we built some trust."

I'm certain *this* is bullshit—his men are likely positioned as strategically as mine—but I let my stony expression soften slightly as I release his hand. "I couldn't agree more."

"Good." He sits back down at the table and motions for me to do so as well. "Please."

I take a seat and assume an impassive expression. "So, is the asset in place?"

Novak nods, maintaining his smug little smile. "She's on the way to Esguerra's compound as we speak."

My pulse speeds up. Time and date of the asset's transport—this is already something I can use. "Congratulations. That's quite an achievement," I say, keeping my voice even.

Novak accepts the praise as his due. "Thank you. It took a lot of work, but I did it."

"So tell me about her, this mysterious asset of yours," I say.

He drums his pale fingers on the table for several long seconds, then says, "Are you familiar with the financial structure of Esguerra's organization?"

I stare at him. "No. Not particularly. I was his security consultant, not financial advisor." This is not where I was expecting Novak to go. Could the asset be someone connected to Esguerra's portfolio manager? I know the guy resides somewhere in Chicago, but I don't see—

"So you don't know that legally and practically, Esguerra's wife is his business partner and stands to inherit everything in the event of his death?"

"No, but it wouldn't surprise me," I say slowly. Even back then, when I was still working for Esguerra, Nora, the American girl he kidnapped and then married, showed an unusual aptitude for her husband's business.

Novak smiles again and opens the folder in front of him. "Yes. The young Mrs. Esguerra is quite something, isn't she? Finished Stanford at the top of her class." He takes out a photo and lays it in front of me. It shows Nora in a voluminous graduation gown accepting a diploma from a university official. Her smiling face is half turned, looking elsewhere, but even from this angle, it's obvious she's ecstatic.

"When was this taken?" I ask, puzzled. If Novak's people were close enough to take that photo, they must've been close to Esguerra himself as well.

The Colombian arms dealer wouldn't let his wife out of his sight for longer than a minute.

"A couple of months ago, at the spring graduation ceremony," Novak answers. "Pretty, isn't she? So small yet so strong…"

His voice is unusually soft as he says this, his touch almost caressing as he takes back the picture and places it in the folder. I lift my eyebrows, waiting to see where he's going with this. Did he somehow develop the hots for Esguerra's petite wife?

It's odd, but stranger things have happened.

Closing the folder, he looks up. "I know what you're thinking," he says. "Why didn't I have him taken out right then and there, at that ceremony? Why bother with you when I had a shot at him back then, all on my own?"

I incline my head. "The question did occur to me, but I assumed Esguerra's security was tighter than your possession of that photo indicates."

Novak's lips stretch in another thin smile. "You're right—the security was impressive. Still, if I really wanted to, I could've attempted it. I would've sustained heavy losses, but there's a small chance I could've gotten through."

"But you didn't want to risk it?"

"Oh, I would've risked it... if Esguerra's death was all I wanted."

Now we're getting to the core of the issue. "You also want her." I nod toward the folder. "Is that part of it?"

Novak's pale gaze hardens. "Yes... but not the way you think. You see, Nora Esguerra is not just a pretty face—she holds the keys to Esguerra's kingdom. If I kill him, she simply takes over, and I have a new enemy to contend with— one with nearly unlimited resources and a very personal grudge against me."

This is getting interesting. "So you want them both eliminated?"

"That was my original thought, but no. You see, Esguerra is smart—much smarter than most in our business. Nearly all of his holdings are legally titled, and everything is buried behind layers upon layers of shell corporations. If both Esguerras are killed, it will take me years to untangle the mess, and while I will have achieved the elimination of a rival, I won't have access to what I really want."

"His business holdings."

"Yes. That's exactly right." He leans forward. "I don't just want Esguerra gone—I want what he has… his wife included."

I cock my head. "So you want Julian Esguerra killed but his wife kidnapped?"

"Yes, and not just his wife." His smile is chilling. "You see, she's useless to me without some kind of leverage."

"Leverage? You mean something like a family member?"

"Yes, precisely. And not just any family member. I need someone she'd do anything for… even embrace her husband's killer."

My face remains unchanged, but my blood turns to icy sludge. Is this a roundabout hint that he knows about my obsession with Sara? If so, I'll kill him on the spot, his hidden goons be damned. If he so much as threatens her, I'll peel his fucking skin off and—

"You see," Novak continues, oblivious to my rising rage, "I need Nora, and I need her completely under my control. I considered using her parents for that, but it might not be enough. After all, parents usually sacrifice for their children, not the other way around."

I rein in my bloodthirsty thoughts. "What do you have in mind, then?" He might not be talking about Sara; at least, he fucking better not be. Going on the assumption that he's not stupid enough to threaten me so obliquely, I decide to take him at face value and say, "As far as I know, other than her parents, Nora doesn't have—"

"Yes, exactly. As far as you know." Novak leans back, clearly enjoying his moment of superiority. "You and all the rest of the world, a select few people excluded."

I stare at him, my thoughts jumping from one fact to another. "Your asset," I say slowly. "The eight-month time-line... Are you saying that Esguerra has a—"

"Child? Yes." His bland face animates. "A daughter, in fact, born last Tuesday in Switzerland, some two weeks ahead of schedule. Elizabeth Esguerra—Lizzie, for short. Pretty name, no?"

"Yes, very," I manage to say. My heart is threatening to erupt from my ribcage, and under the table, my hands form into fists.

A baby. A fucking newborn. That's his plan, his asset. He's right in that it would be the perfect way to control Nora. A mother would do anything for her child; she'd give up an empire and her own life if need be.

It shouldn't matter to me—Esguerra is no friend of mine—but for some reason, the involvement of an infant makes Novak's plan downright obscene to me.

It makes me glad I was going to double-cross the fucker all along.

But wait. He mentioned that his asset would be able to assist in the hit. That means the child is not it. However... "Is it a nanny?" I ask evenly. "Your asset—she's connected to the child, isn't she?"

Novak nods, his hand flexing on the table in front of him. "Yes, but not a nanny," he says, his expression smoothing out. "A pediatrician—one that comes highly recommended by the Swiss clinic doctors Esguerra favors."

Of course. I suspected Novak might have some connection to that place. "You bribed the clinic staff?"

"I tried, but sadly, no." He sighs. "They're so frightened of their patients that they're next to impossible to bribe. I had to hack into their computers instead."

"I see." All the pieces are falling into place now. "That's how you knew about Nora's pregnancy so early."

He nods. "Esguerra brought her there to be examined as soon as she missed her period. And as soon as they knew, I knew—and I reached out to you."

I suppress the urge to reach across the table and break his neck. Maybe it's because I know Nora, or maybe it's because when I think of infants, I picture my son at that age, but the mere notion of a newborn being used like that makes me ill.

Keeping my tone steady, I say, "So you want me to kill Esguerra, kidnap Nora and her baby, and bring them to you, so in one fell swoop, you'd eliminate your biggest rival and gain control over his holdings."

Novak's smile is all teeth. "Exactly."

"That's very clever." I inject an admiring note into my voice. "If you just took Nora and the child to control Esguerra, he'd find a way to fuck you over and get them back—he's done that before. But his wife—his widow, I should say—will be easier to handle, especially with a baby to keep her in line. Are you planning to make it legal with her?"

"Yes, of course. Marriage is the easiest way to bypass all those pesky ownership hurdles. I will adopt the daughter as well."

"And raise her as your own?"

He shrugs. "More or less. Any children I breed with Nora will obviously take priority, but as long as her mother behaves, I have no intention of harming the child."

"Very generous of you."

He either misses the sarcasm in my voice or chooses to ignore it. "Yes. I think we'll all benefit in the long term—as will you. A hundred million will go far in assisting with your little vendetta."

I'm not the least bit surprised that he knows about that. "Yes, it will," I say without blinking.

"Good. Do you already have an idea of how you'll go about getting into Esguerra's compound?"

"Yes," I say and look him straight in the eye. "I'm going to reach out to Lucas Kent and have him bring me to Esguerra. I'm going to tell him that I want to bury the hatchet—and that I'm willing to reveal a traitor to make that happen."

CHAPTER 28
SARA

I don't sleep all night again, and by morning, I'm so exhausted I all but crawl to the kitchen for coffee. If today was a workday, I would've had to call in sick. However, it's that most rare of all days.

A Saturday when I have absolutely nothing scheduled.

If this was pre-PN (Peter's note), I might've gone to the clinic to help out for a few hours, or surprised my parents by popping over for breakfast. However, this is post-PN, and between the lack of sleep and the ever-present anxious waiting, it's all I can do to plop on the couch and turn on a cooking show.

I've been watching a lot of those lately. They remind me of Peter.

As always, when I think about him, my mind starts going in circles. It's now been eight months since he brought me home—eight months during which my only word from him was that note. Two months ago, pre-PN, I was more or less convinced that his obsession with me faded, and that despite his vow, he might never come back for me. Now, however, I don't know what to think.

If he still wants me, why am I here?

What is he waiting for?

Mom is now completely well—or at least as well as she'll ever be. Her left arm is still weak, but she's able to move her fingers and can use that hand to pick up light objects—a much better outcome than initially feared. She's also walking without assistance and has been puttering around her garden ever since the weather improved. Dad is ecstatic about her recovery, and they're both looking forward to their anniversary cruise in September—a gift I was finally able to give them.

As Mom's health improved and the novelty of my return wore off, my visits with them have gone from a daily to a weekly occurrence. My parents are always glad to see me, of course, but they also value their independence. My dad, in particular, takes pride in being self-sufficient, and I don't want to take it away from him by constantly hovering over them like a nursemaid.

My parents love me, but they don't need me as much as I once thought—or so I tell myself to soothe the guilt that inevitably accompanies my craving for Peter.

My perverse wish that he'd come and take me.

I've thought about it so often I can picture it like a movie in my head. I'll enter my apartment one day, and he'll be there, big and dangerous, as lethal and beautiful as ever. He'll be there despite the police patrols outside, despite all of the Feds' precautions.

He'll be waiting to steal me away, and nothing I say will matter.

That's probably the most shameful part of these fantasies: that I never have a choice in them... and that I like that. I want Peter to steal me away, to just come and take me over my objections. Then and only then will I be able to live with the knowledge that I once again disappeared from the lives of the people who love and need me, that I abandoned my family, my patients, my bandmates, and my friends.

I need Peter to be bad, so I can be at least somewhat good.

I have to hate him in order to love him.

I'm beginning to understand that about myself, to embrace the perversity within me, but what I don't understand is why I'm still here if he wants me. It can no longer be about my parents, so it must be about something else—something he hasn't told me.

I've racked my brain for what it could be, and the best I can come up with is something he said when we were parting. I asked him if I'll be home until Mom recovers, and he started to say that he had to finish with something first as well. He didn't disclose what it was, though, nor so much as hint at how long that something would take. The only thing I can imagine being that important to him is his vengeance, but I don't know why that would keep him from me for so long.

He was hunting Henderson when we were together, and according to the FBI, that's what he's doing still.

Two months ago, right after I got Peter's note, Ryson had me brought to their downtown office again. I nearly had a panic attack, thinking that the Feds somehow learned about the note, but as it turned out, Ryson wanted to question me because Peter and his men struck again, "interrogating" five more US citizens in their quest to uncover Henderson's whereabouts.

"They were all in Charleston, South Carolina," Ryson told me. "Once again, Sokolov got in and out of the country undetected. We need to know how he's doing it, so we can stop him from wreaking havoc on people's lives."

"I'm sorry, I don't know anything about that," I said truthfully. Peter never spoke much about his connections or how he does the impossible things he does. As awful as I feel about the people he terrified and tortured, I know nothing that can help the Feds in this regard.

Assuming I wanted to help, that is. If Peter was unable to get into the US, he wouldn't be able to hurt more people. However, he also wouldn't be able to retrieve me, and that perverse, contradictory part of me—the one that keeps me awake at night, thinking of that note with a mixture of joy and trepidation—can't stand that possibility.

I need him.

I crave him so much it hurts.

Before that note, I was able to hold the pain in, to be strong as I told myself that it was over, but hearing from Peter—knowing he'll be back—stripped away my fragile new defenses, plunging me back into that endless waiting mode.

"Come back," I whisper, hugging a pillow to my chest as I stare at the TV screen. "Please, Peter, I need you. Come back for me and take me home."

CHAPTER 29
PETER

"You what?" Yan stares at me like I've sprouted a pair of tentacles.

"I contacted Lucas Kent about arranging a meeting with Esguerra," I repeat, stirring the pasta sauce. "Hand me that basil, will you?"

Yan doesn't move, so Ilya silently pushes the chopped basil toward me, and I sprinkle it liberally over the sauce. I'm making Italian food tonight—a cuisine my men feel quite neutral about, but Sara loves.

For you, ptichka. So I feel like you're here with me.

I've started doing that this week, talking to her in my mind. It's probably not healthy, but it makes me feel closer to her, as though she's here with me instead of an ocean away.

Maybe it's because I know I might see her soon, but I've been missing her even more than usual. Each day without her is fucking torture.

"I thought you were going to kill Kent," Yan says, frowning in confusion. "For letting Sara crash."

"And I still might, just not at this time." I dip a long spoon into the sauce and taste it before adding a pinch more salt. "I need him to get me into Esguerra's compound."

Anton comes up to stand next to Yan. "So that's your grand plan? To have Kent hand you on a silver platter to Esguerra? You do remember the guy swore to kill you, right?"

I give him a level look. "He won't kill me if he wants the name of Novak's asset."

"Ah." Yan's expression smooths out. "So you're going to pretend to double-cross Novak to gain access to Esguerra's compound."

"Precisely." *And then I'm going to double-cross him for real*, I think, but I don't say it. As much as I trust my guys, I have to operate on the assumption that Novak has eyes and ears on us at all times. It's highly unlikely in the privacy of this safe house, but I can't afford to risk it.

As it was, I barely managed to convince the Serbian to go along with my plan.

"You're going to what?" He stood up, nearly knocking over the table when I informed him of my intentions in the café. In an instant, his goons appeared from their hiding place in the back, surrounding him like a human wall, their M16s drawn and pointed at me.

"So much for building trust, huh?" I said, amused, and Novak gave me a dark glare before ordering them to stand down.

I sat down and waited for him to do the same before explaining the gist of my plan. It took a while, but he finally understood why that was the only option… why, even with his asset in place, we wouldn't be able to get into Esguerra's compound by force.

"Even if your pediatrician is a tech whizz who manages to disable the drones and the electric fences that protect the compound, we'll still have the guard towers to contend with. Which wouldn't be a problem for my team except that Esguerra has generators and backup drones that would go online within a minute of the main ones being disabled. And then, while we're dealing with the drones firing on us from the sky, Esguerra's backup guards—over a hundred of them—will appear and take us out. The only way past them would be with an even bigger force—say, a couple of hundred mercenaries of our own—but a group that size has no chance of getting near the compound undetected. We wouldn't even be able to enter Colombia without Esguerra hearing about it and intercepting us long before we get anywhere near his place."

"So you plan to sacrifice my asset to gain Esguerra's trust?" Novak asked, frowning, and I nodded, explaining that once I'm in, it won't be all that difficult to get within grabbing distance of Nora—and once I have her as my hostage, I'll have leverage over Esguerra.

He'll give up his life to save her.

"My men will be waiting just outside the compound, so once I have Nora and the baby, I'll disable the perimeter defenses myself and use the confusion of Esguerra's death to make our escape," I told Novak. "It won't be easy, but it's the only chance we've got."

The pasta sauce is finally ready, so as we sit down to eat dinner, I relay the same plan to the guys.

"No fucking way," Anton says when I'm done. "Hostages or not, you're not going to walk out of that compound alive. You're talking about a suicide mission."

"Not necessarily," Yan says softly, winding his fork in the pasta. His green eyes hold a strange gleam. "Esguerra has a weakness now: his wife and daughter. And we're going to use it. Isn't that right?"

"Yes, exactly," I say and remind myself to keep an eye on Yan during this mission.

With everything so precariously balanced, the slightest unforeseen element—like one of my own double-crossing me—could bring it all crashing down.

CHAPTER 30
PETER

The response from Lucas Kent comes almost immediately. He's willing to meet with me, which is the first step to getting near Esguerra.

He proposes his wife's new restaurant in London as a potential meeting place. It's not exactly neutral ground, but I agree. I know what he's thinking: that this might be a ploy to lure him out, so I could punish him and his wife for fucking up with Sara.

Under other circumstances, he wouldn't have been wrong. The image of my ptichka in that hospital, her delicate face pale and bruised, still features in my nightmares. Someday, Kent *will* pay for letting her escape and crash, but for now, I need him.

He's my best shot at reaching out to Esguerra.

Of course, if he turned me down, I had a backup plan. I know Nora Esguerra's email, having communicated in the past with her about my list. However, Esguerra is not exactly rational about his tiny wife and might take it the wrong way if I contact her after all these years.

It's better to go through Kent—Esguerra might be more willing to listen in that case.

———————————

Kent's wife, the beautiful Yulia, is nowhere in sight as I enter the stylish restaurant and make my way to a booth in the corner, where Kent's blond head is visible above the partition.

He stands up to greet me, his hard face wary as he extends his hand. "Sokolov."

I shake his hand, squeezing his fingers with slightly too much force. "Kent."

His eyes narrow, but he releases my hand without retaliating. "I didn't expect to hear from you again," he says as we take a seat and open the menus. "How is your Sara these days?"

"Who? Oh, that." I catch the waiter and tell him to bring me an unopened Guinness bottle with an opener on the side. Kent requests a cup of Earl Grey for himself. I wait for the waiter to leave before telling Kent, "I have no idea how she is. I let her go last year and haven't seen her since."

His eyebrows rise. "Really?"

I shrug. "What can I say? It was time."

"Right." He doesn't seem to believe me, but he turns his attention to the menu and scans it before looking up to ask, "Do you know what you want?"

"I'm not hungry, thanks." Given what happened with Sara and what I'm about to tell him, I no longer trust Kent or the food in his wife's restaurant.

His mouth curls in a dry smile. "I see." Closing the menu, he waits for the waiter to set our drinks on the table and then says, "Why do you want to meet Esguerra? He still hasn't forgiven you for the incident with Nora, you know."

"Yes, I'm aware." I used his wife as bait, letting her get kidnapped in order to find out where a terrorist group was holding him at the time. Back then, I knew he'd be pissed about Nora's involvement, but his rage didn't really make sense to me—after all, it was the only way to save his life.

Now, however, I understand his reaction better. If anyone endangered Sara like that, I wouldn't care about the reasoning behind it.

My life for hers would never be a fair trade.

"I had a very lucrative offer come my way," I tell Kent, opening my Guinness. "As a result, I've come into possession of some information Esguerra might appreciate."

Kent frowns and picks up his cup of tea. "Oh? And what information is that?"

"There's a traitor in his compound," I say and take a large swig as Kent's frown deepens. "A traitor who's supposed to aid me in my assignment."

Kent puts down his tea. "Someone hired you to carry out a hit on Esguerra?" At my confirming nod, he asks sharply, "Who?"

I open my mouth to tell him, but he reaches the correct conclusion on his own.

"Novak," he spits out, pushing the tea away. His jaw flexes violently. "Of course. Who else would fucking dare?"

I take another swig of my beer. "A hundred million euro is his offer, but I'm willing to let Esguerra match it—if you bring me to Colombia to talk to him. I want bygones to be bygones. Well, that and a hundred million," I clarify, lest he think I'm all about making peace.

Kent stares at me, eyes narrowed. "You know he might not go for it, right? Now that we know there's a traitor, we'll figure out who that is. It's only a matter of time."

"Sure. But time matters—especially when a vulnerable newborn is involved."

Kent's face turns to stone. "What the fuck do you know about newborns?" His voice is dangerously soft. "Because if you're trying to imply that—"

"Lizzie is in danger? I'm not implying, I'm telling you. Novak knows all about the recent addition to Esguerra's family, and he has plans for her." I'm taking a risk revealing so much, but I can't afford to pussyfoot around.

I have to get Esguerra to listen to me.

My future with Sara depends on it.

The waiter approaches to take our order, but Kent shoos him away with a curt wave. "What if Esguerra just wires the hundred million to you?" he asks, picking up his tea again. "A hundred million for a name, all at zero risk to you."

"No go," I say and finish my beer. "I don't need to spend the rest of my life looking over my shoulder, waiting for Esguerra to carry out his revenge on me. He either hears me out in person, or I take the job. It's up to him."

Getting up, I walk out of the restaurant, my stomach rumbling at the delicious smells emanating from the kitchen.

If all goes well, I'll eat here for real one day... with Sara by my side.

CHAPTER 31
PETER

I don't have to wait long for Esguerra's answer. His email is in my inbox by the time I get back to my hotel.

Tonight at seven, the message reads. *Lucas will pick you up.*

Seven is only a half hour away, so I swiftly notify my guys and get ready.

Kent shows up at my hotel room promptly at seven. I'm not at all surprised that he knows where I'm staying; I knew I was being tailed from the second I left the restaurant.

Kent's face might as well be hewn from granite. "No weapons," he says, and I lift my arms, letting him frisk me from head to toe.

He finds the knife in my boot, the two knives in my pockets, and the small revolver tucked into the inner pocket of my leather jacket. However, he doesn't notice the razor blade in the hem of my jeans or the coil of wire sewn into my jacket collar.

Camp Larko taught me well.

"Let's go," he says when he's satisfied that I'm clean, and I follow him out of the hotel and into an armored limo.

The ride to the airport passes in silence. I expect Kent to deliver me to Esguerra's private plane and take off, but he goes in with me.

"You're piloting?" I ask, and he nods curtly.

"Esguerra requested that I bring you myself."

He doesn't sound too pleased about that, and I smile as I take a seat on the cream-colored leather couch in the cabin. Kent being pissed about the disruption to his routine is a bonus as far as I'm concerned.

I can't yet kill him for letting Sara crash, but I can certainly enjoy screwing up his plans.

I spend part of the eleven-hour flight napping and the rest emailing with my team. They're on their way to Colombia too, and will be waiting for me outside the compound as per our Novak-approved plan. If all goes well, I won't need them, but if things go sideways, they might be able to help get me out.

Assuming I'm still alive to get out, that is.

Esguerra's enormous estate is in the southeast part of Colombia, right on the edge of the Amazon rainforest. It's night when we land on the small airstrip inside the compound, and the humid air is warm and completely still as we step off the plane.

I recognize the driver of the car waiting for us. He was one of the guards here when I was in Esguerra's employ.

"Hey, Diego," I greet him, and he grins, white teeth flashing.

"Sokolov. Never thought I'd see you again, man." His Spanish accent is not as thick as I remember, but still quite noticeable. "What have you been up to?" Then he notices the blond man at my side. "Hey, Lucas. Where's Yu—"

"Just drive," Kent snaps, getting into the car, and I follow suit.

Looks like we're dispensing with the niceties. Oh, well.

Instead of bringing me to the mansion where Esguerra and his wife reside, Diego takes us to a shed on the outer edge of the compound. I recognize the place—it's where I once helped Esguerra interrogate his enemies—and despite myself, a chill roughens my skin.

There's nothing to prevent the Colombian arms dealer from stringing me up and trying to torture the name of the traitor out of me.

Nothing but the fact that Esguerra knows me—and hopefully realizes I won't be easy to crack.

He steps out of the shed as Kent and I get out of the car, and as the headlights of the car illuminate his face, I see that he still has his movie-star looks, even with the artificial eye that replaced the one gouged out by his enemies. I haven't seen him since that time—I knew he'd be pissed over the method of his rescue, so I left before he could have me killed—but he's the same as I remember.

Still dangerous as fuck and lacking all empathy... except when it comes to his wife.

And now possibly his infant daughter.

"You've got balls," he says softly, stopping in front of me. His English is of the American variety, without a trace of a Spanish accent. His mother was American, I recall—a model of some kind.

"I wanted to talk to you in a secure location," I say, meeting his piercing blue gaze without flinching. I'm not afraid, though I probably should be. Julian Esguerra is one of the cruelest men I know, a true sadist. I've seen him skin men alive and take great pleasure in it, and I've often wondered how his young wife handles that aspect of her husband's nature.

He loves her, but I doubt he spares her.

"Why?" he asks in that same lethally soft tone. "Why would you want to come here, of all places?"

"Because I want to make a deal with you," I say calmly as Kent walks over to stand next to Esguerra. "And I'm certain Novak doesn't have eyes and ears here." As I say this, I'm cognizant of Diego sitting in the car with the motor still running—likely to produce enough noise to drown out our conversation.

It looks like Kent is the only person my former employer fully trusts.

"You think Novak doesn't know you approached Lucas?" Esguerra says, his mouth twisting derisively. "That he wasn't notified the moment my plane took off with you on it?"

"Oh, he was." I smile coldly. "In fact, he knew about my plan all along."

Neither Kent nor Esguerra blink, but I can sense their surprise. "He knew you were going to double-cross him?" Kent asks, frowning.

"Yes. I told him that as soon as he disclosed the name of the asset."

Esguerra's jaw flexes. "You told him you were going to betray him?"

"Not exactly. I told him I was going to pretend to betray him in order to gain access to your compound. He knows about the deal I told Kent I want to make: peace with you and a hundred million for the name of Novak's asset."

Kent's frown deepens, but Esguerra tilts his head, regarding me thoughtfully. "The deal you told Kent you want to make," he says slowly. "Which, I presume, is not the actual deal you're after."

"Correct." I become aware of painful tension in my neck and shoulders and consciously relax those muscles. "Or at least, it's not the full deal."

Esguerra folds his arms over his chest. "What is the full deal, then?"

"I will give you Novak's asset inside your compound… and I'll deliver to you Novak himself, so you'll never have to worry about him again."

Esguerra's eyes narrow. "In exchange for what?"

"The peace and the hundred million I already mentioned—and just one other thing."

"What thing?" Kent asks, not bothering to hide his curiosity.

"Amnesty," I say, looking from the Colombian arms dealer to his partner and back. "I want global amnesty for all crimes of which I'm being accused, as well as immunity from further prosecution. I want to be taken off all the wanted lists—and I want you to make it happen."

CHAPTER 32

SARA

I dream of him again that night. He comes to me like a phantom, shrouding me in his darkness, holding me tight as I weep and struggle to free myself. I don't know if I'm fighting him or my own craving, but either way, before long, I lose.

I meld into him, let his darkness surround me, chasing away all loneliness and light.

He takes me then, driving into me with punishing fury, and I embrace him, screaming his name as my body convulses with torrid pleasure, with bliss so agonizing and exquisite it threatens to tear me apart. We make love over and over again, until I'm drained and sore.

Until I have nothing more to give and he leaves.

Leaves because he no longer wants me.

Because he's bored with me.

I wake up with my pillow drenched with tears and my sex slick and throbbing with need. I know the dream was just a manifestation of my fears, that none of it was real, but I still feel shattered, destroyed by Peter's rejection.

By the return of the terrible loneliness that's my companion at night.

Getting up, I find my handbag and fish out the note Peter left for me. It's getting worn around the edges, so I smooth it out as I open it and read the words, repeating them to myself over and over again.

Remember, ptichka. For as long as we're both alive.

I bring the note with me and put it under my pillow before going back to sleep.

Peter is coming. I have to believe that.

One way or another, he'll be back for me.

CHAPTER 33
PETER

Esguerra stares at me, as if unable to believe his ears, then lets out a sharp bark of laughter. "Amnesty and immunity? For you?"

Kent remains silent at his side, but I see the comprehension in his gaze.

He knows what this is about.

He and Yulia have seen me with Sara.

"Actually, for me and my guys," I tell Esguerra. "They're not as popular with the law enforcement, but they're still on their shit lists. You get your CIA friends to get us off those lists, and you can forget about Novak for good."

"Really?" he says, still chuckling. "Assuming I could even perform this miracle for you, since when do you give a fuck about being hunted?"

Kent could answer that, but to my relief, he keeps his mouth shut as I say, "That's none of your business. This is the deal I'm offering. Take it or leave it."

All traces of humor disappear from Esguerra's face. "Fuck that. You're going to tell me who the traitor is, and you're going to do it now."

It's my turn to laugh. "And in return, you'll grant me a quick, merciful death?"

Esguerra's smile is razor sharp. "That's the best deal you're going to get. You know I'm going to get that name from you one way or another."

"I know you're going to try—and eventually, you might even succeed. But it will cost you."

His eyes narrow. "How so?"

"Long before you get that name out of me," I say softly, "my team will activate the asset. Maybe they'll succeed in the assignment without me, or maybe they won't, but that's a risk you'll be taking. How old is Lizzie now? Eight, ten days? Maybe you're not that attached to her yet, but Novak has plans for Nora, too. Big plans—"

Esguerra is on me before I finish speaking, his perfect features twisted in a feral mask of fury. He often trains with his guards, so he's fast and lethal, but I was expecting the attack. At the last instant, I twist, and his fist grazes my cheekbone instead of crushing my nose. However, there's no way to avoid his other fist, and the blow reverberates through my solar plexus, knocking the air out of my lungs.

If I hadn't trained for this, I'd be bent over, wheezing. However, I know how to push through the pain. Instead of fighting for air as my body demands, I shut out all awareness of the discomfort and go on attack, coming back at him with my own series of blows.

We're evenly matched in size and strength, and he's good at this—maybe as good as my guys. But I have the cooler head in this fight. Each of my strikes is calculated to disable and deflect, whereas he's acting on instinct, letting his rage guide him.

I evade most of his blows, but the few that land hurt like hell. Ignoring the pain, I pummel him back, and after a minute, I manage to knock him off his feet. The fucker doesn't give up, though. Instead of trying to get up, he catches my foot and yanks on it, dropping me on top of him.

At the last second, I twist, so my elbow lands on his ribcage. My arm explodes with pain, but he grunts, so I must've cracked a rib. In the next moment, however, something shiny flashes in my peripheral vision, and I react on instinct, grabbing his wrist to catch the blade coming at me. He uses the moment of distraction to land a blow to the side of my face, but I keep my focus on the knife and twist the wrist, determined to—

"That's enough." Strong hands grab me from behind, pulling me off Esguerra before I can break his wrist. My instinct is to lash out at the new attacker, but I retain enough presence of mind not to struggle.

Killing either Kent or Esguerra would be counterproductive to my goal.

Esguerra is on his feet before Kent releases me, but he doesn't attack again. Instead, he wipes the blood trickling from his nose and says in a guttural voice, "What fucking plans?"

Of course. He wants to know the specifics of the threat to Nora.

"Novak wants to use her to control all your assets," I say as Kent lets me go and comes around to stand next to Esguerra. My face and elbow are throbbing like a son of a bitch, and my mouth tastes like copper, but I ignore it.

Given the knife Esguerra pulled from fucking nowhere, it could've been much worse.

"How?" Esguerra demands, and I'm pleased to see that one side of his face is already swelling up. "How the fuck does he think he'll accomplish that?"

"By marrying her. How else?" I spit out the blood pooling under my tongue. "He waited until your daughter was born, so he'd have failsafe leverage over Nora. He wants them both, you see—your wife for his own, and your daughter as a tool to control your wife. Who at that point would be *his* wife, but you get the picture."

For a moment, I'm convinced Esguerra will fly at me again, but he restrains himself this time. Barely. Not that I can blame him.

If someone tried to take Sara from me, I'd chop his balls into little pieces and feed them to the local wildlife.

I strongly suspect Esguerra is tempted to do just that with me, so I say, "I can get Novak for you, and I can do it quickly. I know you're capable of dealing with him on your own, but it will take time for you to track him down and get through his defenses—just like it will take time for you to get the name of his asset from me... assuming you'd even succeed in that. In the meantime, your wife and daughter are in danger. If my team fails, Novak will find someone else to come after you, some other way to get through to Nora and the baby. I've met the guy—he's not going to stop. He wants what you have—everything you have, Nora included—and he'll keep coming until you kill him. Or until I do it for you—something that can happen as soon as the end of this week."

Esguerra is all but vibrating with rage, but he must see the wisdom in what I'm saying because he remains in place, hands flexing convulsively at his sides. I can sense the war going on inside him, but finally, he says harshly, "Fifty million. And I want Novak brought to me alive."

My pulse leaps, but I keep my tone even. "Seventy-five. It's the best I can do."

Actually, I'd accept zero—Sara's happiness is worth everything to me—but at least this way, I can compensate my teammates for the upcoming dissolution of our business.

Once I'm no longer a fugitive, we won't be carrying out hits.

"Deal," Esguerra says between clenched teeth. "Seventy-five million, and I do my best to get you and your men immunity in exchange for both Novak and the traitor."

"You get us immunity," I correct. "No immunity, no deal."

"You've been on a fucking global murder spree for years. I can't guarantee any—"

"Yes, you can. Our crimes are no worse than what you and Kent"—I nod toward the blond man silently observing the proceedings—"do every day, and no one touches you.

Make it happen, Julian. Call in whatever favors you need to, and I will give you Novak on a silver platter."

Esguerra stares at me, fingers still twitching. "All right," he says after a moment, his tone noticeably calmer. "You've got yourself a deal. Now tell me who the traitor is."

I assess his expression and make a split-second decision. "Bring me to Nora, and I will."

Esguerra's face hardens, and Kent noticeably tenses—likely getting ready to restrain him.

"Why?" Esguerra grits out. "What the fuck does she have to do with it?"

"Nothing... except she might like to know," I say evenly. "And once she knows, I think she'll have a problem with you killing me despite the deal we just made."

His nostrils flare. "You calling me a liar?"

I shrug. "You'd do anything to protect your family, as I would mine. In any case, I haven't forgotten that it was your wife who came through with my list, not you. Take me to see Nora, and I'll tell you both what I know. On that, you have my word."

And I wait, muscles coiled for combat, as Esguerra makes his decision.

CHAPTER 34
PETER

I'm frisked from head to toe five more times, twice by Kent and Diego, and once by Esguerra himself. On the third search, they find the razor blade and the string, so I'm left truly weaponless—if one ignores my body and its capabilities, that is.

The ride to Esguerra's mansion passes in explosive silence, and I know it would take the tiniest spark to set off my host. He's as edgy as I've ever seen him, the violence inside him on the verge of boiling over.

A contingent of twenty-some guards meets us at the white, colonial-style mansion and follows us into the tastefully decorated living room. Esguerra leaves me and Kent with them and disappears upstairs—presumably to wake his newly post-partum wife.

With a traitor on the loose, he couldn't wait until morning.

For a couple of minutes, all I hear are the guards breathing and shifting from foot to foot. Then a baby's cry pierces the silence, the sound strong and sweet and so familiar my heart clenches in my chest.

Pasha used to wail like that when he was an infant. It was his hungry cry—a demand for food that was always met within minutes.

The grief that hits me is as sharp as in the beginning, during those dark days when rage was the only thing that kept me going. For a second, I can't breathe from the pain of it, from the agony so acute it feels like a blade through my spine.

My son. My little boy who never got the chance to grow, to go from toy cars to the real thing.

If I had any qualms about what I'm doing, they evaporate in this moment. I'm double-crossing a client, but it's worth it. Even without the deal I made with Esguerra, I'd never hurt that helpless baby.

Not with Pasha's face fresh in my mind.

It takes a couple of minutes before the crying stops and nearly a half hour before Esguerra returns, his arm wrapped around a petite, dark-haired girl dressed in a thick terrycloth robe that covers her from head to toe.

Esguerra's very own obsession.

Nora, his wife.

Her small face lights up when she sees me. Unlike her husband, she bears me no ill will for the rescue that endangered her—nor should she, as it was her idea.

"Peter!" She makes as though to come forward to greet me, only to be restrained by her husband's possessive grip.

Sheepishly, she stops and smiles instead. "How have you been?"

"Fine, thank you." Despite the guards all around us and my face feeling like a giant bruise from Esguerra's pummeling, I can't help smiling back. It's hard to believe someone this young and delicate-looking could be a mother—or survive someone as ruthless as Esguerra. "Congratulations on the recent addition to your family."

Her smile widens. "Thank you. I'd introduce you, but you know…" She glances up at her husband, whose thunderous expression grew even more forbidding during our exchange.

Sure enough, he's reached the end of his patience. Tucking his small wife tighter against his side, he asks with lethal softness, "Are you going to tell me who it is or not?"

This is it. Time for me to give up my trump card. Despite Nora's presence and the deal we made, he might still order me killed as soon as he learns the name.

Oh, well. No risk, no reward.

Meeting Esguerra's icy gaze, I say calmly, "I don't know her name, but it's your pediatrician. She is Novak's asset."

CHAPTER 35
SARA

"You know, Joe's been asking about you," Mom says, smearing the honey I brought from the farmer's market on her toast. "You haven't heard from him recently, have you?"

"Mom, please." I fight the urge to roll my eyes like an overgrown teenager. For whatever reason, our Saturday morning breakfast is when this topic inevitably comes up. "He's just being nice, that's all. There's nothing between us, I promise."

"But why not, darling?" Lines of concern crease Mom's forehead as Dad sighs into his coffee. "You've been back for almost nine months, and you have yet to go on a single date with anyone. You don't owe that criminal anything. You know that, right? Clearly, whatever you two had is over, and you have to move on. He won't be back."

He will, judging by that note, but I can't tell my parents about that. Despite my best efforts to convince them that I was with my abductor voluntarily and the whole FBI manhunt was a big misunderstanding, Peter will always be "that criminal" to them. I don't know if it's because they somehow caught wind of my official story to the FBI, or they just have a normal law-abiding citizens' distrust of anyone on the outs with the authorities, but they're convinced that Peter is evil and whatever feelings I had for him were of the Stockholm Syndrome variety.

Not that they're all that wrong—at least, they wouldn't have been wrong nine months ago. My attraction to Peter *was* unnatural and toxic, and I fought against it with everything I had. I fought up until the very end, when I nearly lost my life in that crash.

No. That's not entirely true.

It was up until he put my needs above his own and let me go. That was the true turning point for me, though it's only recently that I've let myself think about that... about the fact that I've somehow managed to accept the feelings I've developed for my husband's killer, that when I think about him now, he's "Peter" in my mind.

The man who loves me, not the man who murdered George.

My parents don't know about that last part—at least I hope they don't—but they still hate Peter for keeping me away from them for so long. They think he's as dangerous as the FBI say, and it makes me sick to think how upset they'll be when Peter steals me away again.

Still, I can't stop myself from wanting it.

From wanting him and everything he is.

"I'm just not ready, Mom," I tell her and get up to pour myself more coffee. "Please understand. I'm still in love with Peter, and when it's all resolved, he *will* be back. You'll see."

And with that, I change the topic, launching into a story about my latest performance with my band.

It's better than continuing to lie. Nothing will ever be resolved because there is no misunderstanding.

Peter *is* a criminal, and when he returns, it will be to take me with him.

To take me away for good.

CHAPTER 36
PETER

I spend the night in the shed where Esguerra keeps his prisoners, with one ankle chained to the metal ring in the middle of the floor.

"Just a precaution," Kent explained when the guards locked the chain in place. "Not that we don't trust you…"

"Right." The chain is about two meters long, which means I can lie down on the cot the guards dragged into the shed. So all in all, it's not that bad. I'd obviously rather not be chained, but considering what I just saw Esguerra do to the pediatrician, I'm not complaining.

It'll take a while to get the woman's screams out of my mind.

She cracked instantly, pretty much as soon as the Esguerras, accompanied by me and the guards, entered her room. I don't know what she expected—to win brownie points for her honesty?—but she admitted her guilt right away, profusely apologizing to both Esguerra and his wife, swearing that she meant no real harm, that she didn't really know them or Lizzie when she took the bribe.

It's like she thought that once she confessed, all would be forgiven and forgotten, that being fired without a reference was the worst that could happen to her.

Maybe because I watched Esguerra literally fillet the idiot when Nora left to feed the baby, or maybe because I'm so close to my goal, but my sleep is again restless, filled with nightmares. Twice, I dream of finding my son's body in a pile of corpses, and at least twice more, that body turns out to be Sara's.

Still, by morning, I'm bleary-eyed but cautiously optimistic. The fact that I'm still alive is encouraging—a sign that Esguerra might stick to his side of the bargain. There are no guarantees, of course, but I suspect Nora has a fair amount of sway with her husband these days—plus, he owes me for the pediatrician.

In any case, I'm not surprised when Esguerra and Kent show up together to unchain me.

"What's your plan?" Esguerra asks as Kent unlocks the manacle around my ankle. "How are you going to get to him? You realize that the moment you show up without Nora and the baby in tow, he'll know you double-crossed him. That, or you failed—either way, he won't be pleased."

I take a deep breath. Here comes another tricky part. "Yes. I've considered that. And that's why I need to borrow your wife for this part of the operation. She'll be in no—"

"Absolutely not." Esguerra's jaw muscles twitch. "Nora is not stepping a foot off this compound."

Disappointing but not unexpected. "Okay, then do you think you can find somebody who looks like Nora? At least a little bit?"

Esguerra frowns, and I sense he's about to say no when Kent says, "There's no one on the estate, but I can have the guards scour the nearby settlements for a potential candidate. It shouldn't be that hard to find a dark-haired girl about Nora's size. Her coloring is not exactly unusual in these parts."

That's true. If we needed a body double for Kent's blond, blue-eyed wife, we'd be in trouble, but Nora is part Mexican, with dark eyes and a tan complexion. "You might want to look for someone really young," I suggest. "Maybe a schoolgirl of some kind, to match Nora's build. Like I started to tell you, she won't be in any danger—I just need Novak to find out that I got off the plane with a woman resembling Nora and her infant in tow. A doll will do for the latter; the girl will just need to keep it wrapped up tight."

Kent looks at Esguerra, and he nods. "Do it. And if possible, find an infant as well—we don't want this to fall apart over a doll."

I open my mouth to refuse, but then I decide against it.

I didn't lie about the lack of danger to "Nora," so we might as well use an actual child.

Whatever it takes to bait the trap and end Novak for good.

Eight hours later, I leave the compound on foot, armed with an M16 that I "stole" from a guard, and with a terrified sixteen-year-old and her two-month-old sister in tow. The girls' family will be well compensated for their acting gig, but the prospect of pretty clothes and tuition money for college is not enough to keep the sixteen-year-old calm.

She's scared out of her mind, and that's perfect.

The real Nora would be as well.

Kent's guards found a teenager who resembles Mrs. Esguerra to an uncanny degree—at least from the back and side. From the front, the girl's face is rounder, with a thicker nose and smaller, deep-set eyes, so we used makeup to disguise those features.

Thanks to skillfully applied eyeshadow, blush, lipstick, and dark-toned foundation, Nora's doppelgänger now sports two black eyes, a split lip, and several yellowish bruises that disguise the childish fullness of her cheeks.

She speaks a little bit of English too, but her accent is thick, so we told her not to talk under any circumstances. "You can either cry or be silent," Esguerra instructed her, and the girl nodded, chin quivering.

"Sí, señor. I be silent."

So far, she's kept her word. We've been trudging through the jungle for over two hours, with her holding her screaming baby sister the entire time, and she hasn't uttered a single complaint—though there's much to complain about.

It hasn't rained today yet, and the humid heat is stifling, the air so thick it feels like a wet blanket on the skin. We had the girl put on one of Nora's usual outfits—a casual white sundress and a pair of flat sandals—and I can see the painful welts on her feet where she stepped into an ant pile a couple of miles back. We're both dripping with sweat, and tiny gnats buzz all around us, biting every centimeter of exposed flesh.

This is sheer misery, and that's a good thing.

It looks more authentic that way.

After another torturous hour, we meet up with my guys at the designated rendezvous point. I can see the shock on their faces as I push the girl forward, with the crying infant clutched tightly against her chest.

"You made it out." Yan's disbelieving gaze swings from me to my hostage and back. "You actually fucking did it."

"Yep. Wasn't easy, but here we are."

My Nora substitute remains silent, giving a good imitation of a traumatized, terrified captive. Her waterproof makeup smeared a little during our journey, but she still looks believably bruised and beaten, her dark gaze dulled by dehydration and exhaustion. None of my guys have seen the real Mrs. Esguerra, only pictures of her, so they have no reason to doubt her authenticity.

The "bruises" are doing their job.

The baby keeps crying, and I make a mental note to give her the bottle of formula I had my guys purchase for the plane, just in case "Nora" had trouble breastfeeding. We got diapers on the plane, too, along with other baby paraphernalia.

"Is he dead?" Anton asks in Russian, and I nod, glancing at the girl as though concerned about her reaction.

"Yeah, I got the bastard. She might not know that yet, though, so keep it on the down low. She fought like a witch for that baby as is."

Ilya looks disgusted but doesn't say anything as we head for the plane. He doesn't like what I'm doing, and I can't blame him. Stealing a newborn and her newly post-partum mother feels wrong, even to remorseless killers like us. And that's exactly what I'm counting on. The subtle disapproval emanating from my men will give this operation the authentic edge it needs.

I want Novak to feel the discord among us.

I want him to sense the reluctance of my guys to hand over a traumatized young woman and her baby into his cruel, greedy grasp.

CHAPTER 37
PETER

I give the formula to the girl as soon as we're on the plane, and she feeds her baby sister, shooting frightened looks at us the entire time. She's overdoing it a bit—the real Mrs. Esguerra wouldn't let her fear show—but since my guys don't know Nora and everything she's been through, it works.

"How did you do it?" Yan asks quietly when the baby finally falls asleep and the girl has calmed down enough to look out the window instead of at the couch where I'm sitting with the twins. "How did you get Esguerra?"

"I shot him." My reply is curt and matter-of-fact, but I'm not going to make up an elaborate story for this. "Blew his head off."

"Did you get the proof?" Ilya asks, frowning. "Because Novak will need—"

"Here." I pull out a phone that I also "stole" from a guard and show a picture of a dark-haired man lying sprawled on the ground in a pool of blood. Half of his skull appears to be missing, but the other half is unmistakably Esguerra.

It took an hour to get a shot that good; for all his male-model looks, my former employer sucks at posing.

Yan looks at me, then at the picture and back at me. I stare back at him stonily. Can he tell that the "blood" is ketchup mixed with a lot of dirt, or that the missing half of the skull is Nora's skilled Photoshopping? I know the picture is fake, so it's hard for me to be objective.

To my relief, Yan hands the phone back to me without saying anything, and Ilya turns away, focusing on transferring the bribe to the Serbian air controller's private bank account in Switzerland. It's how we get in and out of that country—and many others, US included.

It's tempting to talk to my guys and tell them the real plan, but I refrain. I can't take the risk that they might balk at the last minute. We've built a lucrative business on the strength of our reputation, and what I'm about to do—double-cross a paying client—more or less ensures there will be no further job offers.

We've talked about retiring one day, but I don't know if they're ready for that day to be now.

In any case, if all goes well, my team won't suffer financially. In addition to Novak's hundred million—half of which is already in our bank accounts—we'll have the seventy-five-million payment from Esguerra. Even if we don't get the other half from Novak before I nab him, we'll have enough for the rest of our lives.

All we need is to get through this.

A few more days, and I'll have Sara.

I can't fucking wait.

Ilya and I meet Novak in his warehouse just outside Belgrade—as per his request. As usual, he arrives with a full contingent of mercenaries and enough firepower to level a small building.

"Where are they?" he demands as soon as he sees us standing there. "You said you had them. Where are they?"

"Safe and secure with my team," I say and pull out the guard's phone to show him the photos we took an hour ago. They're of the surrogate Nora and her infant, surrounded by my men and looking all bruised and fragile.

He snatches the phone from me and studies them with undisguised lust before looking up at me. "Is Esguerra—"

"Here." I take the phone from him and flip through the "Nora" photos to the one of Esguerra in a puddle of ketchup. "Head blown off."

Novak's pale eyes glint. "Good job. I knew I could count on you. Now take me to Nora and the child."

I cross my arms over my chest. "Payment first."

That fifty million might not be necessary, strictly speaking, but it would definitely be nice to have.

Novak's mouth thins, but he picks up his phone and calls his accountant. "Make the transfer," he orders in Serbian, and I wait until he nods at me, then check the account on my phone.

"All good," I tell him and glance over at Ilya, whose lack of expression still somehow manages to convey disapproval.

Novak must notice it too, because he smiles again. He likes the idea of us being on the outs; he thinks it makes us vulnerable, easier to control.

"Let's go," I tell him, pretending to be oblivious to all the undercurrents. "I'll take you to Nora and the baby."

Ilya and I head briskly toward the exit, and Novak hurries to catch up to us. His guards rush to form their usual protective circle, but the three of us step outside first.

It's just for a couple of seconds, but that's all the time I need.

Grabbing Novak by the arm, I yell, "Duck!" and dive behind a dumpster, shoving Ilya in front of me.

We hit the pavement hard, skidding on our stomachs as Esguerra's men open fire, riddling the warehouse and all of Novak's guards with hundreds of machine gun rounds.

CHAPTER 38
PETER

I give the formula to the girl as soon as we're on the plane, and she feeds her baby sister, shooting frightened looks at us the entire time. She's overdoing it a bit—the real Mrs. Esguerra wouldn't let her fear show—but since my guys don't know Nora and everything she's been through, it works.

"How did you do it?" Yan asks quietly when the baby finally falls asleep and the girl has calmed down enough to look out the window instead of at the couch where I'm sitting with the twins. "How did you get Esguerra?"

"I shot him." My reply is curt and matter-of-fact, but I'm not going to make up an elaborate story for this. "Blew his head off."

"Did you get the proof?" Ilya asks, frowning. "Because Novak will need—"

"Here." I pull out a phone that I also "stole" from a guard and show a picture of a dark-haired man lying sprawled on the ground in a pool of blood. Half of his skull appears to be missing, but the other half is unmistakably Esguerra.

It took an hour to get a shot that good; for all his male-model looks, my former employer sucks at posing.

Yan looks at me, then at the picture and back at me. I stare back at him stonily. Can he tell that the "blood" is ketchup mixed with a lot of dirt, or that the missing half of the skull is Nora's skilled Photoshopping? I know the picture is fake, so it's hard for me to be objective.

To my relief, Yan hands the phone back to me without saying anything, and Ilya turns away, focusing on transferring the bribe to the Serbian air controller's private bank account in Switzerland. It's how we get in and out of that country—and many others, US included.

It's tempting to talk to my guys and tell them the real plan, but I refrain. I can't take the risk that they might balk at the last minute. We've built a lucrative business on the strength of our reputation, and what I'm about to do—double-cross a paying client—more or less ensures there will be no further job offers.

We've talked about retiring one day, but I don't know if they're ready for that day to be now.

In any case, if all goes well, my team won't suffer financially. In addition to Novak's hundred million—half of which is already in our bank accounts—we'll have the seventy-five-million payment from Esguerra. Even if we don't get the other half from Novak before I nab him, we'll have enough for the rest of our lives.

All we need is to get through this.

A few more days, and I'll have Sara.

I can't fucking wait.

Ilya and I meet Novak in his warehouse just outside Belgrade—as per his request. As usual, he arrives with a full contingent of mercenaries and enough firepower to level a small building.

"Where are they?" he demands as soon as he sees us standing there. "You said you had them. Where are they?"

"Safe and secure with my team," I say and pull out the guard's phone to show him the photos we took an hour ago. They're of the surrogate Nora and her infant, surrounded by my men and looking all bruised and fragile.

He snatches the phone from me and studies them with undisguised lust before looking up at me. "Is Esguerra—"

"Here." I take the phone from him and flip through the "Nora" photos to the one of Esguerra in a puddle of ketchup. "Head blown off."

Novak's pale eyes glint. "Good job. I knew I could count on you. Now take me to Nora and the child."

I cross my arms over my chest. "Payment first."

That fifty million might not be necessary, strictly speaking, but it would definitely be nice to have.

Novak's mouth thins, but he picks up his phone and calls his accountant. "Make the transfer," he orders in Serbian, and I wait until he nods at me, then check the account on my phone.

"All good," I tell him and glance over at Ilya, whose lack of expression still somehow manages to convey disapproval.

Novak must notice it too, because he smiles again. He likes the idea of us being on the outs; he thinks it makes us vulnerable, easier to control.

"Let's go," I tell him, pretending to be oblivious to all the undercurrents. "I'll take you to Nora and the baby."

Ilya and I head briskly toward the exit, and Novak hurries to catch up to us. His guards rush to form their usual protective circle, but the three of us step outside first.

It's just for a couple of seconds, but that's all the time I need.

Grabbing Novak by the arm, I yell, "Duck!" and dive behind a dumpster, shoving Ilya in front of me.

We hit the pavement hard, skidding on our stomachs as Esguerra's men open fire, riddling the warehouse and all of Novak's guards with hundreds of machine gun rounds.

CHAPTER 39
PETER

Esguerra wants me back at his compound, so after I catch up with my men, I board his Boeing C-17 and accompany Novak and the guards to Colombia. Ilya, Yan, and Anton go separately in our plane. I still don't completely trust my former employer, so my teammates agreed to provide support in case things go south last minute. I don't expect a double-cross from Esguerra at this point—for one thing, the seventy-five million is already in our accounts—but it doesn't hurt to be cautious.

I also got my team to agree to continue assisting me in the search for Henderson. As the last name on my list, he's unfinished business, and I have every intention of dealing with him in due time.

First, though, I need to get Sara.

She's more important than anything.

Esguerra himself greets us when we land, his face set in hard, savage lines as he watches the guards drag Novak off the plane. The Serbian is barely walking—they didn't bother feeding him or treating his injuries on the flight—but it doesn't matter. He's not long for this earth.

Esguerra won't just kill him—he'll take him apart.

Slowly.

Piece by piece.

I'd feel bad for the bastard, but he brought this on himself. If he'd confined himself to making inroads into Esguerra's business, he'd have lived much longer—at least another year or two. But he went after Esguerra's family... after Nora and her child.

There's no love lost between me and Esguerra, but I do like Nora.

"Where's Kent?" I ask when Esguerra comes up to me after ordering the guards to take Novak to the shed. "Did he go back to Cyprus?"

He nods. "He left right after you did." He doesn't elaborate, and I decide against prying further. I still haven't forgiven Kent for what happened with Sara, but at the moment, I have bigger fish to fry.

"Did you reach out to them?" I fall into step beside Esguerra as we head toward a waiting limo. "Your CIA contacts?"

He casts me a sideways glance. "I did."

"And?" I step in front of him, forcing him to stop. "Did they agree?"

His jaw flexes. "Let's talk about it in the car."

Shit. That doesn't sound good. "Let's talk about it now."

His eyes glint dangerously. "Fine. Here's the deal—the only deal they'll make. You and your team will get amnesty for your crimes and immunity from further prosecution, provided no further crimes are committed. Whoever slips up will be arrested and prosecuted for *all* crimes, past and present."

I consider that and nod. "Sounds fair." I'm almost certain I can live as a law-abiding citizen—or at least give the appearance of one. We'll need to be careful not to get caught when we finally locate Henderson, but I'm sure I'm not the only enemy the former general has. Alternatively, we can make it look like an accident; there are all sorts of ways to carry out a hit without it looking like—

"And there's one more thing," Esguerra says. "One other condition that's nonnegotiable."

"What?" I ask, my stomach tightening with a premonition as my hands curl at my sides. This better not be what—

"That retired general, the one you've been hunting," Esguerra says, confirming my hunch. "You have to let it go. For good. Your immunity is contingent upon his continued health and well-being. If he or anyone close to him so much as gets food poisoning, the deal is off, and all four of you will be on the Most Wanted lists again."

Fuck. Fuck, fuck, fuck!

I suppose I should've known this was a possibility, given Henderson's connections, but I somehow blocked it from my mind. I was so focused on eliminating the main obstacle to a life with Sara—my fugitive status—I didn't even consider that it might come at a price.

Well, a price aside from the end of my business and the risk I took by approaching Esguerra. Those costs I knew and was prepared to pay. But this? Out of everyone on my list, Henderson is the one most directly responsible for the tragedy that befell my wife and son. He's the one who gave the orders that resulted in the village massacre.

If anyone deserves to pay for Tamila and Pasha's deaths, it's Henderson.

He can't be allowed to go back to living his normal, happy life after what he's done.

"I can't take that deal." My voice is harsh and guttural. "You know I can't."

For the first time, some semblance of human emotion warms the blue ice of Esguerra's gaze. "I know," he says quietly. "I figured as much. But they won't budge on it, Peter. I tried."

I pivot on my heel and stride toward the limo, the rage and grief I thought I'd buried bubbling up like magma in my throat. I breathe in, trying to calm myself, but instead of tropical vegetation, I smell death and ashes, charred flesh and stale blood. I taste metal on my tongue and see a pile of corpses, of body parts two meters high.

And that little hand, curled around a toy car.

I barely remember the first few days after the massacre. I know I got away from the task force soldiers who dragged me out of the village, but I don't recall how or when—or if I hurt anyone as I escaped. I assume I did, because my own people started hunting me soon after, even before I killed my superiors for ending the investigation within weeks.

Vengeance was all that kept me going in those days—and in the months and years that followed. I promised my dead son and wife that their killers would pay with their lives, and I kept that promise.

I got them all except Henderson.

"You could just take her again," Esguerra says, catching up to me, and I glance at him, unsurprised that he now knows about Sara. Kent must've told him about her—that or he heard about the kidnapping from his CIA sources. And once he knew that, it was a simple matter of putting two and two together.

Despite that, my first instinct is to threaten him and all he holds dear if he so much as breathes her way. But if he knows Sara is my weakness, then he must know what I'd do if someone came after her.

It's the same thing he'd do if someone went after Nora.

What he's about to do to Novak, in fact.

"She has a life there," I reply instead. "Parents, career, friends."

He shrugs. "She'd adjust. Nora did."

I get in the back of the limo and he joins me there, taking a seat across from me.

"Sara is not Nora," I say as the limo starts moving. "Her roots go too deep. She won't be happy like this." I don't know if I'm trying to convince Esguerra or myself—or that dark, callous part of me that has been wanting this for months.

That has been telling me to forget this mad plan and take back what belongs to me.

"And you will be?" Esguerra tilts his head, regarding me with peculiar curiosity. "You think you'll enjoy that half-life? Thrive in the cage of all those rules and laws?"

I shrug. "Maybe." It's not a concern of mine, but if it ever becomes a problem, I'll deal with it then.

One thing at a time.

"So what then?" Esguerra asks when I remain silent. "Are you going to let her go for good? Or take the deal?"

"I'm not letting her go." The words are instinctive, automatic. Life without Sara—that's not even a possibility in my mind. The past eight months have been hell, almost as bad in their own way as the dark weeks after my family's deaths.

I'd sooner die than let my ptichka go for good.

She's mine, and she's staying mine.

A mocking smile curves Esguerra's mouth. "Well, then," he says softly. "Seems like you don't have much of a choice."

It chokes me to admit it, but he's right.

I either take Sara, or I accept the deal. Her happiness or my vengeance.

I can't have both.

PART IV

CHAPTER 40
SARA

I first sense that something is off when I drive home alone after my evening shift at the clinic.

No government-issue car follows me home, and no one surreptitiously watches me as I park my car in front of my apartment building and walk in.

Telling myself I'm being crazy—that I'm just tired and not properly registering things—I shower and fall into bed. There's no point in worrying about this. Even if I'm not having some weird reverse paranoia, maybe the Feds had to take the night off—babysit their kids or something. It hasn't happened since my return, but that doesn't mean it's impossible.

FBI agents are human too.

Still, I toss and turn, unable to fall asleep despite my total exhaustion. I try to think back to whether I felt watched at all today, but I can't recall. Either my invisible stalkers have become even better at their job, or I've gotten so used to their presence I no longer notice it.

The last time I truly experienced that itchy feeling was when I got Peter's note a couple of months back.

Could it be?

Am I no longer being watched at all?

My stomach pitches precipitously. Given Peter's note, there's only one reason why I would suddenly cease to be of interest to both the Feds and Peter's hires.

No. I slam the door on that terrifying thought.

Peter is not dead or captured.

He can't be.

I close my eyes and force myself to take slow, deep breaths. One night doesn't make a pattern, and there's every chance that when I wake up in the morning to go to work—at this point, less than five hours from now—the Feds will be circling my block in their gray sedan.

I just have to believe it.

But the Feds aren't there when I drive to work, and as hard as I try, I can't figure out if I'm being watched by anyone at all.

I go through my day in a state of barely suppressed panic. Fortunately, all I have today are patient appointments, and since we're double-booked, I don't have much time to think. I just rush from patient to patient, performing examinations, writing birth control prescriptions, and discussing prenatal care—all the while reminding myself to keep breathing, to stay calm and ignore the fact that the Feds are gone.

That for the first time since my return, I'm on my own.

Just as I'm about to head home, Phil, our guitarist, calls to inform me about an upcoming performance, and I impulsively ask if he wants to round up the guys and go out for a drink. It's a Tuesday night and I have both a full workday and a clinic shift tomorrow, but I don't want to be alone with my thoughts.

To my relief, Phil agrees, and we meet at a bar in Uptown Chicago. Only Rory is able to join us—Simon is attending a local book signing—but after we each order a beer, we settle into the same comfortable dynamic as always, with Phil launching into his weekly tour persuasion speech.

"Don't you ever want to just chuck it all?" he says, waving his beer around. "To get something more out of life? Something invigorating and exciting?"

"Dude, you sound like an infomercial," Rory tells him, and we all laugh. I can hear the desperate edge in my laughter, but to my relief, I seem to be the only one. My bandmates are oblivious to my growing turmoil, bantering and carrying on as though the world isn't ending.

As though it's just another Tuesday night.

And for them, it is—the kind of normal, predictable Tuesday night that Phil wants to escape. The kind I haven't had in a long time, because from the moment I met Peter, nothing about my life has been either normal or predictable.

I wonder what Phil would think if he learned about that—about how my husband's killer forced me to "chuck it all" by keeping me captive in Japan. Would he find my reluctant romance with an assassin exciting? Invigorating in some twisted way?

This outing is meant to be a distraction from my anxiety-riddled thoughts, but I can't stop thinking about Peter, and I find my eyes wandering from one person to another, looking for that one guy who doesn't fit... for any clue that I'm still of interest to the Feds.

"Are you waiting for someone?" Rory asks, noticing my persistent rubbernecking.

I force myself to smile and stop looking around like an idiot. "No, sorry. Just thought I saw an old friend."

Phil immediately perks up. "Ooh, an old friend. Of the male or female variety? Because I have to say, that Marsha friend of yours is *muah!*" He dramatically kisses the tips of his fingers, and we all laugh again.

Marsha, Andy, and Tonya came to one of our performances a couple of weeks ago, and we all went out afterward. Naturally, Marsha hit it off with my bandmates, as she always does with men.

One of these days, I'd love to meet a guy who doesn't fall head over heels for her blond bombshell looks—or at least doesn't try to get into her pants right away.

"Your Tonya is not too bad either," Rory says when the laughter partially dies down. "Is she single?"

I grin. "Yep, pretty sure." I don't know the young nurse that well, but I'm almost certain she doesn't have a boyfriend—or if she does, he's fine with her partying with Marsha from dusk 'till dawn.

"Dude, you sure you don't want the redhead?" Phil says with a straight face. "Just think of how pretty your kids would be. Carrot tops galore."

"Oh, fuck off. You're just jealous I still have this." Rory fluffs up his dramatic mane, and I nearly choke on my beer as Phil instinctively touches his receding hairline before flipping Rory the bird.

"That's enough, you guys," I gasp out when I manage to stop laughing. "Andy is taken in any case, and—"

I freeze, the words dying in my throat as I notice the man coming up behind Phil.

I blink, unable to believe my eyes, but the apparition doesn't go away.

Instead, his sculpted lips curve in a magnetic smile. "Hello, Sara," he says in the deep, faintly accented voice that haunts my dreams. "Aren't you going to introduce me to your friends?"

CHAPTER 41

PETER

Sara's heart-shaped face leaches of all color. She doesn't look like she'll be able to speak any time soon, so I turn to the two men gaping at me.

"Peter Garin," I say, using my new identity, and extend my hand. "And you two are?"

I know who they are, of course, but if I'm to integrate myself into Sara's life for good, I need to act like a regular citizen, not someone who does extensive background checks on every person close to my ptichka. That also means I can't put my blade against their throats and slice deep enough that they'd never salivate over her again.

Not in the middle of the bar, at least.

The chubby one recovers first, reaching over to shake my hand. "Hi. I'm Phil Hudson."

"Nice to meet you," I say and resist the urge to crush the bones in that ridiculously soft palm.

"Rory O'Rourke." The redhead's grip is firmer, his hand nearly as callused as mine—though for vastly different reasons.

He lifts weights in the gym to win trophies, while I train to stay alive.

Trained to stay alive, I correct myself. If all goes according to plan, I won't need to do as much of that.

Sara touches my arm, drawing my attention to her. "What—" Her melodious voice cracks. "What are you doing here, Peter?"

I've deliberately avoided looking directly at her, because being this close without grabbing her and fucking her on the spot is a special kind of torture. Her touch on my arm, as light as it is, is like being shot with a Taser. My whole body is vibrating with awareness, all my senses in overdrive. She's half a meter away, and we're both fully dressed, yet I can feel her as intensely as if she were pressed against me naked.

In fact, my cock is convinced we should be naked and is doing its best to burst out of my suddenly-too-tight jeans.

I should've probably waited for her at her apartment, where we could've been alone for this meeting, but I was too impatient. After a month of bureaucratic bullshit, I finally got the all-clear from the US government, along with my new identity and citizenship papers, and I hopped on the plane right away—only to learn that instead of coming home, Sara decided to go out.

With two men who habitually drool over her, no less.

I take a deep breath and remind myself that integration is the name of the game. This is what I've been working for all these months, the reason why I agreed to let fucking Henderson live—a promise that still fills my throat with bile. It would be stupid to blow it all just because Sara is gazing up at me with those hazel doe eyes, looking so heartbreakingly beautiful that I want to wrap her in a potato sack and carry her off to my lair—after first ripping the balls off every man who so much as dares to glance her way.

"I got a chance to come home early," I tell her, and despite my best efforts, my voice is far too husky for a public venue. "In fact, I quit my job."

"You… what?" Her eyes grow huge. "How can you—"

"It's a long story, ptichka." I fight the urge to reach over and gather her against me. "Let's go home, and I'll explain."

The redhead—Rory—clears his throat. "Are you two… together?" Both he and Phil are staring at me incredulously—and more than a little enviously.

The fuckers are beyond lucky I'm law-abiding these days.

"Yes," I tell them, and something in my tone makes them blanch regardless. "We are." I turn to Sara. "Ready to go home, my love? We have a lot to discuss."

And firmly clasping her delicate hand, I lead her outside, leaving her stunned bandmates in the bar.

CHAPTER 42

SARA

I feel like I'm in a dream. Or maybe a nightmare—I can't decide. Peter and I are walking on a crowded street together... without the slightest hint of subterfuge on his part. He's somehow even bigger than I remember, his broad shoulders straining the seams of his soft-looking black T-shirt and his powerful legs flexing in the tight confines of his well-worn jeans. His dark hair is longer than before, waving slightly in the warm evening breeze, and my fingers itch to bury themselves in that soft, thick mass, to clutch fistfuls of it as he goes down on me, his skilled tongue driving me to completion.

A lightning-hot tingle zings through me at the thought, intensifying the burn under my skin. My heart is pounding so violently it might burst, and I'm no longer cold. No longer frozen inside. My body came to life from the moment he spoke, and it's been humming with need ever since... even as I drown in confusion.

"Are you kidnapping me?" My voice is thin and much too high, but I'm having trouble processing this... whatever *this* is. How can he just show up out of the blue, after more than nine months, and introduce himself to my friends like some long-lost boyfriend? Out of all the ways I imagined my second abduction, this scenario—where he'd just walk into a bar and lead me out by the hand—never even blipped on my radar. I was ready for a needle in my neck, or a hood over my head—or at least a rough wake-up in the middle of the night. Not a casual stroll down North Broadway in Uptown Chicago. How can he be out in the open like this? He used a different name at the bar, but his face is unchanged. Where are the Feds? After all the months of watching my every move, they just suddenly—

"I'm not kidnapping you. I'm taking you home." His hand tightens on mine, engulfing it with its heat... just like I feel his will wrapping around me, strong and unbending, as inescapable as a force of nature.

I shake my head in a futile attempt to clear it. "Home?" Does he mean Japan? Because if so, I need to tell him that—

"Your apartment." His metallic eyes gleam as he captures my gaze. "For now, at least, since you have all your things there. Later, we can move back to the house if you want—or get a new one closer to your work."

I feel like I'm either drunk or stoned out of my mind. Was there something in the beer I just had? "What are you talking about?"

He stops walking, and I realize we're next to my car. Releasing my hand, he frames my cheek with his big, rough palm and says tenderly, "Us, my love. I'm talking about us."

And taking my bag from me, he riffles through it, pulls out the car key, and unlocks the car.

CHAPTER 43

SARA

*P*eter is driving, and I'm glad. I don't think I could do it right now—not without crashing, at least.

I don't have that worry with Peter. He handles the car like he does everything else: with calm, lethal competence. As I watch him pull out of the parking spot, it occurs to me that I've never actually seen him behind a wheel before. Whenever we were in a vehicle together, someone else drove and Peter was in the back seat with me. Which brings me to another question: Where are Peter's teammates? Why is he here alone?

And what did he mean by "quit his job?"

My mind is racing in tune with my hammering pulse, but I gather my careening thoughts and try to focus on one thing at a time. "What do you mean by 'us?'" I ask, staring at his strongly etched profile. Or more specifically, devouring it with my gaze. I'd forgotten how strikingly masculine his features are, how beautiful in that dangerously magnetic way. His face is still as lean as when we left the clinic—whatever he was doing, it wasn't rest and relaxation—and his high cheekbones are like twin blades, his stubble-covered jaw so hard it could've been hewed from marble.

I catch a glimpse of his silver gaze and the scar on his left eyebrow as he glances at me before returning his attention to the road. "I mean I'm here for good," he says calmly. "I got full amnesty and immunity—for myself and the rest of my team."

My breath stalls in my lungs. "Amnesty and immunity? As in…"

"As in, I'm no longer a fugitive, yes."

And just like that, I'm careening off a cliff. He's no longer a wanted man? "How? What did you do? How is that even—"

"It's a long story, but I essentially did a favor for a former employer of mine—remember Julian Esguerra, Kent's partner?"

I inhale sharply. "The one who wanted to kill you for endangering his wife?"

"That's the one," Peter confirms as we merge onto the highway and pass a slow-moving truck. "In any case, in exchange for that favor, Esguerra used his leverage with various governments to get the hounds off our trail."

I stare at him, speechless. I had no idea illegal arms dealers had that kind of pull, though I guess I should've suspected. Lucas Kent even talked about some CIA contact of theirs—John, Jeff Somebody?—when we all had dinner at his Cyprus mansion.

"Wow. That must've been some favor," I finally manage, and Peter nods, looking straight ahead.

"It was." He doesn't elaborate, and I don't press him. I have more important things to cover first.

Balling my damp palms on my lap, I try to sound casual. "So, when you say you're here for good, what exactly do you mean?"

The corner of his mouth lifts slightly. "What do you think I mean, my love? You wanted a dog behind a picket fence? Barbecues and children in the park? Well, I can now give you that—or rather, Peter Garin can." He switches into the right lane and gets on the exit ramp. "That different world you wanted, that life—it's yours, ptichka... and so am I."

My heart stutters in my chest. "You want to date me? Here? Like a normal couple?"

"No, ptichka. I don't want to date you." He takes a right turn and pulls into a nearby gas station—which is when I notice the gas tank is nearly empty.

"I'll be right back," he says, turning off the car and stepping out. I watch numbly as he expertly fills up my Toyota, paying at the pump with a fancy-looking black credit card.

My Russian assassin has a credit card, and he's using it to pay for gas.

The sheer improbability of that—of Peter suddenly here, doing something so utterly mundane—adds to the sense of unreality I've been battling since we left the bar. I can't shake the feeling that I'm in some bizarre dream and will wake up at any moment, cold and alone in my bed.

But no. The driver's door opens, bringing with it a wave of humid summer air and the pungent odor of gasoline as Peter gets back into the car, folding his long frame behind the wheel.

If it's a dream, it's the most realistic I've ever had.

"What do you mean you don't want to date me?" I ask as we pull out of the gas station and turn onto a two-lane road. "What *do* you want, then?"

He stops at a red light and looks at me. "I want everything, Sara." His deep voice is low and soft, his gray eyes reflecting the streetlights around us. "I want your days and nights, your hours and minutes. I want to share your joys and sorrows, your triumphs and frustrations. I want to fall asleep with you in my arms every night and wake up every morning smelling your hair on my pillow. I want *you*, ptichka—with me for all time, in all ways."

I stare at him, my ribcage tightening with every word he speaks. "What…" I swallow to moisten my dry throat. "What are you saying, Peter?"

The light must've changed to green, because he returns his attention to the road and the car moves forward.

To my surprise, a few moments later, we stop again, and I realize he's pulled over to the side of the road. Calmly, he puts the car in "Park" and turns toward me.

I blink, my pulse speeding up as he unfastens his seatbelt and reaches into his front jeans pocket, pulling out a small velvet pouch.

"This is what I'm saying," he says quietly, and I stop breathing as he opens the pouch to take out a diamond ring—an exquisitely cut solitaire that looks to be at least a few karats in size. Set in a delicate circle of either white gold or platinum, it's simple yet striking—exactly what I would've chosen if I had a hundred grand to spare.

Stunned, I lift my gaze to meet his. "Peter..."

"I want you as my wife, Sara," he says softly, reaching over to pick up my left hand. His fingers are warm and dry on my chilled skin, his gaze shadowed in the dim interior of the car. It's as if we're all alone in the darkness, as if the rest of the world no longer exists as he slides the ring onto my left ring finger, its cool, metallic weight like a manacle clamping around my heart.

My breath escapes in a shaky exhale.

Oh God. This is happening.

It's actually happening.

Reflexively, I try to pull my hand back, but he tightens his grip, refusing to release me.

"I want to own you, legally and in every other way," he continues, and this time, I hear the steel behind the softness, feel the prick of the barbed wire wrapped in silk. "You're already mine, ptichka, and I want to make it official," he says, his lips curving in a dark smile. "I want you to marry me, and soon."

CHAPTER 44
SARA

I spend the remainder of the ride home in a haze, the ring on my finger both hot and icy on my skin. I didn't respond to Peter's side-of-the-road proposal—I couldn't—and thankfully, he didn't press me.

He just pulled back out onto the road and continued driving.

When we park in front of my building, Peter walks around and opens my door, taking my hand to help me out of the car. His grip is both solicitous and possessive, his gaze roving over me with a hunger that spikes my pulse and sets off alarm bells in my mind.

He's not going to wait to take me.

He's going to be on me—and in me—as soon as we get inside.

"Wait," I say, suddenly desperate to slow things down. As much as I want him—as much as I physically missed him—I'm not ready for this. It's been too long, and there are too many unanswered questions.

Pulling my hand out of his grasp, I step back until I'm pressed against the car.

His jaw tightens and he comes forward, gripping the top of the car to cage me between his muscular arms. "You think I haven't waited?" He leans over me, silver eyes gleaming, and even though we aren't touching, I feel the heat coming off his powerful body. "You think I haven't been patient all these fucking months?"

My pulse shoots up at the barely contained anger in his voice, and an answering fury—one that's been gradually building during his long absence—erupts in me. All these months of worrying and waiting to be stolen, of not knowing if he was hurt or captured, all the lies and half-truths and sleepless nights, and he just waltzes into a bar like nothing happened? Puts a ring on my finger as if after torture and kidnapping, marriage is the natural next step?

Teeth clenched, I punch up with the heel of my palms, striking the front of his shoulders. "Then where the hell have you been?" I shout as he reflexively jerks back, surprised by my outburst. "Why did it take you so long? I was also fucking waiting—and waiting and waiting and waiting—"

His lips crash against mine, his hands gripping both sides of my face as he crushes me against the car. It's not a kiss so much as a conquest, his tongue invading the inside of my mouth ruthlessly, without mercy. I taste blood where my teeth cut into my lip, but it's overlaid by the familiar taste of him, by the dark heat and violence of his desire.

It should've been too much, but my body comes alive with answering fierceness, my hands clutching fistfuls of his shirt as I kiss him back, sucking on that invading tongue, retaliating with an invasion of my own. This, right here, is what I've been dreaming about all those nights, what my body's been burning for.

Why I haven't been able to so much as look at another man, much less imagine myself with him.

After a minute, his lips soften and his hands release my face to roam over the rest of me, one big palm squeezing my breast while the other grips my ass. Despite the gentler kiss, his touch is unrestrained, unapologetically posses-sive—a king reclaiming his birthright. I feel the thick bulge in his jeans as he grinds it against my stomach, and waves of heat pulse through my body as his mouth trails off to my neck, branding me with hot, biting kisses while his hand leaves my ass to wind my hair around his fist.

"You are fucking mine," he growls in my ear, arching my head back, and I shudder, gooseflesh rising on my arms as he nips my earlobe and wedges his knee between my legs, making me straddle his hard-muscled thigh. Even through the layers of my jeans and his, the pressure on my sex is sudden and intense, and as he squeezes my breast again, rubbing the fabric of my bra against my peaked nip-ple, the pulsing heat moves down to my clit, a familiar ten-sion coiling deep within my core. As I helplessly ride his leg, I'm viscerally aware of the starkly male scent and taste of him, of the potent size and hardness of his body, and as his hand delves under my shirt, his rough, warm palm slid-ing over my bare skin, the tension violently spikes.

With a choked cry, I come, the pent-up need releasing all at once as my body spasms and contracts, the blast of ecstasy curling my toes inside my shoes. Dazedly, I'm aware of distant laughter, and then I'm abruptly horizontal, being carried in impossibly strong arms.

Startled, I open my eyes, looping my arms around Peter's neck. He's walking fast, and we're already halfway across the parking lot, but I still catch a glimpse of three teenage boys on the other side of the lot. They must've seen us, I realize, flushing all over as the orgasm-induced haze clears from my mind.

"Peter, they—"

"I know." His jaw is tight as he covers the pavement with long, sure strides, carrying me as easily as if I were a child. "We need to get inside."

The teenagers' wolf whistles and hooting reach my ears again, and I push at his shoulders. "Put me down. Please, I can walk."

The last thing I need is to be carried through the lobby like some kind of underdressed bride.

To my relief, Peter listens, lowering me to my feet as we reach my building's entrance. It's just in time, too. We don't have a doorman, but I do see my neighbors—two young women dressed up for a night out. They're coming out just as we're coming in, and their curious gazes swing from me to Peter, who's maintaining a possessive grip on my arm.

I don't know them that well—we've only exchanged pleasantries about the weather—so I smile awkwardly and wish them a good evening.

"You too," one of the women says, openly staring at Peter as her roommate starts giggling like a schoolgirl. "Have a very nice evening indeed."

My face flushes brighter as they continue down the lobby, whispering and giggling with their heads bent close together, and for the first time, I'm glad my building doesn't have much of a community dynamic. There are a lot of renters, like me, and with the high turnover in the apartments, people don't bother to get to know their neighbors—or gossip about them.

"Friends of yours?" Peter asks, releasing my arm to press the elevator button, and I shake my head.

"Not really." I look up at him, frowning. "Don't you know that? Weren't you having me followed?"

His gray eyes gleam with dark amusement. "Of course. But they couldn't get that close to you with the Feds watching your every move and regularly sweeping for bugs."

"Oh." That makes sense—and explains why I only ever saw the Feds.

The elevator doors slide open, and he ushers me in, his hand on my lower back warm and gentle—and as inflexible as steel. My heart skips a beat, then settles into a heavy, pounding rhythm.

He's herding me.

Literally shepherding me to my apartment so we can fuck.

"You didn't really think I'd leave you alone, did you?" he says softly as the elevator starts moving, and I shake my head again, looking away from his penetrating stare. My gaze falls on the sizable bulge in his jeans, and the heat in my cheeks intensifies.

Has he been sporting that erection this whole time?

No wonder my neighbors went into estrogen overload.

I force myself to look up and to the side, but that way lies disaster too. The inside of the elevator is mirrored on two sides, and the sight of my reflection makes me want to sink through the floor. Thanks to our impromptu make-out session in the parking lot, not only is my underwear damp, but my lower lip is swollen to twice its normal size, my cheeks are bright pink, and my hair is sticking up on one side.

I look like I'm coming home from an orgy.

In desperation, I look away, catching Peter's gaze again. "So you never told me... Why did it take you so long to return for me?"

His jaw flexes. "Because that favor I did for Esguerra—it took a long time. I wanted to come for you sooner, ptichka, believe me." He gives me an arrested stare. "Did you miss me? Were you hoping I'd come?"

I swallow and look away as the elevator doors open, sparing me from having to reply. I thought I'd reconciled my contradictory feelings for Peter, had come to terms with the fact that my husband's killer managed to steal my heart, but all of a sudden, I'm not so sure. This—Peter here, in my regular life—is too unexpected, too terrifyingly real. I can't wrap my mind around the logistics of it, the sheer number of complications involved in attempting a normal relationship—*a marriage*—with a former assassin who once tortured and kidnapped me. If this is really happening, what am I going to tell my parents who still think of him as "that criminal?" Or Marsha, who knows not only the official FBI story that paints Peter as a monster, but also that he killed George? And will the FBI really leave us alone? How can they, when the man standing in the elevator with me has to be one of the most dangerous people they know?

Whenever I imagined us together, it was elsewhere, with me as his now-willing prisoner. I was ready to accept my fate as his captive, to embrace my tormentor as my destiny, but I wasn't ready for this.

The ring is cold and heavy on my finger as we step out of the elevator and Peter leads me down the hallway to my apartment. He's never been to my building before—at least, I assume he hasn't—yet there's no trace of hesitation in his movements, no sense that he's lost or uncertain in any way. He's as confident in navigating an unfamiliar hallway as he is in everything he does, and I can't help envying that.

I myself feel hopelessly adrift, like a rudderless ship in a storm.

We reach my door, and I fumble for the apartment keys in my purse, acutely aware of Peter's gaze on me. He doesn't look impatient, but I sense it in him, feel the violent need he's holding in check. My breathing grows shallow, my palms dampening as I finally close my hand around the elusive object.

"Here, let me." He takes the keys from me and unerringly finds the right one, opening the door on the first try.

We step in, and he closes the door behind us as I flip on the living room lights. I hear the click of the lock, and I turn to face him, heart hammering. "Peter…"

He's on me before I can utter another word. His big hands frame my face as he backs me up against the couch, his mouth slanting greedily across mine as we fall onto the soft cushions in a tangle of limbs and unrestrained need.

Whatever doubts I might've had are swept away, drowned by a wave of lust so intense it feels like fire in my veins. The orgasm in the parking lot just whetted my appetite, leaving my sex sensitized and swollen, desperately aching for more. My nipples are agonizingly tight, and I literally throb between my legs as he rips off my shirt and moves to undo my zipper, his hands rough with urgency, with the same hunger that's tormented me for months.

I meet him kiss for kiss, my hands ripping at his shirt as he yanks the jeans off me, growling in frustration as they get caught on my ballerina flats. I manage to kick them off my feet along with the bunched-up jeans as he unsnaps my bra, and then I'm naked, sprawled on the couch underneath him as he reaches for his zipper.

There are no pretty words, no sweet caresses—just the primal feel of him as he ruthlessly pushes into me, face taut with lust and eyes glittering darkly as he catches my wrists and pins them above my head. I suck in a breath at the relentless invasion, my inner muscles quivering, struggling to adjust to the impossible thickness of him, to the way my flesh stretches to accept him. My body has somehow forgotten this part, and it feels like our first time all over again, only the shame and guilt are now just dim shadows in my mind.

I need this—I need *him*—and I can't deny it.

When he bottoms out inside me, he stops, giving me a moment to get used to him, and I see him fighting for control, reining in that savage part of him so he won't hurt me.

"It's okay," I whisper, squeezing my pelvic muscles around his thick length. "It's okay, Peter... I can take it."

I want to take it, in fact.

His pupils dilate, and in the depths of his metallic eyes, I see the monster surface. With a low, guttural growl, he surges deeper into me, and I cry out, arching, as he sets a savage rhythm.

He takes me violently, pounding into me without mercy, and my cries grow in volume as pain edges into pleasure, blanketing my mind with white noise, silencing the incessant buzzing of my thoughts. There's no mental room for guilt or worry, no space for doubts and questions. There's just this, just us, and as the tension inside me spirals, I scream out his name, cognizant of nothing but the agony and ecstasy splintering me apart.

He comes at nearly the same time, his powerful neck cording as he arches his head back, hips grinding into me. The pressure triggers a wave of aftershocks for me, and I cry out again, my inner muscles squeezing and contracting, feeling every hard inch inside me as he groans and floods me with his seed.

I might've zoned out after that, or closed my eyes, because the next thing I know, I'm being carried again, this time to my bathroom.

I blink, instinctively looping my arms around Peter's neck as he steps into the tub and lowers me to my feet.

"Are you okay?" he murmurs, steadying me as I let go, and I nod, still too overwhelmed to speak.

"Good."

He steps out of the tub and strips off the clothes he was still wearing. Greedily, I devour his nakedness, taking in the powerful lines of his tall, broad body as he steps back into the tub with me, draws the curtain closed, and turns on the faucet. Every chiseled muscle in his back flexes as he moves, his ass tight and round as he bends over to test the temperature of the water. His balls swing heavily between his legs, his big cock still semi-hard, and warmth creeps along my neck as I notice the gleaming slickness of our combined body fluids on his skin.

No condom again. For some reason, I'm not particularly horrified—or the least bit surprised. If Peter really intends to do this—to settle down with me here, where we can live a normal life—then children are not that insane of a notion. Given that he admitted to wanting me pregnant, I shouldn't expect condoms at all going forward. We're both clean, unless—

"Did you sleep with anyone?" I blurt out, horrified at the possibility that just popped into my mind. "When you were away, I mean?"

I'm shocked this didn't occur to me before. Peter is a highly sexual male in his prime, with the kind of looks and lethal appeal that's bound to cream panties. Case in point, my neighbors—both women in their mid-to-late twenties—giggling like eighth-graders. There's no reason to assume he's been faithful to me this whole time. Nine months of celibacy for someone like Peter is—

"What?" He pivots to face me, dark eyebrows pulled low over his eyes. "Are you serious?"

I shrug and try to sound casual, as if the mere of idea of him touching some other woman doesn't make me want to vomit. "Nine months is a long time, and it's not like we're—"

"Like we're what?" His voice is dangerously soft as he grips my arms. "Like we're what, Sara?"

My mouth goes dry at the look in his metallic eyes. "You know..." I swallow thickly. "In a committed relationship."

"Are you telling me you slept with someone else?" His fingers bite into my skin as a tiny muscle starts ticking in his temple. "Let some other—"

"No!" How can he even think this? "Of course I didn't! Besides, I'm sure your spies would've told you. You said they couldn't get that close, but they wouldn't have missed *that*."

His punishing grip on my arms eases slightly. "No, they probably wouldn't have," he agrees after a moment's consideration. Releasing me, he turns around to twist the knob that directs the water from the faucet to the showerhead above.

I blink water out of my eyes and watch him adjust the spray so it hits lower. Then he faces me again, blocking most of the water with his back.

"I haven't fucked anything other than my fist since I dropped you off," he says evenly. "In fact, since we met,

I haven't so much as brushed against another woman in a crowd. You are it for me, ptichka—all I want, now and forever. Every night for the past nine months, I'd lie in bed, dick so hard it hurt, and think of you. Only you. You're every wet dream of mine, every fantasy and daydream. I want to fuck you all the time, no matter where we are or what we're doing. Even when we're oceans apart, *you* are the only one I want—the only one I'll ever want."

My throat tightens, trapping air inside my lungs. I believe him. How could I not? He's never lied to me, never tried to hide his feelings. From the very beginning, I've known the depths of his obsession with me, and while it used to scare me, it's now perversely reassuring.

For as long as we're both alive.

Something clicks for me, like a light flipping on, cutting through the fog of shock and post-sex daze. "Peter..." My voice shakes as I reach over to capture his hand between my palms. "Did you do it for me?"

He cocks his head, gray eyes puzzled. "Do what, ptichka?"

"This favor for Esguerra so he'd take you off the wanted lists... that thing that kept you away for so long." Squeezing his hand, I bring it up to my chest, where a peculiar tightness constricts my pounding heart. "Am I the reason? Did you do it so you could be here with me?"

He frowns, covering my clasped palms with his other hand. "Of course, ptichka. Isn't this what you wanted? A life where I'm not a fugitive, where we could be together without you losing your family and your career?"

I stare up at him, finally comprehending the enormity of what he's done. It *is* what I wanted, what I've been longing for in the deepest recesses of my heart. It's my darkest, most shameful fantasy—an actual life with my tormentor—and he's made it a reality.

He's done the impossible, pulled God knows how many strings—and all for me.

The steam filling the bathroom is making my eyes burn, and the vise around my heart squeezes tighter.

Peter loves me.

Really, truly loves me.

It's no longer theoretical, what he'd do for me.

It's real. He's done it.

"Isn't this what you wanted, Sara?" he repeats, frown deepening, and I find myself nodding like a marionette, still unable to speak.

"Good." He gently extricates his hand from my grip and turns sideways, so that I'm under the water spray. Picking up my shampoo, he pours it into his palm and starts massaging it into my scalp, as though that's what one does after that kind of revelation.

As though that's all there is to say.

And maybe that's true. Maybe we should revisit this conversation when I don't feel so blindsided, so overwhelmed by his sudden return and all that's bound to go along with it. Because I still don't know what to say to him, how to explain the way I feel.

How to tell him that though I'm overjoyed to have him here, I'm terrified in equal measures.

He washes my hair thoroughly, his strong fingers massaging my scalp and neck, and then he applies conditioner and lets it sit while he washes the rest of me, his soapy, calloused hands sliding all over my body, stroking and caressing my skin with just the right amount of tenderness and roughness.

It feels amazing, like the most exquisite spa treatment, and when he finally rinses the soap off me, I pick up the body wash and do the same to him, enjoying the feel of his sleek, hair-roughened skin as I run my hands over his large, hard-muscled body.

He's always taken care of me, pampered me like a princess, but I've never done it for him, I realize. Returning my tormentor's affection has always felt like a betrayal of George and everything else that mattered, and while I couldn't help myself in bed, I kept myself aloof at other times, accepting Peter's ministrations but never reciprocating them.

I still feel some of that guilt, that sense of wrongness, but it's no longer the suffocating pressure it once was. As the months passed and the shock of George's violent death faded, I've been able to think about it more rationally, to analyze the events from a different perspective.

For one thing, George wasn't truly alive when Peter put a bullet in his head. He'd been in a coma for eighteen months, and given the extent of damage to his brain, there'd been almost no chance he'd ever emerge from it. At some point, I would've had to make the excruciating decision to take him off life support—something I'd been avoiding thinking about, especially since I'd been convinced that George's accident was partially my fault.

In a way, Peter took that awful responsibility from me—something I've only recently let myself consider.

There's also the fact that George betrayed *me*. The drinking that ruined our marriage was bad enough, but all along, he'd also led a double life, had a career as a spy that I knew nothing about. It's taken me all this time to absorb it fully, but I now see George's actions for the gross betrayal that they were, and the love I thought I felt for him now seems like a chimera.

Not that any of this justifies Peter's actions—not by a long stretch. He's still the amoral assassin who's killed more people than I can wrap my mind around, still the man who once tortured, stalked, and kidnapped me. But now he's also the man who loves me, who's demonstrated in the clearest way possible that I matter to him.

That he's willing to do whatever it takes not just to have me, but to make me happy.

Finishing with his chest and stomach, I wash his underarms and the top of his broad shoulders, then massage the thick, heavy muscles around his neck with my soapy hands. He seems to enjoy that, arching into my touch like a big cat, so I knead the area some more, then crouch and wash his legs. His thighs are like steel, with zero give in the powerful muscles, his glutes as round and hard as a bodybuilder's. Unable to help myself, I squeeze those tight globes and look up, blinking at the water spray, to see his eyes closed and his head tipped back in purely masculine bliss.

He likes what I'm doing. Likes it very much, judging by the rapid hardening of his cock.

Impulsively, I close my soapy fist around that thickening column and cup his balls with my other hand, then glance up through the water spray again. He's staring down at me now, the rapturous look replaced by one of predatory hunger.

"Keep doing that," he says hoarsely, slipping his hand into my hair. "And take it into your mouth." Closing his fist around the wet strands, he guides my face to his groin, the pressure gentle but inescapable.

I obediently close my lips around his now-fully-erect cock, tasting water and the faint remnants of soap as I shift forward onto my knees. Despite my earlier orgasms, heat is curling deep within my core, my sex beginning to pulse anew. I might've started it this time, but he's taking over, taking charge as he always does. Unbidden, the recollection of the time he punished me comes to mind, and my inner muscles clench on a surge of need, the images in my head more erotic than any pornographic movie.

He fucked my mouth that time. Tied my hands behind my back and took it without mercy, controlling my breath, my very life. It had been brutal, utterly crushing, yet it made me ache with this same agonizing arousal, made me crave more of the darkness.

I don't fully understand why his roughness turns me on so much, why I enjoy being in his control like this. Prior to meeting Peter, my sexual fantasies rarely involved any element of force or coercion; vanilla was my comfort zone, even in my mind. Could the trauma of our first encounter in my kitchen have transformed me somehow? Maybe some wires got crossed in the aftermath, and the violence I experienced at his hands became linked with pleasure in my mind?

Either way, whatever the reason, I burn as he pushes his cock deeper into my mouth, so deep I almost gag. Reflexively, I brace myself on the steely columns of his thighs, but I don't fight him, not even when he starts to move his hips, thrusting into my mouth with increasing savagery. I just stare up at him, blinking away the water spray, and when the pulsing ache between my thighs grows unbearable, I slip one hand there and rub my clit, letting his thrusts pace my fingers' movements.

He notices, and his hard features tighten, the predatory look intensifying. "Yes, that's it, ptichka." His voice is a low, thick rumble as he pushes deep into my throat, cutting off my air. "Keep doing that. Let me see you come."

Eyes watering, I obey, rubbing my clit faster as I hold his gaze. My other hand clenches on his thigh, my heart rate surging as my body catches on to the lack of air.

I'm not breathing.

I'm not breathing, and there's water on my face.

My entire body stiffens, my eyes squeezing shut and my muscles locking up as my mind flashes back to the torture in my kitchen, when he had me drowning in the sink. The recollection chills me, but doesn't cool the fire in my core. Somehow, the terror intensifies it all, ramping up the tension, and even as I claw at Peter's thigh in panic, my other hand frantically works my clit.

I come so hard I see explosions of light behind my tightly closed eyelids. The spasms rack my body, making me scream, and it's only when I slump against Peter's legs that I realize my mouth is free and I'm breathing.

Dazed, I look up and find him fisting his cock, a savage grimace on his face. Then, with a harsh groan, he comes, spurting ropes of cum all over my face and hair. I blink up at him, wiping it off my forehead with a shaky hand, and he helps me up to my feet, his grip strong, though he must also still be recovering from his orgasm.

I don't say anything and neither does he as he washes my hair for the second time. It's not until we step out of the shower and he's toweling me off that he speaks.

"You never gave me your answer, you know." His tone is calm, but I see slivers of darkness in the cool gray of his gaze as he wraps the towel around me, then reaches to the side to grab one for himself.

I blink, gripping the edges of the towel. "Was there a question?"

I know what he's talking about, of course—the ring is still heavy on my finger—but I'm nowhere near ready for that discussion. I didn't even think this discussion would happen. He didn't ask me to marry him; he told me that's what's happening. So it's not like I was supposed to—

"Don't, Sara." He drops the towel and steps close, backing me against the vanity counter. "Don't play games with me." His jaw flexes as he grips the smooth stone on both sides of me and leans in. "Are you going to marry me?"

I stare up at him, frozen, unable to speak or think. I didn't expect that he'd demand an answer. That he'd want an answer at all. From the very beginning, he's made all the decisions in this strange relationship of ours, and it's hard to believe that he's giving me a choice in this.

That he's giving me the option of not marrying him.

"What if…" I swallow, gripping the towel harder. "What if I don't want to?"

His face tightens. "Is that a no?"

Yes. No. I don't know. How can I answer when my brain is mush from his sudden return and all the orgasms he's wrung from my body? I want to slink away, crawl under my covers and sleep so I can wake up with some magical clarity, but even in this foggy state, I know it'll never happen. There will never be a clear yes or no when it comes to Peter, never an easy decision to be made. What we have together is a shrink's wet dream, and I could sleep for a week straight without gaining any insight into our mutual insanity.

Yes or no. Do I marry the assassin who once tortured me? He loves me, and I'm almost certain I love him. The "almost" is there because a tiny part of me still cringes away in terror, in the toxic sludge of guilt, self-loathing, and shame. Even if I eventually forgive him for George's death, I can never forget that he's a killer—that in the name of vengeance, he's inflicted massive suffering and pain.

That he himself has suffered more than I can comprehend.

I hold his gaze, feeling the temperature in the humid bathroom dropping, sensing the growing darkness in the hard metal of his gaze. "Yes. It's a yes." The words leave my lips of their own volition, like some demon yanked me by the tongue. Yet as soon as I say it, it feels right.

It feels like it was fated.

The dangerous tension leaves his face, though I still sense the menace deep within. "Good," he says softly, pushing away from the counter. Turning, he walks out of the bathroom, and I slump over the sink, taking deep breaths to calm the churning in my stomach.

I said yes.

I agreed to marry my tormentor.

Oh dear God. What have I done?

CHAPTER 45
PETER

I watch my beautiful fiancée sleep, alternating between joy and dark satisfaction. Her fine-featured face is particularly sweet and delicate in her repose, with one slender hand tucked in a half-open fist under her cheek and plush lips slightly parted.

I should probably turn off the bedside light and go to sleep as well, but that would mean missing this. Some irrational part of me is afraid that if I close my eyes, it'll all turn out to be a dream, a fantasy like the ones that sustained me all these months.

My Sara.

Finally, I have her.

She's mine, and soon, the whole world will know it.

She was completely worn out by the time I finally brought her to bed, so tired she fell asleep right away. I held her for about an hour, ignoring the renewed stirrings of my body, and then I got on her laptop to start making the appropriate arrangements.

She agreed to marry me. The elation I feel at the thought is almost violent. I'd been prepared to resort to harsher measures to convince her, but I didn't have to.

She said yes.

She's still wearing my ring on her left hand, the one that's currently tucked inside a blanket. I'm tempted to pull the blanket away so I can look at it again, but that might wake her, and I want her to get good sleep.

After all, this Saturday is our wedding.

Over the past month, while I waited for the bureaucrats to get their paperwork in order, I had time to plan it all out and grease all the requisite palms. So unless Sara hates what I've chosen, we're all set in terms of venue, dress, flowers, photographers, and nearly everything else that goes along with a small, private wedding. There are still a few small decisions to be made—like who'd officiate the ceremony—but I want Sara, and hopefully her parents, to weigh in on those.

It really does help that she agreed.

Taking a deep breath, I climb into bed next to her and turn off the light, then curve my body around her from the back, holding her tight as she mumbles something in her sleep.

My ptichka.

She's not a fantasy anymore.

This is as real as it gets, and when I wake up, she'll still be here.

She better fucking be.

CHAPTER 46

SARA

I wake up to the mouthwatering smell of eggs and bacon, mixed with some kind of baked goods. Pancakes? Biscuits, maybe?

Did I fall asleep at my parents' house again?

Prying open my heavy eyelids, I roll over onto my back and stare at the ceiling.

My apartment's plain white ceiling.

Instantly, the memories rush in, and I sit up with a gasp, throwing off my blanket.

Was last night real? Is Peter here?

A flash of something bright catches my attention, and I glance down at my left hand, where a giant diamond is sparkling in the barely-there sunlight seeping through the lowered blinds.

Holy shit. It *is* real.

Peter is here.

I'm officially engaged to him.

Throwing on a robe, I run to the kitchen, where I not only smell but hear the sizzle of frying bacon.

The sight that greets me stops me in my tracks.

Dressed in nothing but a pair of dark jeans, Peter is standing over the stove, expertly flipping over an omelet. On another frying pan are bacon strips, and on a plate by the oven is a stack of pancakes. The muscles in his broad back ripple as he moves, the jeans riding low on his narrow hips, and I literally have to swallow my saliva as he turns around to face me, revealing a solid eight-pack and a powerfully built chest dusted with dark hair.

The few pounds he lost only refined his incredible physique, made him even harder, more dangerous.

"Good morning, ptichka." His deep voice is like a tiger's purr as he looks me over, his gaze traveling from the tips of my bare toes to the top of my sleep-mussed hair. The tattoos on his left arm flex as he sets the spatula down on the counter and starts toward me.

"Oh, um… good morning." I back away, realizing I rushed in without so much as splashing water on my face. "I'll be right back."

I beeline for the bathroom before he can stop me. Swiftly, I brush my teeth, then jump into the shower for a quick rinse. My heart is galloping in my chest, and my breathing is fast and shallow.

Peter is *here*.

In my kitchen, cooking up a storm.

I should probably take a moment to calm myself, but I don't want all that delicious food to get cold.

After all, my *fiancé* made it for me.

My stomach flips, my heart rate accelerating further, and I force myself to take deep breaths as I towel off and put the robe back on.

Then, squaring my shoulders, I head back into the kitchen.

CHAPTER 47
SARA

"What time do you have to be at work?" Peter asks, serving me an artfully arranged plate of vegetable omelet with strips of bacon and a side of pancakes.

I glance up at the clock on the wall. "In about forty minutes." I'm lucky I woke up when I did, because I completely spaced out on the alarm last night.

I'm probably spacing out on something right now, because even though I'm outwardly calm, on the inside, I'm a hyperventilating mess.

Peter is *here.*

He's here, and we're *engaged.*

"I'll walk you to your office," he says, sitting down across from me with his own plate. "Unless you're taking the car?"

I cautiously spear a piece of pancake with my fork. "I was planning to go from there straight to the clinic, so yeah…"

He doesn't blink. "Okay. I'll ride with you and then go grocery shopping. Your fridge is nearly empty. How late are you going to be at the clinic?" He begins consuming his omelet with obvious hunger.

"I'm scheduled to be there until ten, but if there's any kind of an emergency, I might end up staying later," I say, watching him warily. Is he going to object? Try to control this portion of my life? George was understanding about my long hours, as he often worked late himself and had to travel a lot for work, but I don't know how Peter feels about it. He didn't stop me from working a lot before, but that was different.

Back then, he was just biding his time before stealing me away.

"Okay. I'll pick you up there." He gets up and walks over to the counter, where my handbag is sitting. Reaching in, he fishes out my phone and starts typing on it.

"What are you doing?" I ask, puzzled.

"Giving you my number." Finishing his task, he slips my phone back into my bag and returns to the table. "So you can call me when you're close to being done at the clinic. I don't want you in that area alone at night."

"You're not having me watched anymore?"

"I am, but they keep their distance—and I won't." He cuts into a piece of bacon, then looks up. "It's for your safety, ptichka."

His voice is soft but firm, utterly inflexible. He's not going to compromise on this, and for some reason, I'm okay with that. Instead of making me feel restrained and controlled, his pathological need to protect me fills me with a kind of bubbly warmth. I'll never forget how it felt when the two methheads tried to rob me by the clinic, and as traumatic as it was when Peter killed them, in hindsight, I'm grateful he was there. Besides—

"Are you expecting any trouble?" I ask as the thought pops into my head. "I mean, you must have quite a few enemies, with your former profession and all…"

He puts down his fork and meets my gaze. "It's always a possibility, ptichka, I can't lie. That's why I'm not going to take the security team off you—and why I created a new identity before coming here. I didn't want anyone in my former life to connect Peter Garin in the suburbs of Chicago with Peter Sokolov the assassin. In fact, part of the deal I made with the authorities is that Peter Sokolov no longer exists. He's listed as deceased in FBI, CIA, and Interpol records, as are Yan and Ilya Ivanov and Anton Rezov. The amnesty deal itself is highly classified, with only a few high-ranking individuals in the FBI and CIA privy to all the terms. The rest, like Agent Ryson, were told to just back off and keep their mouths shut. Of course, Esguerra and Kent know who I am, and there's always a chance I'll be spotted and identified by a former client or some such. However, unlike my name, my face wasn't widely known, and in any case, the chance of a random encounter with someone from my former life is small—especially in this part of the world."

"Oh. Wow." Until this moment, I didn't realize the full scope of the impossible deal he made. "How did you get them to agree to all this? I mean, I know you said this Esguerra has leverage, but…" I trail off as Peter's expression noticeably darkens.

"Your government had conditions of their own for me," he says tightly. "But it's nothing that needs to concern you, ptichka. Suffice it to say, the US military is one of Esguerra's biggest clients, and they want to maintain that amicable relationship, both because they want the weapons he produces and because they want to keep those weapons out of others' hands."

"By buying them up themselves?"

Peter nods and resumes eating. "Exactly."

There's a grim edge to his expression, and as much as I want to pry further, I know I need to back off. Watching him finish his food, I have the unsettling sensation that a wild animal has invaded my cramped kitchen, a predator who belongs out in the jungle. I've seen him in domestic settings before, of course, but it feels different this time, knowing that he's here for good, that this big, lethal man is going to be part of my regular life… part of my family.

My mind starts to spin again, and I push my nearly empty plate away. "Peter… How is this going to work?" At his questioning look, I clarify, "What am I going to tell my parents? The FBI probably showed them your picture at some point. Even if I introduce you as Peter Garin, they're bound to suspect who you really are—especially since I kept insisting that you'll be back when the misunderstanding with the FBI is resolved."

The grim look leaves his face, replaced by one of dark amusement. "Well, that's just perfect then, isn't it?" Reaching across the table, he covers my hand with his palm. "You'll just tell them that the misunderstanding finally got resolved—and that I got a new last name in the process."

"Uh-huh. And what about their friends, who've heard a version of that same story, and what about *my* friends, who were told a completely different version—one in which you're nothing more than my kidnapper? What are they all going to think when I show up with *this*"—I lift my left hand, displaying my ring—"out of the blue, and introduce a Russian fiancé named Peter who looks suspiciously like a picture FBI agents might've been passing around when I disappeared?"

He squeezes my hand. "Don't worry about them, ptichka. Their opinions don't matter. Just tell them I'm someone you've been secretly dating for a few months, and let them draw their own conclusions."

"What conclusions? That I'm fucked in the head? Or that I have a fetish for Russian men who share the same darkly handsome looks and happen to be named Peter?"

He grins and gets up, picking up his plate and mine. "Either way works. Just don't confirm anything. Let them think I'm in some kind of witness protection program, and you can't really talk about it."

That's actually not a bad idea. Marsha and anyone else who suspects Peter's real identity will think I'm completely nuts, but as long as I don't confirm their suspicions, there will be room for doubt. After all, how crazy is it that the man who murdered George and kidnapped me got full amnesty and is now about to marry me? My friends might as well think I've got some kind of masochistic tendencies and have decided to hook up with a man who shares many of my tormentor's traits.

It's certainly a simpler explanation.

"So we tell my parents the truth, and stick to the Peter Garin story with everyone else," I say, getting up to help him clear the table.

"That's what makes sense to me," he says and glances at the clock. "You should get dressed and going, ptichka. You don't want to be late."

Right. For my job. I almost forgot about that.

"Here, let me help you," I say, walking over to put away the leftovers, but he waves me away.

"I've got it, don't worry. Just go get ready for work." And dropping a quick kiss on my forehead, he starts loading the dishwasher.

CHAPTER 48
PETER

I drive Sara to her office and leave the car with her, so she can go to the clinic after work as planned. It's only a ten-minute walk from her office to her apartment building, and the grocery store is on the way, so I stop by and load up on the basics for tonight's dinner. It's not a lot, only what I can easily carry in one hand—I like my gun hand always free—and I make a mental note that we'll need a second car, just like everyone in the suburbs.

That's not the only thing we'll need, either. The fridge in Sara's tiny kitchen is only a meter tall, and the kitchen itself is barely usable. I spent my formative years in a freezing, crumbling cell in Siberia, so I'm not picky about living quarters, but I see no reason for us to continue with an apartment that was clearly designed for a single occupant.

Tonight, when Sara returns, we'll discuss living arrangements, as well as our upcoming wedding on Saturday.

Of course, I know why cars, apartments, and wedding details are on my mind. Thinking about logistics is distracting me from the urge to grab Sara and lock her in my bedroom, so I can fuck her all day long. And then all night. And then for a week after that.

In fact, I want to chain her to my bed and always keep her there.

I don't know what I expected when I returned, but it wasn't this. I didn't expect it to be so hard for me to let Sara go about her routine, to go back to the way we lived before Japan. Back then, I also wanted her with me all the time, but letting her leave for work didn't tear me apart like this, didn't activate this maddening need to cage her and throw away the key. It was all I could do to act normally this morning, to kiss her on the forehead and drop her off at the office like a good husband-to-be instead of a savage who wants nothing more than to cart her away to his cave.

It's the one variable I didn't account for in my planning.

My intensifying obsession with Sara—the one thing that can fuck it all up.

I'm hoping it's a temporary situation, that I'm feeling this way because we've just spent nine months apart and I've missed her so intensely. That over time, as the memory of those hellish months fades, separating from her for a few hours will get better, easier... less like torture.

The other possibility—that in Japan, I got used to having Sara with me twenty-four-seven and may not be able to readjust to the old routine—is infinitely worse. The reason why I did all this is to make Sara happy, to give her the ability to retain her career, her relationships with her family and friends. It was impossible when I was a fugitive, but now I can be a part of her life without taking it all away from her.

I can give her everything—if only I can overcome my selfish need to keep her to myself.

CHAPTER 49

SARA

I spend the majority of my workday oscillating between heart-pounding joy and spurts of panic.

Peter is alive.

He's back and we're together—without me getting kidnapped, no less.

Despite what Peter said about his deal, I half expect the FBI to show up and charge me with aiding and abetting. Nobody comes, however. Everything is normal—or as normal as can be when one is engaged to a former assassin.

I'm not ready to answer my coworkers' questions, so I hid my hand in my pocket and took off the ring as soon as I had a moment of privacy. Now the huge diamond is sitting at the bottom of my handbag, forcing me to carry the bag with me everywhere.

I don't know how much the ring cost, but I suspect it was well into six figures.

Did Peter buy or steal it? It's probably the former—he's rich enough to afford it—but I'll ask to be sure. I doubt he'll be offended; he's done much worse, that's for certain.

That I'm even thinking about that, wondering if my millionaire fiancé could've stolen my engagement ring, would've given any normal person pause. However, I'm no longer in the "normal" camp. Compared to killing my husband, a diamond heist is nothing more than a misdemeanor, one for which I can easily forgive Peter. In general, now that I've had time to recover from the shock of his arrival, the sporadic panic assailing me at the thought of marrying him is less intense, almost manageable. Toward the evening, as I get in the car to drive to the clinic, I even start thinking that we could visit my parents this weekend, and depending on their reaction, tell them that we're getting married soon.

Maybe as soon as this winter.

My heart starts racing again, and I have to take calming breaths before getting out of the car. No, winter is definitely too soon; there's far too much to plan in such a short span of time. Next spring would be better... maybe even next summer.

A summer wedding is always in fashion.

Yes, that's it, I decide, walking into the clinic. A year-long engagement would be perfect. We'd have a chance to acclimate to each other, settle into a regular life together. I have no idea if Peter is even capable of living like this, without the adrenaline and danger of his missions. He admitted to me once that he likes killing, that he enjoys the power and control that comes along with dealing death.

Addictive, he called it, and I knew then that he'd never give it up.

That the darkness is a part of him, one that can never be erased.

Except he did give it up for me. He quit his job, he said. I haven't had a chance to question him about that, but there's only one way to interpret what he said.

He's going straight.

For me.

So I wouldn't have to give up everything for him.

My eyes prickle, and it's all I can do to smile and wave at Lydia as I hurry into the room where the patient is already waiting for me. She's a sixteen-year-old girl, here with her mom for her first Pap smear, and I force myself to push my emotions aside and focus, to give the patient the attention she deserves.

Fortunately, her exam shows nothing untoward, though when the mom leaves the room, the girl admits to having been sexually active since last year. I surreptitiously give her a box of condoms, and when the mom returns, I recommend an IUD—to regulate the daughter's painful periods and provide protection against unplanned pregnancy in case she does become sexually active in the future.

"My daughter ain't no slut," the woman snaps and drags the girl away, making me glad I at least gave her daughter those condoms.

Parents like that can be their kids' worst enemies.

My next patient is a pregnant woman in her thirties. She has a history of miscarriages and no health insurance.

After her, I see another teenage girl—she turns out to have chlamydia—and then it's time for my last patient.

Finally.

For the first time in forever, I'm eager to go home.

Getting out my phone, I look up Peter's new number—*Peter Garin*, it says in my Contacts—and text him that I'll be ready to leave in about twenty minutes, in case he wants to meet me at the clinic. I don't know how exactly he'd do that, since I'm the one with the car, but knowing Peter, he'll manage.

Putting the phone away, I stick my head out of the exam room and tell Lydia I'm ready for the next patient.

I'm jotting down a few notes about the girl with chlamydia when the door opens and the last patient walks in.

I look up and freeze in shock.

I recognize this girl.

It's Monica Jackson, the seventeen-year-old I helped after her stepfather raped her.

Her small round face is covered with purplish bruises, and one corner of her puffy lips is crusted with blood. "Hi, Dr. Cobakis," she says tremulously, and before I can answer, she breaks down crying.

It takes me a solid fifteen minutes to calm her down and learn that the stepfather got out of jail last week. "He was supposed to be away for s-seven years," she tells me, her voice shaking. "And we were doing so, so well. With the money you gave us, we got a new place, I graduated and have been working full-time, and Bobby—that's my baby brother—he started school, a really good one, where they have computers and everything. And Mom.... she was doing better too, only drinking a little in the morning. I thought we finally had our shit together, and then *he* got out on a technicality and…"

She starts crying again, and I wait until she calms a little before asking carefully, "Did he do this to you? Did he hurt you?"

She nods, wiping the tears off her face with one small fist. "Mom went on a drinking binge as soon as she heard he's out, and when I came home the day before yesterday, he was there, home with her, drinking together like old times. I got into an argument with him, told him to get out, and then he—" She breaks off, her shoulders beginning to shake again.

It takes all my training to maintain a physician's required distance instead of hugging her. "Did you report this to the police?" I ask gently when she regains some composure, and she shakes her head, looking down at the floor.

"He said he'll sue Mom for custody of Bobby if I say anything, and he's got connections now. That's how he got out early. Some drug-dealer friend of his pulled some strings."

"Even if he does sue, that doesn't mean he'll win," I say, but Monica adamantly shakes her head again.

"He might not win, but he'll drag her through the mud," she says, looking up to meet my gaze. "She's got priors too, for public intoxication and prostitution, and Child Services is bound to get involved. I'm eighteen now, so I could also sue for custody, but my job pays minimum wage and there's no guarantee I'd win. And if I don't, Bobby will end up in a foster home." A fierce protectiveness kindles in her brown eyes. "I can't let that happen, Dr. Cobakis. I've been through that, and I can't have that for my brother. He's got special needs; he won't survive the system. I can't take that risk, believe me."

My heart breaks for her all over again. I still feel she should go to the police, but I can see I won't be able to convince her of that. And this time, I can't cut her a check and make it go away.

Five thousand dollars won't fix this, and I finally understand what it's like to hate someone enough to wish him dead.

If a car hit her bastard of a stepfather tomorrow, I'd be the first to cheer.

Swallowing my anger, I reach deep to find the distance necessary to do my job. "Okay, Monica, I understand. Climb up on that table, please, and let's make sure you're not injured inside."

She complies, wiping away the remnants of her tears, and I carefully examine her. Though the assault took place two days ago, there are still signs of vaginal bruising and tearing, so I collect a rape kit, just in case any DNA evidence remains and she later changes her mind about going to the police. I also give her emergency contraception and check for STDs after she admits that her assailant didn't use a condom.

"Can you also please give me one of those copper things?" she asks when I'm done. "I don't want to get pregnant for a long time."

"Of course."

She's eighteen, so it's easy. I schedule her for an IUD insertion next week, to give her time to heal.

"Do you have someplace to go? Other than your mom's place?" I ask as she prepares to leave.

She better not be going home to her stepfather.

"I'm staying with a friend right now," she says to my relief. "He's got a couch I can crash on."

"What about your brother?"

Her narrow shoulders tense. "There's no room for Bobby at my friend's place. I pick him up in the morning to take him to school, and then I bring him home."

"To your mom who's drunk? Is your stepfather there when you return with Bobby?"

She looks away. "I have to go, Dr. Cobakis. Thank you for everything."

And before I can question her further, she hurries out of the room.

CHAPTER 50

SARA

I thought I did a good job fixing my smeared mascara before leaving the clinic, but as soon as I step outside and lay eyes on Peter's tall, broad-shouldered figure, the smile on his hard face disappears.

"What's wrong?" he asks sharply, stepping forward to grip my hands. "Did someone hurt you?"

I attempt a smile. "No, of course not. Everything's fine."

His eyes narrow dangerously. "Don't lie. You've been crying." His gaze drops to my bare left hand. "Where is your ring?"

"I... didn't want to have to explain." Despite my best efforts, my voice is overly thick, and I see his expression darken further.

"Did someone say something?" he demands, and I shake my head, pulling my hands out of his grip and taking half a step back.

"No, it's nothing like that." I glance around us, but the street is dark and quiet, deserted except for an SUV idling by the curb on the other side. His ride, maybe? Looking up, I meet Peter's gaze. "I just got upset over a patient, that's all."

His harsh expression eases slightly. "I see. I'm sorry, ptichka. Did someone get hurt?"

I swallow against a fresh influx of tears. "It's a long story. Let's just go home." I start turning toward my parked car, but he catches my arm.

"I'll have it taken home, don't worry," he says and leads me toward the idling car—a black Mercedes SUV with suspiciously thick tinted windows.

The driver rolls down his window as we approach.

"Take her car home," Peter orders, and a big, hard-looking man climbs out of the vehicle and hands over the keys to Peter.

I blink as he walks by without so much as a nod to me. "Is that—"

"One of the security experts I've had watching you? Yes." Peter leads me around the car to the passenger side and opens the door for me, helping me climb inside before walking back to the driver's seat.

"I've decided that instead of us getting another car, Danny will be your driver going forward," he says as he starts the car and pulls away from the curb. "I'll still pick you up most of the time, but if I can't get here in time or you need to leave right away, I'll know you're safe regardless."

I open my mouth to argue, then stop. I don't have the energy for this right now—not with my heart in pieces over Monica's tragic story.

Not when I know that tomorrow morning, she'll be picking up her brother and confronting her assailant in the process.

"What happened, ptichka?" Peter's big, warm palm covers my thigh, massaging the tense muscle before withdrawing. "What got you so upset?"

I hesitate for a second, then capitulate. Who cares if Peter knows the whole story? So I tell him everything, from Monica's visit to the clinic before my kidnapping to what happened today.

Peter listens expressionlessly until I finish. Then he asks softly, "So this girl is the reason you were assaulted by that alley that night?"

I sit up straight, jolted by a sudden fear. "It's not her fault!" The last thing I need is for my overprotective assassin to blame Monica for the methheads who tried to rob me.

"Not saying that it is." He pulls off the highway onto my exit and stops at a red light. "Just want to make sure I have all the facts."

My heart skips a beat. This is not going in the direction I expected.

"Why?" I ask, staring at his hard profile. "What do you need that for?"

He doesn't look at me. "Don't worry about it, my love. Your patient will be fine, I promise."

My mouth goes dry. Is he saying what I think he's saying? I didn't tell him Monica's name, but it wouldn't be hard for someone with Peter's knack of finding people to triangulate who she is.

"Peter…"

The light switches to green, and he presses on the gas, still not looking at me.

My pulse speeds up further. "Peter, please tell me you're not going to…"

"Going to what?" He turns onto my street. "I told you, you have nothing to worry about. She's going to be fine, this girl you helped. You don't need to worry about her."

She will be fine… but what about her stepfather?

I want to ask, but I can't bring my mouth to form the words. If I say it out loud, it will make it real, instead of just a terrifying possibility in my mind.

It will make me culpable.

We pull into the parking lot of my building, and I exit the car before Peter has a chance to walk around and open the door for me. My heart is hammering in an audible rhythm, and my palms are sweating even though I tell myself I'm likely misinterpreting the situation.

Peter might just be soothing me, telling me what he thinks will calm me down.

I want to believe it, and with any other man, I *would* believe it. If this were Joe Levinson or any one of my band-mates, I'd take those words as nothing more than an empty reassurance, a kind of "there, there, all will be well." But this is Peter, and I can't make that kind of assumption.

I have to—

"When are we going to see your parents?" Peter asks, and I look up, startled, to find him standing next to me. Reaching over, he gathers my hand in his big palm and starts leading me toward the building, saying, "We need to discuss the arrangements for this Saturday with them."

I stare up at him in confusion. Did I already tell him about my idea of visiting my parents this weekend? But no, I just thought of that at work, and— "This Saturday?"

He nods, glancing at me with a smile. "That's when I've booked everything for our wedding. We just need to discuss a few small details, and we're all set."

I stop in my tracks. "What?"

Did he just say *our wedding*?

He releases my hand and turns to face me. "If you call them tonight, maybe we can have dinner with them tomorrow. That way, they'll have a chance to invite a few friends. And you can already talk to your coworkers and whoever else you want to be there. We should keep it small, for security reasons, but the venue will accommodate up to a hundred people."

My tongue unglues from the roof of my mouth. "You want us to marry this Saturday? As in, three days from now?"

He tilts his head. "Is that a problem? I wanted to do it sooner, but I figured the weekend is better than mid-week as far as getting your friends to attend."

I gape at him, feeling like I got hit by a freight train. "Next *year* would be better," I finally manage. "This weekend is just… It's impossible."

"Why?" He takes my hand again and resumes walking, as though we're discussing what to eat for dinner and not our freaking wedding.

A wedding he wants to have in *three days*.

"Because… because we can't." I scramble for ways to convince him. "What about invitations? We don't have time to send them and—"

"You can just call the people you want to invite. It's more personal like that, anyway."

"What about food? And photographers? And the dress?"

"All taken care of. I hired an excellent catering company and a highly recommended florist, and the photographer is booked for all day Saturday, as is the videographer. For the dress, they're going to come to your office to measure you tomorrow, and you'll choose a design you like from their catalog. They promised me it won't take longer than a half hour, so you could do it on your lunch break. The hair and makeup people will come to our apartment first thing Saturday morning, and for the music, I hired a band that's currently on tour in Chicago—The C-Zone Boys, I believe they're called. I think I've heard you sing their songs?"

If my jaw weren't attached, I'd be picking it up off the floor. He hired The C-Zone Boys for our impromptu wedding? As in, the band whose singles have been topping the charts for the past two years?

"Why not Rihanna or The Black-Eyed Peas?" I ask when I can speak again, and he shoots me a sidelong glance as we enter the lobby.

"Is that what you want? I can see if we can—"

"No! I just…" I shake my head, unable to even find the words to explain. "Never mind that. C-Zone is perfect. What's the venue?"

"It's Silver Lake Country Club, over in Orland Park. The weather is supposed to be perfect, so we'll have both the ceremony and the reception outdoors, right by the lake. Unless you want to take it inside? It's not too late to do that."

"No, that's… The lakeside will work."

He shepherds me into the elevator, and I numbly press the button for my floor, feeling like that freight train is dragging me along at madness-inducing speed. How could he have done all this? When? And why didn't he consult me?

Is this what our life together is always going to be like?

Before I tackle that thorny issue, I need to voice one last rational argument.

"What if no one comes?" I ask as we exit the elevator. "It's already Wednesday. Most people have weekend plans, and—"

"They'll change them." He reaches into his pocket and takes out a set of keys—a set he must've had made today, as I have mine in my bag. Opening the door, he lets me in and closes it behind us.

I kick off my sandals. "And if they can't?"

"Then they'll miss out." He removes his own shoes and turns to face me. "Do you really care, ptichka? Your parents will be there, and so will you and I. Who else do you need?"

No one—not really—but that's not the point.

"Peter..." I take a deep breath. "I can't marry you this weekend. It's just too soon."

His gaze hardens. "Too soon how? I told you, we have all the logistics covered."

"It's not about the logistics!" My voice spikes in volume, and I take another breath in an attempt to regain control. Striving for a calmer tone, I say, "I haven't seen you for over nine months, and before that, we didn't exactly have a... normal relationship."

"So what?" His eyes narrow. "We have that now."

"You railroading me into marriage and making all the decisions about our wedding is not normal, Peter. Not by a long stretch." I'm proud of my composure so far. "We need time to get to know each other in *this* context, to see if we can make this work..." I trail off, seeing the storm gathering in the reflective silver of his gaze.

"Why wouldn't we make it work?" His voice is dangerously low as he steps toward me. "This isn't a trial run, a wait-and-see college roommate situation. Do you really think that if we argue over dishes, I'm going to let you walk away?"

My pulse spikes again. Of course he wouldn't. Not after everything he's done to get us here. Still, he has to realize that marrying me *this weekend*—and not giving me any choice about it—is not the way to go after a nine-month-long absence preceded by a forced relationship involving murder, torture, and abduction.

"How about a winter wedding?" I say in desperation. "We could do it right around the December holidays, so the season will always be extra festive for us. We could plan a honeymoon around that time, too. I'll be able to take a week or two off work, and—"

"We can do the honeymoon whenever." Reaching for me, he slides his hands under my blouse, resting warm palms on my bare sides. His metallic eyes take on a heated gleam as his thumbs rasp across the sensitive skin underneath my ribcage, stroking back and forth. "If you can't or don't want to take time off next week, you don't have to. I'm okay with waiting until winter for the honeymoon."

"Then why not the wedding?" I hold his gaze, trying to focus on the topic at hand instead of the way the slow, hypnotic stroking of those thumbs is heating up my skin and making my insides quiver. "What harm will it do if we get married then, too?"

His mouth takes on a sensuous curve, and he bends his head, inhaling deeply, as if breathing in my scent. "You mean other than all my planning going to waste?" he murmurs, his lips brushing across the top of my ear.

"Y-yes." I close my eyes as he pulls me closer, nuzzling against the side of my neck as my head instinctively falls back, granting him better access. My breathing quickens, a melting sensation softening my bones as the hard ridge of his arousal presses against my stomach, making me aware of an empty ache deep within.

"Well…" He lightly bites my neck, then soothes the tiny sting by licking the wounded spot. "For one thing, I want you as my wife, and I want it today, not tomorrow or three days from now." His mint-scented breath is warm on my skin, sending electric tingles down my body. "I want you to wear my ring at all times, everywhere, so everyone knows you're mine." He places another biting lick behind my ear, his voice deepening further as he murmurs, "It's not rational, ptichka, but I need this—need you. And I can't wait. Not after being apart from you for so long."

"What about…" It's getting harder to gather my thoughts as he continues to inflict those sensuous little bites all over my neck and shoulder juncture. With monumental effort, I force myself to focus. "What about kids? And where will we live? And what—" I gasp as he undoes my zipper and slides his hand into my soaked panties. "What about"—I begin to pant as his fingers find my clit and start manipulating it with unerring skill—"your job?"

"I told you, I quit." His breathing is just as ragged as mine as he sinks one long finger into me, then uses the resulting slickness to paint wet circles on my throbbing clit. "It's over."

"But… oh, God." My hips are now shimmying in a circle, chasing after the movement of that teasing finger. The pressure is building inside me so rapidly I can no longer form a single thought. "Oh, God, Peter, I'm going to—"

With a choked cry, I explode, every muscle in my body clenching on a violent wave of pleasure. The orgasm is so strong that my mind goes blank, flooded with purely physical sensations. I'm dimly cognizant of being moved, of my pants and underwear being pushed down my legs, and then I'm bent over the sofa and he's pushing into me, his big cock penetrating deep in one hard stroke.

The shock of it jolts me to the bone, and my still-quivering muscles lock tight, clamping in an instinctive effort to halt the invasion. But that only makes him feel thicker, more massive inside me, and I find myself panting again as he grips my hips and starts thrusting, his pelvis slamming against my ass with each merciless stroke.

"Peter…" I feel the wave gathering again, threatening to swamp me in white-hot bliss. "Peter, wait…"

He doesn't slow down; if anything, his punishing thrusts speed up. "Come with me," he commands hoarsely. "I want to feel you milk my cock."

I'm there before he finishes speaking, the wave cresting with tsunami-like force. The pleasure batters my senses, eviscerating the last shreds of my resistance. I don't know if I'm screaming or if it's the blood roaring in my ears, but the rest of the sounds fade out.

All I hear, all I feel, all I sense is the ecstasy and him.

CHAPTER 51
PETER

*M*y ptichka is quiet as I bring her to the bathroom and lower her into the bubble bath I prepared before leaving to pick her up. The tub is too small for us both, so I use the sink to wash up and then perch on the side of the tub, watching her rosy nipples play peekaboo with the bubbles. With her head resting on the edge of the tub, her eyes closed, and her delicate features pink with post-orgasmic glow, she looks so tempting I want her all over again.

Tonight, I promise myself.

As soon as Sara is done with her bath, we're going to eat, and then she's mine all night long.

Sensing my gaze on her, she opens her eyes. "Thank you for this," she murmurs, moving one graceful hand through the bubbles. "I can't remember the last time I did this."

I fight the urge to reach in and capture that hand, to haul her against me so I can feel her bubble-slick body rubbing against mine. "You're going to marry me on Saturday," I say, my tone harsher than I intended. "That's nonnegotiable."

She visibly stiffens and sits up. "Peter, that's not—"

"Or it can be tonight. I'm not averse to flying to Vegas with you after dinner." I do my best to keep my eyes off the soft white breasts exposed above the water.

This is too important to get distracted by my lust.

As if sensing my thoughts, Sara sinks back into the water, letting the bubbles shield those tempting breasts from view. "You have a plane on standby?"

"More or less." I let my teammates keep our plane for now, but I can charter a private jet on a couple of hours' notice.

With enough money, anything is possible.

"Peter..." She sits up again, this time covering her breasts with one slender arm. "We need to talk about this—about everything, really. You just came back yesterday, and I still don't really know where you've been or what you've been doing. Where are Anton and the twins? Are they here with you?"

"No." I take a deep breath and tamp down on the instinct that demands I carry her off to Vegas this very second. Sara is right; there's a lot we haven't discussed. "They're in Europe, but they'll fly in for our wedding," I explain and stand up.

She follows my example, and I wrap a towel around her as she steps out of the tub. She looks impossibly small like this, with her head bent and the thick towel wrapped all around her slender body.

It makes me aware of how defenseless she is, how breakable.

Reminds me of how I once wanted to punish her... and how I still sometimes do.

"Let's eat and talk," I say, reining in the dark impulse. "I'll tell you everything."

None of it, though, will change what's about to happen.

Before the end of this week, one way or another, Sara will be my wife.

CHAPTER 52

SARA

*O*ur dinner tonight is a mix of Russian and Asian cuisine, with juicy *pelmeni*—Russian-style meat dumplings—served with sour cream as an appetizer and a vegetable stir-fry topped with chili-marinated tofu as the main dish.

Lunch was forever ago, and the bout of intense sex combined with the hot bath further depleted my stores of energy. I'm so ravenous that as soon as Peter sets the food on the table, I dig in, devouring five large dumplings and two servings of the spicy stir-fry before looking up from my plate.

"Hungry?" Peter asks wryly as I go in for serving number three, and I flush, realizing I've been so focused on the food I've barely said a word.

"This is really good," I say apologetically, and he grins, his metallic eyes as warm as I've ever seen them.

"Enjoy, ptichka. I love seeing you eat the food I've made."

"You're an amazing cook," I tell him sincerely, and his smile widens further.

"I'm glad you think so, my love."

"What if you open a restaurant?" I ask impulsively. "You know, like Yulia did? Or a café of some kind?"

He laughs again, shaking his head. "No, ptichka. That's not for me. But I will feed you anytime you want."

"No, but seriously.... what *are* you going to do here?" I put down my fork and study him intently. "Do you have some ideas of what you'd like to do career-wise? You said you quit your job. I assume that means you're no longer a... um..."

For some reason, the word sticks in my throat, and he lifts his eyebrows, looking deeply amused.

"An assassin? No, ptichka. I'm done with that part of my life." He spears a piece of bok choy with his fork. "I'm a law-abiding citizen going forward."

"Really?" I stare at him, both hopeful and disbelieving. I initially thought he might be going straight, but then we had that conversation about Monica. Does that mean I misunderstood? I could've sworn there was an implicit promise to do something to the stepfather, but if Peter says he's going legit, then maybe those were just empty, soothing words, the kind that any guy might say to calm his girlfriend.

Thinking about Monica instantly sours my mood, killing what remained of my appetite, and I push my plate away as Peter grins and says, "Really. That's one of the conditions of the deal: no more crimes going forward."

"Oh. Good."

His eyebrows lift again. "You don't sound too enthusiastic."

"What? No!" I force away the heavy feeling blanketing my chest at the thought of Monica and smile brightly. "I'm ecstatic you're going straight. How could I not be?"

I mean it, too, even if I have to squash that tiny kernel of guilt-tinged hope about a permanent solution for Monica's dilemma.

There's no way I wanted that.

I refuse to believe it.

"I don't know, ptichka." Peter cocks his head, regarding me thoughtfully. "Is there something that worries you about that?"

"Everything worries me," I say bluntly. "How are you going to handle this kind of life? What are you going to do with your time? You say you want to marry me this Saturday, but then what? And what about your revenge? Did you find that last—"

"It's over." His tone is bolt-cutter sharp, his face darkening abruptly. "There's nothing to discuss on that front."

I stare at him, the food I ate turning into a boulder in my stomach. "What happened?"

He stands up and picks up his half-empty plate, then mine. "Nothing." Striding to the sink, he deposits the dishes so hard they rattle, then returns to the table to get more.

I get up too, my nerves strung tight as I watch him prowl around the kitchen with poorly controlled violence.

"Peter...." Gathering my courage, I catch his wrist the next time he strides by me. "What happened?" I repeat softly, looking up to meet his steely gaze.

The tendons in his thick wrist flex, and I know it would be child's play for him to break my grip. "Nothing," he answers instead, and this time, I catch the undertone of bitter grief and rage. "Absolutely fucking nothing."

I dampen my dry lips. "What does that mean? You didn't find him?"

His mouth twists, and he carefully extricates himself from my grip. "Let's just drop it, ptichka."

I want to, but I can't. Not if we're to build a life together.

I won't marry another man whose secrets could destroy us.

"Please, Peter." I recapture his hand, squeezing it between my palms. Holding his gaze, I say quietly, "Just tell me the truth."

His fingers curl in my grasp, and he closes his eyes, breathing deeply. When he opens them, the bitter rage is gone, veiled by a lack of expression. "I told you—nothing happened," he says evenly. "And nothing will. Henderson will go back to his regular life, safe and sound, because that's part of the deal I made." And as I stare at him, stunned, he says, "It's over, Sara. There's nothing more to say."

I start to speak and stop, unable to come up with the right words. With any words, really. My heart feels like it's crumbling into pieces, my chest so tight I can't pull in a breath.

He gave up a chance to fully avenge his family.

For me.

He did all this for me.

"Don't," he says tightly, and I realize I can feel a trickle of wetness on my face. The watery blur in front of my vision must be tears.

"I'm sorry." I let go of his hand and swipe the back of my hand across my cheeks. "I'm just… It's fine."

He stares at me, then turns away, resuming kitchen cleanup like nothing happened.

Like he didn't just rip my heart out of my chest and put it in his pocket.

I give myself a couple of minutes to calm down, and then I walk over to my bag and pick up my phone.

"What are you doing?" Peter asks as I press my parents' number, and I hold up my finger to my lips in a universal silencing gesture.

"Hi, Mom," I say when I hear the familiar hello. "How are you? How are you feeling?"

"I'm good, honey." She sounds puzzled. "What's going on? Everything okay?"

I look up at the clock and wince when I see it's after ten. "Yeah, everything is fine. Sorry to call so late—I had a shift at the clinic and lost track of time. I didn't wake you, did I?"

"Me? Oh, no. I was just reading before bed. Your dad is already asleep, though. Did you want to talk to him? I can wake him up if you—"

"No, no, it's fine. Let him sleep." I take a deep breath. "Mom, what are you and Dad doing tomorrow night? Are you free for dinner?"

Out of the corner of my eye, I see Peter go still, then resume loading the dishwasher.

"Well, we were thinking of going to Bingo Night, but we don't have to," Mom says. "Why, honey? You're not working tomorrow?"

"I have a light schedule," I say, and it's almost true. I'm not on call tomorrow, nor do I have any surgical procedures. And as far as my clinic shift goes, I'll reschedule it for another day. "Do you guys want to come over for dinner?"

A moment of silence, then: "To your place?"

"Yes. There's someone I'd like you to meet," I say as Peter turns to look at me.

This will be only the second time my parents visit my new apartment. I've never been particularly good at hosting, so usually, I either come over to their house or we go out for lunch or brunch. With Peter in the picture, though, I figure it's best if we're at my place.

My parents are more likely to be on their best behavior this way.

"Oh." Mom's voice fills with obvious excitement. "Yes, of course, honey, we'd love to. Do you want us to bring anything, or will we order in?"

"We got it, Mom. Don't worry about anything," I say as Peter continues staring at me. "See you tomorrow at six, okay?"

I hang up, and he comes toward me, his movements slow and vaguely predatory, like the lazy stride of a jungle cat.

"That was my mom," I say, instinctively backing up. "I invited them here for dinner tomorrow. You don't mind, do you? We can order in, or—" My words end on a squeak as Peter picks me up and places me on the counter, then pulls apart my robe.

"Peter, wait…" I lick my lips as he pushes the robe down my arms, baring me completely. "We should decide what we're going to—ahh…" I moan, my head falling back as he kisses the sensitive area around my collarbone at the same time as his hand invades the aching nook between my legs, two rough fingers pushing into me without mercy. I'm not yet wet and it hurts, yet my body clenches on a flash of heat, on a burst of violent sensation.

"You're marrying me. This Saturday," he growls, fucking me with those fingers, and I moan my agreement, my body igniting anew.

This Saturday, tonight, tomorrow—it doesn't matter anymore. I'm done fighting, done resisting.

He was right all along.

I'm his, and he's mine.

This was meant to be.

CHAPTER 53
PETER

She's sleeping, exhausted, when I carefully climb out of bed and gather the clothes I left folded on a chair. I dress quietly, taking care not to wake her, and then I pad out of the bedroom on sock-clad feet.

My boots are by the entrance, so I pull them on and pat my jacket pocket to make sure my phone is there.

I'll need it to navigate to the current location of one Mr. Samson "Sonny" Pearson, Monica Jackson's stepfather.

Danny is already waiting for me in the parking lot, so I pull up the email from my hackers and give him an address a few blocks away from where Pearson lives—which happens to be at his ex-wife's apartment.

Monica's mother clearly has no qualms about letting her daughter's rapist crash with her.

It's a risk I'm taking, doing this myself. It would've been smarter to hire someone to carry out a discreet hit in a few months, when no one could possibly connect Pearson's death to his stepdaughter's visit to the nonprofit women's clinic. However, my *ptichka* was crying today—crying because of this *ublyudok*—and I can't let that stand.

He's going to die tonight, and his stepdaughter will finally be free.

"Drop me off here," I tell Danny when we reach the address I gave him, a building that's a few blocks from my real destination. The guy is loyal and quite willing to operate outside the law, but I don't trust him like I do my own men.

It's better if I do this alone, with no witnesses.

Amira Pearson's apartment is on the second floor of a rundown four-story building. There is a faint smell of piss and vomit in the lobby, and the paint on the stairs is chipping, reminding me of Soviet-era buildings back in Russia. However, the apartment door I stop in front of is made of regular wood, not two layers of steel as is common in my corruption-ridden home country.

I could break this door with a single kick if I were so inclined.

I press my ear to the wood instead and listen. I can hear the low murmur of voices, so my information is correct. Sonny got a job unloading grocery store trucks at three in the morning and will be leaving for his shift shortly.

I go back down and step outside to wait. I could've broken in while the fucker was sleeping, but Monica's mother and brother are in the apartment, so it's better to wait.

It's better if I catch Sonny on his own and make it look like a robbery gone wrong.

It's nearly a half hour before he comes out, but I stay sharp and alert, the adrenaline pumping steadily through my veins. I can't deny the dark anticipation I'm feeling, the bloodlust fueling me like jugs of coffee.

I'm a predator, a monster, and I know it.

Now Sonny Pearson will know it too.

I stay half-hidden in an alley, and as he passes by, I reach out and grab him by the front of his shirt, pulling him in.

"Hey!" He tries to take a swing at me but freezes as soon as I press my blade to his throat.

"Don't move," I whisper, leaning in. "Don't even breathe."

The Adam's apple in his thick neck bobs dangerously close to my blade. "W-what do you want, man? I ain't got no m-money."

"I know." I don't have to see him blanch to know my smile is chilling. "That's not what I'm after."

And with that, I slice my blade across his throat. His warm blood bathes my fingers, and the stench of evacuating bowels fills the air. I watch the life fade from his mud-brown eyes, and then I say softly, "Monica sends her regards."

Letting his body drop to the pavement, I wipe my hand and my blade on the cleanest part of his shirt, extract his wallet from his pocket, and step out of the alley, heading back to where Danny is waiting.

We'll have to stop by a motel on the way back.

I need a shower before returning home.

CHAPTER 54

SARA

I'm still not ready to openly wear my ring in the office, but at lunchtime, when the dress people—two stylish women about my age—show up, I lead them through the main lobby, ignoring the receptionist's curious stare. We go into one of the exam rooms, and they measure me from head to toe—a process that takes mere minutes with their skilled hands.

"You're very slender, which is great," a tall, dark-haired woman who introduced herself as Suzie says. "We have a gorgeous Monique Lhuillier that will fit you with minimal alterations. Pam, do you have a picture?"

Pam, a short, curly-haired blonde, pulls out her phone and shows me a sleek, mermaid-style dress hanging on a mannequin. Covered with delicate lace, it's strapless with a square neckline and a row of pearl buttons in the back—simple yet so perfect that I can only stare and drool.

"We have many other styles as well," Suzie says, incorrectly interpreting my speechlessness. "Is there anything specific that you'd—"

"No, this is great." I tear my gaze away from the phone screen. "How much is it?"

Suzie blinks and glances at Pam.

"Mr. Garin told us there's no set budget," Pam says carefully. "Is that not the case?"

"Oh, um... sure. I'm just asking out of curiosity." Finances is yet another thing I haven't discussed with Peter, so I do my best to hide my discomfort behind a brighter smile.

"Oh, I see." Pam beams back at me. "Well, rest assured that your fiancé is a very generous man. This dress is a one-of-a-kind runway edition with handmade lace, and it retails for thirty-three thousand plus tax. We're throwing in the alterations for free, though."

"That's... very nice of you." My voice sounds choked, but I can't help it. I'm no Cinderella—even after the pay cut at my new job, my salary is solidly in the six figures—but thirty-three thousand is still an eye-popping sum for a dress I'll wear exactly once.

I thought the twelve-hundred-dollar dress at my first wedding was expensive.

"You'll need shoes and accessories as well," Suzie says, pulling a shiny catalog out of her oversized handbag. "Do you want to flip through this"—she holds up the catalog—"or would you rather we recommended something?"

"I'd appreciate a recommendation," I say, and they swiftly find me a pair of white Louboutin pumps with delicate straps around the ankles, and a pearl necklace to go along with two pearl-and-diamond studs for my hair.

"You're going to want an updo, of course," Pam says, flipping through the catalog to point at a few intricate hairstyles on the models. "It's going to really bring it all together."

"Thank you. I'll be sure to do that," I say as they pack up and head out. True to their word, the whole process took just under thirty minutes—a fraction of the time I spent shopping for a dress and accessories for my first wedding.

Maybe there's some benefit to Peter railroading me like this, I think wryly as I step out to grab a quick lunch in the half hour I have left before my next patient. My first wedding was a big production, with George inviting everyone we knew and spending money we didn't really have. We had two hundred people at the reception, and it took a year to plan—and I, swamped with residency at the time, hated every minute of that planning.

A small wedding where all I have to do is show up might be exactly up my alley.

"Who were those people?" the office receptionist, Annabelle, asks when I return from lunch, and I take a breath, realizing I do have one important task on my plate.

I have to invite my friends and colleagues, enduring their surprised questions in the process.

"They were here to measure me for a dress," I say, deciding there's no time like the present. Slipping my left hand into my bag, I surreptitiously put on my ring and take my hand out, displaying the large diamond to Annabelle. "You see, I'm engaged, and the wedding is—"

An excited squeal drowns out my words before I can say "this Saturday." Annabelle, a no-nonsense woman in her late fifties who handles insurance companies and difficult patients with equal aplomb, jumps to her feet as spryly as a teen and grabs my hand to gape at the ring, chattering the whole time.

"Oh my God, look at that rock! Who's the lucky guy? How did you meet him? I didn't even know you were dating!"

When she pauses for breath, I tell her that Peter and I have been dating on and off for some time, but that our relationship wasn't serious because of his job, which required a lot of travel abroad. Now, however, he's going to be doing something else, so we decided to take the next step and got engaged.

"We're not planning a big wedding," I say before she can launch into the next set of questions. "Instead, we're going to have a small ceremony this Saturday, and I would love it if you and your husband could attend. I know it's short notice, but—"

She squeals again and hugs me. "Oh, thank you, honey—I'm so honored! We'll definitely be there. Did you already tell Bill and Wendy?"

I grin at her excited face. "No, I'm about to."

"Oh, then go do that. Right now. I can't wait to see the look on Bill's face when he finds out I was right." At my raised eyebrows, she explains, "I bet him twenty bucks that a pretty girl like you must have a boyfriend." And as I burst out laughing, she sticks her head out to the waiting area and says, "I don't see your patient yet, so you have a couple of minutes."

"Thanks, Annabelle." I laugh as she makes shooing motions with her hands. "I'm going, I promise."

I hurry to my bosses' office before Annabelle can physically drag me there, and knock on the door.

"Wendy? Bill? Do you guys have a second?"

Wendy opens the door a second later. "Of course, my dear. How can I help you?" Her smile is as soft as the white hair puffing out around her kind face. Everything about the female Dr. Otterman is kind, from the gentle tone of her voice to the way she regularly calls her patients to check up on them.

Working with her is an absolute pleasure, even with her grouchy husband always at her side.

"Is Bill here?" I ask, then see him sitting behind her, chowing down on a sandwich nearly as big as his mustache.

He gives me his customary glare and puts down the sandwich. "What is it?"

If I didn't know better, I'd think he hates me. But he's like this with everyone, patients included, so I don't take it personally.

According to the nurses, the more he glowers at you, the more he likes you.

"Well…" Out of the corner of my eye, I see Annabelle come up to stand next to me. She clearly can't resist seeing the aforementioned look on Bill's face firsthand. "I was wondering if you guys have plans this Saturday," I say, figuring it's best not to make a big deal of it. "I'm getting married in a small, low-key ceremony, and—"

"You what?" Bill's grizzled mustache quivers as his gaze falls to my left hand. "You're engaged?"

"As of yesterday," I say, lifting my hand to display the ring. "I know it's short notice, so if you have other plans, it's totally—"

"Oh, no, we'll be there, my dear. Congratulations." Wendy beams at me and reaches out to squeeze my right hand. "Who's the lucky gentleman?" She peers at my left hand. "That's a beautiful ring he gave you."

Bill's mustache refuses to stop moving. "You have a boyfriend?" His glower deepens as he gets to his feet. "We didn't know you had a boyfriend."

I smile and repeat my explanation about us being on and off and Peter traveling a lot before. "So now we're ready to take the next step," I conclude and glance up at the clock on the wall. "Oh, look at that. My patient is probably here now," I say, and watch as grinning Annabelle hurries back to her post.

"Sorry, I have to run," I tell my bosses. "So you'll be there?"

"With bells and whistles on," Bill says sourly.

I take that to mean he's happy for me as well, and with a cheerful wave at Wendy, I hurry off, pleased that this part of my task, at least, went off without a hitch.

Now I just have to tell everyone else—and then explain it to my parents.

I have an appointment cancellation in the second half of the afternoon, so I use that time to start making the necessary calls.

Simon and Rory don't pick up, so I leave them a voicemail to call me. Phil, however, must already be done with his workday at school, because he picks up on the first ring.

"Hey, there you are. We thought your mystery boyfriend might've carried you off," he says, and I laugh, hoping he can't hear the semi-hysterical note in the sound.

He's joking, but Peter could've easily made me disappear.

That's what I thought was going to happen when I left the bar with him.

"Still here," I say when I stop laughing. "But I do have some news."

"Don't tell me." Phil mock-gasps into the phone. "You're preggers."

"Um, no…" Or at least if I am, I don't know it yet. It's not impossible after two days of unprotected sex, but it's definitely too soon to tell. "I *am* getting married, though."

There's dead silence on the phone. Then: "WHAT?"

"Yeah, it's kind of a long story," I say and launch into the same explanation I gave my coworkers about my on-and-off relationship and Peter's travels.

"But why didn't you tell us about him?" Phil still sounds stunned. "We all thought you didn't date because of your husband."

"It was a bit complicated at times. And since I wasn't sure it was going anywhere…" I trail off, hoping Phil fills in the blanks on his own. "In any case, we *are* getting married, and it's happening this Saturday, so—"

"WHAT?"

I grin, picturing his bulging eyes. "Yes, I know. We decided against a long engagement. In any case, I know it's super short notice, so if you have other plans this Saturday, I completely understand. But if you *can* make it, we'd love to have you there, and obviously, you're welcome to bring a date."

"You're getting married. This Saturday."

"That's what I just said." I pause to give him a chance to emote more, but he seems to have lost his tongue, so I plow ahead. "You don't have to tell me right now, but if you get a chance, I'd love to know by tomorrow if you'd be able to attend. Peter booked a catering company and everything, so it's going to be small but hopefully nice."

"Where..." Phil clears his throat. "Where is the wedding going to be?"

"At Silver Lake Country Club," I say. "You know it?"

"Yes, of course. My cousin got married there a couple of years ago. Beautiful spot."

"Oh, good." I smile, though he can't see it. "So can you tell me if you'll be there, or do you need until tomorrow?"

"Are you kidding me? Of course I'll be there. Did you already tell Rory and Simon?"

"Left them voicemails," I say and look at the clock. I better hurry if I'm to call Marsha before my next patient. "Thanks a lot, Phil, and sorry to spring this on you," I tell him. "See you Saturday."

"Yeah. See you," he says, still sounding stunned as I hang up.

Marsha is next on my list, and it's a conversation I'm dreading nearly as much as the upcoming dinner with my parents. As I dial her number, I'm half hoping she doesn't pick up, but she grabs the phone on the first ring.

"Hey, hon."

I take a deep breath. "Hey, Marsha. How's it going?"

"Eh, you know. Just about to head in for my evening shift. Andy pulled the short straw this week, but her boyfriend threw a hissy fit because it's their anniversary today, so she asked me to swap with her. How's it going with you? What are you up to this weekend? Tonya and I were going to hit up a couple of bars on Saturday. Want to join us? You don't have a performance, do you?"

"No, but actually, about this Saturday..." I grip the phone tighter. "I have some news."

"Oh?"

"There's a guy I've been seeing for a while. Kind of on and off."

"Really?" Marsha's voice perks up. "Who? Not that red-headed bodybuilder from your band, is it?"

"Rory? No, not at all."

"Oh, good. Because Tonya really liked him and thought it might be mutual. Who then? Have I met him?"

"No, you haven't." I take another deep breath. "It's gotten very serious between us, though."

"Really?" Her interest level is clearly spiking. "Serious how?"

I brace myself and rattle out, "We're getting married this Saturday."

"You're *what*?"

The cat is out of the bag, so I repeat as calmly as I can, "I'm getting married. This Saturday. And if you can, I'd love for you to be there."

"This is a joke, right?"

I pinch the bridge of my nose with my free hand. "No. We decided against a big formal ceremony, so we're just inviting a few people. It's going to be at Silver Lake Country Club. You know, over in Orland Park?"

"Uh-huh. And I'm going on *Dancing with the Stars*."

"Marsha... I'm not joking."

There are a few moments of heavy silence. Then: "You're getting *married*?"

"Yes. This Saturday."

"What the fuck? Are you serious? When did you two meet and how? What's his name? How come you never mentioned him to me?"

"It's a long story. We were on and off for a while, and then—"

"What do you mean *for a while*? How long is a while? Weeks? Months?"

I wince internally. "Um, months. Definitely months." Technically, this October will mark two years since Peter waterboarded me in my kitchen, but in terms of actual time spent together, it's probably closer to seven or eight months in total.

"Wow. Okay. Just... wow." Marsha falls silent for a second, then asks in a vaguely hurt tone, "Why didn't you say anything? You know we all thought you were single after… well, you know."

"I know, I'm sorry. Because we were so on and off, I didn't think it was that serious at first. He traveled a lot for work. But now he's done with that, so we decided to go ahead and take the next step."

"And the next step is *marriage*? What happened to just dating and living together? Sara, hon…" Her voice takes on a concerned note. "What's going on? Is everything okay?"

This is the hard part, because unlike Phil and my new coworkers, Marsha has known me for years. She knows I always look before I leap, and she also knows what happened with Peter.

Well, the darker parts of it, at least.

"Everything is fine." I put as much cheerfulness into my voice as I can. "We're just excited that we can finally be together, and we see no reason to wait. Neither one of us wants a big ceremony, so—"

"Okay, okay, whoa. Back up the truck. You still haven't told me his name or what he does."

I take a deep breath. Here goes nothing. "His name is Peter Garin. He used to be a security consultant, but he just retired from that field."

"Peter Garin? Wait a minute…" Marsha's voice grows tense. "Wasn't that Russian assassin who kidnapped you named Peter something?"

"Sokolov—and please, let's not go there." Mostly because I don't want to lie to her any more than I have to. "Anyway, as I was telling you, we're going to have a small wedding this Saturday, and we'd love it if you could attend. But I know you said you have other plans, so if you can't—"

"Oh, please, Sara. I'll obviously be there. The fucking bars can wait. But I'm still confused. Your guy's name is Peter too? And what kind of name is Garin? Where is he from?"

I drum my fingers on the desk. "He's from… kind of all over. But he was born in Eastern Europe." I can't lie about this; Peter's accent, faint though it is, clearly marks him as being from that part of the world.

That must be why he chose a Russian-sounding last name instead of something like Smith or Johnson.

"What?" Marsha sounds on the verge of flipping out. "Where in Eastern Europe?"

I squeeze my eyes shut. "Russia."

"You're kidding me, right? Tell me you're kidding."

I open my eyes and steal a glance at the clock. To my relief, it's almost time for my next patient.

"Look, Marsha, I have to run. You'll meet Peter on Saturday and learn all about him, I promise. Now I have to see a patient."

"Sara, wait—"

"I'll email you all the details tomorrow," I say and hang up, then mute my phone before she can call me back.

Four invites down, a bunch more to go.

I can handle this.

It's not so bad.

CHAPTER 55
SARA

It *is* that bad, I decide by the time I get off work, having spoken with Rory, Simon, Andy, Tonya, and my coworkers at the clinic during another fortuitous cancellation. After having essentially the same conversation a dozen times in a row, I'm wiped, and I still have to deal with the big kahuna tonight.

Dinner with my parents.

"I got it," Peter told me at breakfast when I offered to pick up takeout on my way from the office. "Just come home on time and don't worry about a thing."

Danny is idling by the curb when I emerge from my building, and I roll my eyes at Peter's overprotectiveness as I get into the car. This morning, the weather was too nice to drive the short distance to my office, so Peter walked me to work. And now I have an escort home as well.

At this rate, I'm going to forget what it's like to be on the street by myself.

Impulsively, I dial Peter's number.

"Hi, ptichka." His deep voice caresses my ears. "Are you on your way home?"

"I'm in the car with Danny." I glance at the driver, who's doing a good job of pretending to be deaf and mute as he pulls out onto the street. "You already knew that, though, right?"

"Danny texted me a minute ago, yes. How was your day, my love?"

"It was good. I invited pretty much everyone I wanted to invite, and Simon is the only one who won't be able to make it. He's got a family thing in South Carolina."

"Very nice." I hear some kind of clanging noise in the background, followed by running water, and then Peter says, "Hold on one sec. Just have to strain this pasta."

"Are you making dinner?" I ask when he picks up the phone again a minute later.

"Yes, Italian. Your parents like that, right?"

"They love it," I say, smiling. "I'm sure they'll be very impressed."

"You mean once they get over the urge to call the FBI? Yeah, you're probably right. This is coming out pretty tasty."

I burst out laughing, my anxiety over the upcoming dinner transforming into pure giddiness. This is happening, really, truly happening.

Peter and I are becoming a normal couple.

"How was your day?" I ask. "What did you do today?"

What *does* a former assassin do with his time?

"I ran a few errands, picked up some more groceries and such," Peter says, and I can hear the warm smile in his voice. "I also scoped out a couple of houses in the area for us to take a look at later. I didn't get a chance to talk to you about it yesterday, but this apartment is probably too small for us—especially this kitchen. And if I'm not mistaken, they don't allow pets, right?"

"Right. It's one of the biggest downsides of this building," I say, my heart tap-dancing in my chest. It's happening, really happening. A life together—house, dog, and all. Tamping down on a spike of giddiness, I say, "I chose it because it was close to both my parents and my work, but I wouldn't mind moving a bit farther now that Mom has recovered."

"That's what I figured," Peter says. "Two of the houses I looked at are close by, and one is about a mile farther from your office. Of course, there's still your old house…"

"They gave it back to you?" I ask and immediately realize it's a silly question. Peter is no longer a fugitive, so the government has no legal right to keep the property they seized when they learned it belongs to him.

"Yes, of course," Peter says. "Think about it and let me know what you want to do with it. Even if we don't move back there, we can keep it just in case, or we can sell it. Your call."

"Oh, really? And here I thought you're making all the decisions," I tease, then realize I'm only partially joking. Once again, Peter has swept into my life like a whirlwind, turning it upside down and wreaking havoc on my peace of mind. His force of will, coupled with his ruthlessness, makes it impossible to pretend that I'm in any way in control of my fate, that I have any real say in where our relationship is going.

And yet... maybe I do. We're here instead of hiding out in some remote part of the world, and I'm about to be his wife, not his captive. Even if his methods are heavy-handed, Peter has demonstrated in the clearest way possible that he cares about what I want.

That my happiness matters to him.

"You mean about the wedding?" Peter asks, taking my teasing at face value. "Because we can still change a few things if there's something you don't like."

"Such as the date?" I ask wryly. At the silence on the phone, I say, "Never mind. I already invited everyone. It's all good."

"Good, I'm glad." There's more clanging in the background as Peter says, "I'll see you home in a couple of minutes, ptichka. Love you."

Love you too. The words are on the tip of my tongue, yet I find myself saying, "See you soon," as I hang up the phone. I'm sure Peter knows how I feel—he's been convinced we belong together from the beginning—but because I've never said the words before, it feels wrong to casually blurt them out.

I do love him, though. I can finally admit it to myself, even though nothing's really changed. He's still a killer, still a monster any sane woman would fear and loathe. But I'm no longer sane, because I love him and I'm about to marry him.

Of my own free will, I'm about to join my life with a man who once tortured and stalked me. Who, technically, still stalks me—if always having me followed fits that definition.

"We're here," Danny says in a gravelly voice, and I look out the window, startled to realize that we're already parked by my building—and that the stone-faced driver actually spoke to me.

"Thank you," I tell him, grabbing my bag, and Danny gives me the slightest of nods as I climb out of the car.

Wow. Progress.

I was just acknowledged by my driver/bodyguard.

The giddiness I'd all but banished returns—at least until I see my parents' car pulling into the parking lot on the other side.

They're early.

A full twenty minutes early.

Frantically, I redial Peter.

"They're here," I say breathlessly as he picks up. "My parents—they're already here."

"That's good," he says, unruffled. "The food is almost ready. See you in a minute."

"Okay, yeah." I hang up and stuff my phone back into the bag. I start to slide the ring off my finger to leave it in the bag as well, but change my mind.

There's no point in hiding anything when they'll meet Peter in a minute.

Taking a deep breath, I approach my parents' car. "Hey, Mom, Dad."

"Oh, hi, darling." Mom opens the door and climbs out with only minimal stiffness. "Are you just coming home from work? Sorry we're a bit early; your dad thought there might be traffic, so he made me leave with lots of time to spare."

"There was *supposed* to be traffic, according to the GPS," Dad corrects and comes around the car to give me a hug.

I hug him back and then kiss Mom on the cheek. "It's all good. Dinner is almost ready."

Mom grins. "It's not takeout?"

"No, afraid not. The man I want you to meet—he's cooking." I look back to see Danny sitting inside the black car, silently guarding us, then turn back to face my parents. "There's something I have to tell you," I say carefully.

"What is it, darling?" Mom reaches out to touch my left hand, and her fingers brush against my ring. Instantly, her gaze hones in on the diamond, and her eyes widen to the size of quarters. "Sara, is that—"

"I was just about to get to that," I say as my dad freezes, staring at my left ring finger in disbelief. "I have some really good news."

"You're engaged?" Mom tears her gaze away from the shiny rock to gape at me. "How? To whom? You weren't even—"

"Mom, Dad." I take each of their hands in one of mine. "Please listen to me and try to remain calm." They stay frozen, staring at me deer-like as I say steadily, "Peter, the man I love, is back. He's finally succeeded in resolving his misunderstanding with the authorities, and he's no longer wanted for questioning. We can finally be together—and yes, we just got engaged."

CHAPTER 56
PETER

I look out the window again, where Sara is talking to her parents in the parking lot. They've been at it for a solid eight minutes, and I wish I had a listening device on Sara so I could hear what they're saying.

Judging by the wild gesticulating by all three, emotions are running high.

Maybe I should plant a bug with listening capabilities on Sara. Maybe even a few—one in her phone, one in her bag, and another couple in her favorite footwear. I already track her phone, so I know where she is at all times, but this would give me an additional peace of mind.

The table is all set, but I hold off on putting out the food. Finally, the Sara-tracking app on my phone informs me that her phone is in the building and approaching the apartment, so I walk over to open the door for her and her parents.

"Mom, Dad, this is Peter," she says as the elderly couple come in behind her and stop, eying me warily. "As I explained, he's made a clean break with his old connections and now goes by the name of Peter Garin. Peter, these are my parents, Lorna and Chuck Weisman."

"Pleasure to meet you both," I say and extend my hand for Sara's father to shake.

"Likewise." Despite the polite response, Chuck's voice is as hard as his grip, and his faded blue eyes are sharp as he glowers at me.

I shake Lorna's hand next, being careful not to crush her fragile fingers.

"You have a lot of explaining to do, *Mr. Garin*," she says softly, looking up at me, and I smile, seeing shades of Sara in the elegant lines of her aged face.

"Of course. I'm happy to explain everything."

"Dinner is ready, so how about we sit down at the table?" Sara suggests, coming up to stand next to me, and warmth fills my chest as her slender arm slips around my elbow in a proprietary gesture.

My ptichka. Finally, she's accepted us as a couple.

"Sure. Whatever's cooking smells good," Lorna says, and I smile at her again, realizing that Sara's mother, at least, is willing to play ball.

When we get to the kitchen, Sara excuses herself to go to the bathroom, and I set the Caesar salad and the antipasti platter I prepared on the table.

"Sara said you like to cook," Lorna says, watching me move around the kitchen, and I nod, taking a seat across from her.

"It's a hobby of mine. I find it very soothing."

"Hobby, huh?" Chuck's glower deepens. "What's your occupation then? We've never been able to get a straight answer from Sara."

"I've done a couple of different things, but most recently, I worked as a security consultant and had a business along those lines," I say and stand up. Picking up the salad tongs, I look at Lorna. "Salad?"

She nods regally. "Please."

I lean over the table and place a sizable portion of salad on her plate, then look at Chuck.

"None for me, thanks." He spears a marinated artichoke with his fork and transfers it from the antipasti platter onto his plate, eyeing me balefully the whole time.

"What kind of business?" he demands as soon as I sit back down. "Sara said you were a contractor of some kind. Was that the security consulting business? Who were your clients, and how does all this tie into your recent troubles with the law?"

I suppress the urge to smile. The old man doesn't pull his punches.

"My background is Spetsnaz—the Russian Special Forces," I say, deciding I can disclose that much. "After I left the military, I traveled all over the world and consulted for a number of organizations and individuals who had reasons to be concerned about security. I can't tell you the specifics of what got me in trouble, as that's classified, but I can assure you that it's all resolved now."

"Resolved how?" Lorna asks as Sara returns to the kitchen, and I smile as my ptichka takes a seat next to me and eagerly reaches for the salad.

"I made a deal with the authorities that was advantageous for both sides," I say as Sara begins eating, apparently content to let me field her parents' questions. "So now I have a new last name and a clean slate—and Sara and I can finally get married."

"A clean slate from what?" Sara's father asks, his nostrils flaring. "I heard people had been killed."

"I can't tell you anything more than what you already know, I'm afraid." I place some salad on my own plate. "It's part of the deal I made."

Chuck's face reddens, and for a moment, I'm convinced he's going to stab me with his fork. However, he must be more civilized than I am, because the only thing he spears is a juicy green olive from the antipasti platter.

"Mr. Garin," Lorna says, putting down her fork. "I hope you—"

"Please, call me Peter. We're about to be family."

Her carefully painted mouth tightens slightly. "Okay, *Peter*. I hope you understand that we have a lot of concerns, both about your background and your connections. Not to mention the fact that Sara disappeared for five months after the two of you... well—"

"Started dating?" Sara helpfully suggests, and her mother frowns at her.

"Right, started dating." Lorna turns her attention back to me, and I recognize the backbone of steel within her. It's the same one her daughter possesses, the one that has enabled my ptichka to handle the kind of trauma that would've destroyed a weaker person.

"Listen to me, Peter." Sara's mother leans forward, and though her voice remains soft, her gaze is as sharp as her husband's. "You might've resolved your 'misunderstanding' with the authorities, but we're not convinced you're not a danger to our daughter. We don't know anything about you, and what we do know is, frankly, quite unsettling. Sara says that the two of you are in love, and that she went with you of her own accord, but we have serious doubts about that. You are not the kind of man our Sara would ever—"

"Mom, please." Sara pushes aside her plate. "I've told you over and over again that Peter is not what you—"

"Your parents are right, ptichka." I cover her hand with my palm and squeeze lightly, then turn to look at her mother. "Mrs. Weisman," I say, using the formal address to show my respect. "I completely understand your reservations. If I were you, I'd be just as concerned because you're absolutely right: your daughter and I come from different worlds."

Lorna and Chuck stare at me, obviously taken aback, and I use the moment to prepare what I'm going to say. I have to be very careful here, walk a fine line between letting them feel like they know me and terrifying them out of their minds.

I decide to start at the beginning. "I grew up in an orphanage in Russia," I say. "I have no idea who my parents were, but I'm almost certain they were nothing like the two of you. Most likely, my mother was a teenager who found herself pregnant, but that's pure speculation on my part. All I know is that I was left on the doorway of the orphanage when I was maybe a few days old."

Sara covers our joined hands with her free one, silently lending me her support as I continue.

"It wasn't a great place to grow up, and as a youth, I was perpetually in trouble," I say as the Weismans continue to stare at me. "However, when I was seventeen, I got recruited into a special counterterrorism unit of Spetsnaz— which is where I served my country for a number of years."

"He was really good at that," Sara interjects, sounding as proud as any fiancée. "At twenty-one, he was already head of his team."

I smile at her, the warmth in my chest intensifying even though I know she's just putting on a show for her parents. Sara knows what I did as part of that unit, and I doubt she's truly proud of how many terrorists and radical insurgents I caught and tortured for my country. Still, it feels good to have her approval, fake though it might be.

"That *is* impressive," Lorna says, and I turn to see her and Chuck regarding me with a slight lessening of hostility.

"Thank you," I say and smile at them. "I *was* good, thanks partially to my misspent youth."

"So why did you leave then?" Chuck asks, reaching over to spear another olive. "How did you end up here?"

My mood darkens, the warmth inside me dissipating despite Sara's continued gentle touch. I didn't know if I would go there—if I could bring myself to go there—but I see now that I have to, that if I omit this important part, the Weismans will sense it and I'll lose a chance to gain their trust.

"A few years into my service, work brought me to a small mountain village in Dagestan, where I met a young woman," I say evenly, pulling my hand out of Sara's hold. "She became pregnant, and we got married."

Lorna's eyes widen. "You have a child?"

"Had," I say, and despite my best efforts, the word comes out harsh, almost bitter. "Pasha, my son, and Tamila, my wife, were killed seven years ago. Daryevo, the village where they lived, was mistakenly thought to be harboring terrorists, and dozens of innocents were killed in a NATO-led strike."

Sara's parents gape at me, their faces pale and eyes full of disbelief.

"I don't understand," Chuck says after a long, heavy moment. "How could something like that happen? And wouldn't that kind of horrible error have been all over the news? What you're saying is..." He shakes his head and reaches for a glass of water with an unsteady hand.

"It's hard to believe, I know, Dad," Sara says. "But I can tell you that it's true. I saw the pictures with my own eyes. It happened, and it *was* horrible."

Lorna stares at her daughter, then turns to me. "I'm so sorry, Peter." Her voice softens further at whatever she must see on my face. "How old was your son?"

"He would've been three the following month." A surge of anguish chokes me, and I stand up, unable to look at Sara's parents. Walking over to the stove, I pick up the pot of pasta and return with it to the table, using the time to compose myself.

"I hope you like this kind of marinara sauce," I say in a calmer tone, putting a solid portion of the sauce-covered linguini onto Sara's plate before doing the same for her parents. "It's a little different from what you'd buy at the store."

Sara's mother winds her fork in the linguini and takes a bite, then gives me a tremulous smile. "It's very good, Peter. Thank you."

"You're welcome."

I feel Sara's delicate hand on my knee, squeezing lightly, and when I look at her, I see that her hazel eyes are much too bright. She doesn't say anything, but the elusive warmth returns, thawing the icy block that formed inside me at the recollections.

Sara's father pointedly clears his throat. "So, um… how did you end up here, then? After, you know."

I take a breath. This is where I have to be careful not to disclose too much.

"There was an investigation," I say, meeting Chuck's gaze. "One that resulted in the guilty being officially absolved of blame and the whole incident being dismissed as 'one of those things that happen in that part of the world.' I didn't accept that outcome, and since my superiors were complicit in the cover-up, I left my job. I then traveled the world, working as a security consultant, and eventually, I ended up in Chicago, where I met your daughter."

"How did you end up in trouble with the authorities, then?" Lorna asks, eyeing me with wariness tinged with a touch of sympathy. "Did it have something to do with what happened to your family?"

"I'm afraid I can't tell you that. As I mentioned before, it's classified." I pause, letting them draw their own conclusions, and when no more questions are immediately thrown at me, I look them both in the eye and say quietly, "Lorna, Chuck—I hope I can call you that?" At Lorna's nod, I continue. "I can't lie to you about the kind of man I am. I didn't grow up in a nice neighborhood, and I didn't go to school to be a doctor or a lawyer. I'm a soldier by training and inclination, and I've seen and done things you most likely can't imagine. But I do love your daughter. I love her with everything I am. She's the only person who matters to me in the world, and I would do anything for her." Turning to Sara, I gather her hand in mine and say with complete truthfulness, "I would give my life to make her happy."

CHAPTER 57

SARA

I have no idea how I thought the dinner would go, but the last thing I expected was for Peter to bare his soul to my parents, to disarm them with sincerity instead of squashing their objections with arrogance and veiled threats.

All through the rest of the dinner, he's polite and respectful, answering their questions with enough detail that when he does gloss over something, it still sounds like the complete truth.

Where did we meet? In a club in Chicago. Was he already a fugitive? Yes. Why did we date in secret? Because of said status as fugitive, which he didn't inform me about until I was already on the plane with him. Why didn't I come home for five months? Because the authorities discovered where he was, and that was the only way for us to be together. What is he planning to do now? Still deciding, but he has enough money for both of us to live on for the rest of our lives. How did he acquire so much money? Through his consulting business—and yes, the specifics of that are classified, too.

At first, I just listen, but when I better understand his strategy, I pitch in with my own answers, carefully following Peter's lead. By the time we get to dessert—bowls of fresh berries topped with homemade tiramisu—my parents appear, if not exactly comfortable with our relationship, then at least more accepting.

It's certainly better than their panicked reaction when I informed them about our engagement in the parking lot. They were on the verge of calling the FBI when I told them our wedding is this coming Saturday, and it took everything I had to convince them to go up and actually meet Peter for themselves.

"I still don't understand why you're rushing into marriage," Mom says, sipping her chamomile tea, and I hide a smile at the resignation in her tone. At least the topic now is the speed of the wedding, not how dangerous Peter is or whether we should be together at all.

"That's my initiative, I'm afraid," Peter says and gives my mom a smile so charming I'm surprised she doesn't melt on the spot. "I've missed your daughter so much that I proposed as soon as we were back together. Life is just too short, you see; when you find the right one, you have to hold on to her—and I know Sara and I are right for each other. Besides"—he glances at me, his gaze heating up—"I'd like us to start a family soon."

My dad nearly knocks over his coffee cup. "You what?"

Peter hands him a napkin. "I'd like us to have children," he says calmly as my dad mops up the spill. "A little girl and a boy—or whatever fate has in store for us."

I blush as Mom's gaze instantly zeroes in on my belly.

"Sara, darling, you're not—"

"No, of course not." I can feel my face reddening further as Mom lifts her eyebrows disbelievingly. "It's too soon—Peter's just returned."

"But you're already trying?" Mom asks, a gleeful grin spreading over her face, and to my shock, I realize she's happy about this development.

The primal urge to have grandkids must outweigh her remaining concerns about Peter.

Dad, on the other hand, looks as uncomfortable as I feel. "Lorna, please. This is none of our business."

"As soon as a baby is on the way, you'll be the first to know," Peter promises my mom, and she shocks me again by nodding conspiratorially.

"Thank you." Lowering her voice, she leans in toward my former kidnapper. "I thought it wouldn't happen in our lifetime."

My face must match the color of the raspberries in my bowl, but my dad appears intrigued. I guess it just occurred to him that all of this—from the unexpected return of my no-longer-criminal lover to our hasty engagement—bodes well for something he's been hinting at ever since my wedding to George.

Like Mom, he wants grandkids, but given his advanced age, he'd all but given up hope he'd see any.

On my end, I'm still rather terrified by the idea, but now is not the time to express those doubts. Besides, I remember how I felt when I got that late period, how the disappointment was so intense it was almost like grief. Maybe I *do* want a child with Peter, even though the rational part of me is screaming that we should wait and see how this all unfolds.

Whether I can really build a normal life with a ruthless killer.

As we finish up dessert, Peter discusses the details of the upcoming wedding with my parents, considerately asking them about their officiant preferences and how many people they'd like to invite themselves. I listen bemusedly as the three of them settle on a local judge my dad knows, and my parents express a desire to invite the Levinsons along with a few more of their friends—something Peter very much supports.

"On my end, I'm only going to have three friends," he says, undoubtedly referring to his Russian teammates, and that seems to calm my parents a bit more—probably because the fact that he has friends further humanizes him in their eyes.

When we finish, Peter starts clearing the table as my parents get ready to head home.

"Thank you. That was delicious," Mom tells him.

"Yes, thanks," Dad echoes grudgingly as my fiancé smiles at them.

"It was my pleasure. We hope to see you again soon," he says, and I put on my shoes to walk my parents down to their car.

"Well, that was not what I expected," Mom says as the elevator doors slide shut. "He's… interesting, this Peter of yours."

I grin at her. "You mean, gorgeous *and* domesticated? Yes, I agree."

Dad snorts. "If that man is domesticated, I'll eat my foot. A savage, that one. Without a doubt."

"Chuck!" Mom frowns at him.

"Didn't you see the way he looked at her?" Dad retorts as the elevator doors open on the first floor. "I'm surprised he didn't club her over the head and drag her off to bed in front of us."

"Dad, please." The blush that had just left my face returns, magnified tenfold. "That's not—"

"Well, of course I saw that," Mom says as though I'm not there. "That's not necessarily a bad thing, though."

"It is when you are dealing with a man like that." Dad glances over his shoulder, as though Peter might be listening—which, knowing his stalker tendencies, he might very well be.

For all I know, there are already cameras in the building and who-knows-what planted on me.

"I don't think he's as bad as that," Mom says as we pass a couple of neighbors in the lobby. "I mean, yes, he's not your average Joe or Harry, but—"

"He's dangerous," Dad says flatly. "Don't fool yourself. Just because the man wants a family doesn't mean he's not capable of things that would make your eyelashes curl. What he's told us today is just the tip of the iceberg, believe me."

"Oh, I believe you," Mom says as we exit into the parking lot. "But I think he does love her, and if all those problems with the FBI are really over—"

"Maybe you guys want to wait two minutes, so you can discuss me in third person when I'm *not* there?" I suggest, trailing behind them. "Otherwise, I can head back up and—"

"No, no, darling." Mom stops and turns around, giving me an apologetic look. "Sorry, we're just trying to come to terms with it all, you understand."

"I do, Mom." I smile and lean in to kiss her soft cheek. "I was just kidding. I know this will take some adjustment."

"Sara, darling." Dad touches my shoulder, and when I face him, he says quietly, "Just promise us one thing."

"What is it?"

"If he ever hurts you, or scares you, or does anything else that worries you, come to us. Don't hide it or try to deal with it on your own, okay?" Dad's gaze is as hard as I've ever seen it. "I know you're in love with this man—I see it—but tigers don't change their stripes. He's dangerous. Maybe not to you, but to everyone else. I see it in his eyes."

"Dad—"

"No, listen to me, Sara. Even if he doesn't bring the horrors of his past into your life—something I doubt very much—he's not going to be like George, content to remain on the fringes of your life. He's not that kind of man, you understand?"

"I do." I understand better than my dad can imagine, because I know exactly what kind of man Peter is. With

George, even when I was part of a couple, I was able to remain my own person, to maintain that little bit of mental distance necessary to protect myself. But Peter is too dominating, too controlling to allow that. I'm going to be his in every sense of the word, and my dad intuitively grasps that.

"Chuck." Mom lays her hand on Dad's arm. "Come. We should go."

"Promise me," Dad insists, not budging, so I nod and smile.

"I promise, Dad. If anything happens, I'll come to you."

Dad nods, satisfied, and we walk together to their car. As I kiss and hug them goodbye, I notice Danny still sitting in his dark car, and I smile, looking up at the lit-up window of my kitchen.

For all their warnings and admonishments, my parents have no idea just how dangerous and controlling my fiancé truly is. I lied when I made that promise to Dad. There's no way I can come to them with Peter-related concerns because there's nothing they, or anyone, can do.

The monster I've grown to love is in my life for good, and I have to figure out how to live with him.

CHAPTER 58
SARA

I go to work on Friday as usual, but I end up spending every minute between patients fielding my coworkers' questions about my upcoming wedding. To avoid sounding as ignorant about the event as I actually am, I tell them we want the details to be a surprise and leave it at that.

They'll see the flowers, the cake, and the dress tomorrow.

My parents keep calling as well, asking about all sorts of minutiae that I can't answer. I give them Peter's number, as he's the official wedding planner, but my mom still calls every hour with some kind of question or concern. I suspect it's because they're afraid I'll disappear again, so I try to be patient, but by the fifth call, it's all I can do to bring myself to pick up the phone and explain yet again that I have no clue if there will be chairs or benches at the ceremony.

It's a busy day at work, too, with a twin-pregnancy C-section scheduled this afternoon, which means I barely have time to get lunch before I have to head over to the hospital to perform the procedure. To speed up matters, I grab a sandwich from a convenience store and consume it in the car.

One perk of having a driver is having both of my hands free for eating.

The patient has already been given the epidural by the time I get to the operating room, and after I examine her, I perform the procedure right away, as she's starting to dilate and one of the twins is positioned the wrong way. The mom-to-be frets the entire time—she's in her early forties and wasn't able to conceive until her sixth IVF cycle—and when I place the two tiny but perfectly healthy boys in her arms, her face lights up with such joy that I have to blink away a few tears.

"Thank you, Dr. Cobakis," she says fervently as the nurses take the babies for their tests. "Thank you so much for everything."

"It was my pleasure, believe me," I tell her as I check her bandages one last time and jot down some notes in her chart. "Some pain and bleeding is expected after the procedure, but if you start to run a fever or are in severe pain, call me, okay?" I give her a strict look. "I mean it. Any time, day or night."

"Will do. You're so kind." Her teary-eyed smile is exhausted but full of joy. "Is it true what I overheard from the nurses? You're getting married this weekend?"

Rumors certainly travel fast.

Stifling a sigh, I say, "Yes, I am. But you can still call me if anything. I'll be around, okay?"

"Oh, thank you! And congratulations. I'm sure you'll be a beautiful bride." She beams at me, and I smile back, enjoying the uncomplicated interaction.

Unlike everyone else in my life, this woman doesn't know that this wedding is coming out of nowhere, or that I'm marrying a man most of my friends haven't met.

"Get some rest and enjoy your sons," I tell the new mom, and then I head back to the office to wrap up the day.

Maybe Peter has the right idea about not dragging this out any longer than we have to.

With any luck, the wedding madness will be over by Monday, and then things will return to normal—or at least as normal as they can be when you're married to the man who once kidnapped you.

CHAPTER 59
PETER

I give Danny an evening off and pick up Sara myself, too eager to see her to wait the extra few minutes necessary for her to get home. I'm glad she's neither volunteering at the clinic tonight nor has a performance, because even the hours she spends at work are too much time apart for me.

I need her with me. Always.

She comes out of her office building, her hazel eyes searching the street—looking for Danny, no doubt—when I open the car door and step out.

Her gaze immediately swings to me, and a smile lights her pretty face as she heads my way. It's a warm summer day, and she's wearing a sleeveless gray dress that hugs her ballerina-like frame. Her shiny chestnut waves bounce around her slender shoulders as she walks, and I'm again reminded of a fifties Hollywood starlet transplanted into modern times.

My beautiful ptichka.

I can't fucking wait until she's my wife.

"Hi," she says breathlessly, stopping in front of me. "Did you get a new car? I didn't know that was—"

I catch her face between my palms and slant my mouth across hers, kissing her deeply. I can't help myself. I crave everything about her, from the sweetness of her scent to the way her slim body arches against mine, her hands clutching helplessly at my biceps. I want to devour that sweetness, drink it in until I quench this raging thirst—though I know there's no quenching it.

I'm going to crave her until the day I die.

Becoming aware of some irritating giggling, I lift my head and pin the offenders—a pair of teenage girls standing a dozen feet away—with a harsh glare. They skitter away instantly, their faces paling under the heavy layer of their makeup, and I turn my attention back to Sara, who's blinking up at me, her soft lips swollen and rosy from the kiss.

"Hi, ptichka." Fighting the urge to reclaim those lips, I lower my hands to her shoulders, squeezing gently. "How was your day?"

"It was good." She still sounds a bit out of breath. "How about you?"

"Also good. I got this new car for us." I nod toward the black Mercedes S-560 behind me. At first glance, it looks like any other luxury sedan. A closer inspection, however, would reveal that the windows are made of bulletproof glass and that the metal frame is unusually sturdy.

It cost me a pretty penny, but it's worth it. I'm not expecting anyone to shoot at us, but one never knows. Plus, this car is pretty much indestructible in a crash—something that's very important to me after what happened with Sara in Cyprus.

"Nice," she says, even as a tiny frown forms between her eyebrows. "What about my old Toyota?"

"I sold it."

She steps out of my hold, her frown deepening. "You didn't think to consult me?"

I'm tempted to haul her to me and kiss her again until she forgets whatever it is that upset her about this. However, we've put on enough of a show for the passersby, so I just ask, "Were you attached to that car, my love? I can get it back if it has some sentimental value."

That doesn't seem to please her either. "No, I don't care about the car. It's just..." She squares her shoulders and looks me in the eye. "Peter, I need you to involve me in decisions that affect me—that affect us both. You told me once that this can be a partnership if I wanted, and I want that now. It's important to me."

I consider her words and nod. "Okay."

She blinks. "Okay?

"I'll ask you before I do anything else with the car," I say and open the passenger door. Clasping her elbow, I help her inside, my jeans growing uncomfortably tight as I catch a glimpse of pale blue underwear when she swings her shapely legs inside.

We might need to reevaluate this dress as a staple of her work wardrobe.

"I'm not just talking about the car," she says when I get behind the wheel. "It's about everything—like wedding arrangements and where we're going to live and what you're going to do work-wise. I want us to make all those decisions together going forward, like any normal married couple."

"I understand." I carefully check the mirrors and pull out onto the street. "You want me to consult with you like a husband should. I get it."

"You do?" She sounds puzzled for some reason. "I thought that—never mind. I'm glad you get it."

I smile and lay my right hand on her slender thigh, enjoying the silkiness of her bare skin. If my ptichka wants me to consult her about such trivia as the car or what I'm going to do with my time, I'm glad to do so.

We can make all the decisions together as long as she understands one simple fact.

She belongs to me, for the rest of our lives.

CHAPTER 60
PETER

$\mathcal{S}$aturday morning dawns warm and clear, with the kind of blue, cloudless sky I would've ordered from a wedding catalog if I could. The weather was the one uncontrollable variable, but as luck would have it, it's cooperating, so the event should go off without a hitch.

I've made sure of that.

Organizing a wedding is not all that different from planning a hit, I've come to realize. You have to be just as methodical about the logistics, and prepare for all eventualities. Of course, the stakes are very different, but it's good to see that some of my skills are applicable in the civilian life.

Esguerra was wrong.

I'm going to make this work.

Sara and I will be happy here.

Her hair and makeup appointments aren't until ten, and I wore her out last night, so I let her sleep while I make breakfast. Then I return to the bedroom with a steaming cup of coffee in my hands.

She either hears me or smells the coffee, because she rolls over onto her back, one slender arm splaying out across the mattress while the other hand scrunches into a delicate fist to cover a big yawn. "Is it morning?" she mumbles without opening her eyes, and I grin as I sit down on the edge of the bed and set the cup of coffee on the nightstand.

"Yes, my love." Leaning in, I nuzzle the warm, fragrant crook of her neck. "It's our wedding day."

Her hair smells sweet and faintly fruity, like the shampoo in her shower. It makes my mouth water. Unbidden, my hand slips under the blanket, closing around one soft, round breast, and my cock hardens, my breathing speeding up as her erect nipple stabs my palm.

Fuck. There's no time for this—not to mention, she might still be sore from the three times I took her last night.

I force myself to straighten and move my hand away. "Your breakfast is ready," I say thickly and stand up, adjusting the uncomfortable bulge in my jeans. I need to cool off before I attack her right here and now, breakfast and wedding appointments be damned.

"Hmm." She yawns again and sits up, holding up a blanket to cover those tempting breasts. Blinking the sleep out of her eyes, she focuses on the cup sitting on the nightstand. "Is that coffee?"

"You bet. And there's breakfast in the kitchen—a vegetable quiche and home fries. You'll need the fuel to last you through the day."

She grins at me. "You're amazing."

My heart clenches—and my cock twitches again—as she jumps out of bed naked and beelines for the bathroom, apparently invigorated by the promise of caffeine and food. This is what I've wanted, what I've fought for all this time: Sara like this, playful and affectionate with me. We'll never be able to erase the darkness of the past, but together, we can build a lighter future.

A future that still feels terrifyingly fragile for some reason.

I shove the thought away as soon as it surfaces. There's no reason to assume that this kind of morning is temporary, that it's anything other than the start of our new life.

Today is our wedding day, and I'm going to make sure it's the best one ever.

It's the least my ptichka deserves after everything I've done.

CHAPTER 61

SARA

The invasion begins just as I finish gobbling down the breakfast Peter prepared for me. What feels like an army of stylists, makeup artists, and hairdressers descends on my tiny one-bedroom apartment, filling the living room with enough hair products, garment bags, and pots of eyeshadow for fifteen brides—or drag queens. Pam and Suzie, the women who measured me for a dress, are there, but so are two of their assistants and at least four hairdressers and makeup people. It's hard to tell exactly how many with all of them coming in and out of the apartment to bring the ever-mushrooming amount of supplies.

Peter promptly abandons me to the torture, claiming that he needs to oversee the security arrangements and other logistics at Silver Lake. His own tux is getting delivered straight there, so I won't even get a chance to see him in it until Danny brings me there later this afternoon.

"So not fair that all you have to do is put on a nice suit," I complain, mock-pouting, and he grins, then drops a quick kiss on my lips, making my pulse jump.

"Behave or else," he warns, silver eyes gleaming with amusement, and I pinch his side in revenge, making him laugh and kiss me again.

"Hair first," a flamboyantly dressed young man announces as soon as Peter leaves, and I let myself be guided to the couch where an array of scary-looking styling tools are already spread out in a row.

My hair is still wet from my morning shower, so it's first blow-dried into submission, then flat-ironed and curled. The updo apparently requires a perfectly smooth cuticle, which my wavy hair doesn't naturally possess. While that's happening, my nails are buffed, trimmed, and painted a soft pink shade, and then it's time for my makeup.

Mom shows up just as the last of the mascara is applied to my lashes. She's already coiffed to the max and dressed in a long peach dress that emphasizes her still-trim frame.

"Wow," she breathes as I get up from the couch, and I grin, walking over to hug her.

"You look amazing, Mom." I draw back to give her a thorough once-over. "I love this dress. When did you get it?"

"Your fiancé had it delivered last night. It's Chanel. Can you believe it? I was just lamenting to your dad yesterday morning that I wouldn't find anything decent on such short notice, and then bam, this dress arrives—and magically fits. Can you imagine? Your dad got a new tux too." She sounds as excited as a teenager going to prom.

"Wow, yeah. That's amazing." Peter must've installed cameras and/or listening devices at my parents' place again—an invasion of privacy we'll need to discuss. For now, though, I'm grateful he was thoughtful enough to include my parents in his insanely thorough brand of wedding planning.

Mom loves to dress up and would've been gutted if she'd had to wear an older dress or something she didn't find sufficiently special.

"How's Dad?" I ask as Pam and Suzie shoo everyone else out of the apartment and make me strip down to my underwear to try on the dress.

"He's good. Still processing all this, but—" Mom gasps as she sees the dress. "Wow, Sara. That's gorgeous!"

"It's Monique Lhuillier," Pam proudly tells her as Suzie helps me put it on and fastens the buttons in the back. "All handmade lace—every inch of it."

"Sara, that's…" Mom blinks several times, then audibly sniffles. "Darling, you look so beautiful… simply out of this world, like some kind of fairy princess."

"Really? Let me look." I wait until Suzie adds the hairclips, then walk over to the mirror in the bathroom.

A striking beauty stares back at me, her green-flecked eyes huge and mysterious in her flawless face. And it is flawless. The forehead scar from my crash—almost invisible these days anyway—is completely gone, and my skin is as smooth and poreless as glass. An hour of makeup, and I look like I'm scarcely wearing any—except that every feature appears as perfect as if it had been Photoshopped.

The hair is what gives the princess impression. Piled high on the crown of my head, it's an artful arrangement of curls and waves, each strand so shiny and smooth I hardly recognize it as my own. Even the color—dark brown with hints of red—is richer and brighter next to the diamond clips, though it could just be the extra glossiness imparted by all those products.

Pam was right about the updo: it's exactly what this dress needed. The lace gives the sleek mermaid dress an ethereal quality, yet it's only in combination with the intricate hairstyle that it takes on that magical, fairy-like look that got my mom all teary-eyed.

As I stare at myself in the mirror, my throat constricts.

I'm getting married.

To Peter.

Today.

The wave of panic is as spontaneous as it is irrational. Sucking in a gasping breath, I shut the bathroom door and lean against it, forgetting all about the fragile lace. My heart is like a war drum in my chest, my breath coming in rapid, shallow pants.

I'm getting married. To Peter.

I don't understand the source of my panic, but that doesn't make it any less intense. I can feel icy sweat popping out on my forehead and dampening my armpits, and it's all I can do to remain upright instead of sinking to the floor.

Peter and I are getting *married*.

"Sara?" Mom knocks on the door, sounding worried. "Are you okay, darling?"

Am I? I should be okay. I should be over the moon, in fact. I'm marrying the man I love, one who's gone to incredible lengths to show me that he loves me... to make me happy despite our inauspicious start.

Is that the issue? Is some part of me still unable to get past what Peter has done?

The flawless face in the mirror holds no answers, so I take a couple of deep breaths and steady my voice. "I'm fine, Mom. Just got a bit of an upset stomach."

"Oh, you poor darling. Do you have any Pepto-Bismol in the house?"

"No, but I'm fine. Just give me a second." I take a few more deep breaths, and when my heart is no longer jack-rabbiting in my chest, I wet a towel and rub under my arms. I then reapply anti-perspirant and pat at the top of my hairline with a tissue, taking care not to smear my makeup.

When the mirror confirms that there are no traces left of my impromptu panic attack, I paste a smile on my lips and step out, assuring Mom yet again that I'm fine.

We return to the living room, which is now startlingly empty.

"They all left," Mom says, smiling at my look of surprise. "While you were in the bathroom."

"Oh." I look at the clock and am shocked to see that it's already two in the afternoon.

No wonder Peter wanted to make sure I ate a hearty breakfast.

"The ceremony starts at four, but Peter said the photographer is coming at three for family pictures," Mom says. "So we should head over there. Your dad is already on his way."

"Right, okay." I curl my hand into a fist to hide the slight tremor in my fingers. My throat still feels too tight, and the thought of it all—the pictures, the ceremony, everyone staring and gossiping—is unbearable, completely overwhelming.

"Mom…" I press my hand to my stomach, which is now genuinely unsettled. "You know, I think I do need some medicine. There's a pharmacy a block away, so I'll just—"

"What? No, don't be crazy." Mom all but pushes me toward the couch. "You can't go anywhere dressed like this. Sit here, relax, and I'll be right back, okay?"

"No, Mom, that's fine. I'll just slip out of the dress and—"

"Sit." Mom's tone brooks no disagreement. "I may be old, but I can walk a block. I'll be back in a few minutes, and you just sit and rest, okay? Maybe eat something, too— you might have low blood sugar."

That's actually a good point. As soon as Mom leaves, I go to the kitchen and pop a few leftovers into the microwave. I remember this from my first wedding: being too busy to eat and feeling faint. This time, there's much less to worry about, thanks to Peter overseeing everything, so I actually have a few minutes to grab a bite.

The photographer can wait.

The doorbell rings just as I'm taking the pasta out of the microwave.

"It's open, Mom," I yell, grabbing a towel to make sure I don't burn myself with the hot plate, and then I realize it's far too soon for her to have returned.

Did one of the makeup people forget something?

Setting down the plate of pasta, I step out of the kitchen and freeze in place.

Agent Ryson is in my living room, his gaze raking over my white dress with derision.

CHAPTER 62
PETER

"You've actually pulled it off," Anton says admiringly as I adjust my black tie in the mirror. "Civilian life, amnesty, the girl, and all. I fucking can't believe it."

"Believe it." I turn around and grin at my former teammates. "How do I look?"

"Not bad." Yan walks around me, studying me critically. "I would've gone with a white tie, though. More formal and goes better with your skin tone."

Anton rolls his eyes at him. "Stop being such a fucking metrosexual. Seriously, Ilya, what did your mother feed this one?"

"Same crap she fed me," Ilya says and steps in front of the mirror to adjust his own tie. Unlike his elegant twin, who looks like he was born to wear a suit, Ilya resembles nothing more than a thug playing dress-up. The jacket strains across his steroid-enhanced shoulders, and the tattoos on his shaved skull gleam menacingly in the bright daylight.

Sara's father might have a heart attack just looking at him—and that's without knowing about the arsenal hidden inside his jacket.

Inside all of our jackets.

There's no real reason to worry, of course, but I'm still uneasy. Back in the good old days, events like this, especially in an outdoor venue, often provided an opportunity for us. Weddings, birthdays, funerals—we loved them all, because our targets, caught up in all the excitement, would invariably forget some key aspect of security.

It's a mistake I have no intention of making, which is why in addition to my usual Sara-watching crew, I've hired twenty more bodyguards and commissioned aerial surveillance via a dozen drones.

No one is getting within a kilometer of the venue without my knowledge.

"So, how's the civilian life so far?" Yan asks, falling into step beside me as I head outside to check if the photographer has arrived. "Is it everything you've dreamed of?"

His tone is mocking, as usual, but when I look at him, I don't see any amusement on his face.

"Yes," I answer, deciding to take the question at face value. "You should try it sometime."

He chuckles, but the sound lacks humor. "No, thanks. I'm enjoying this life too much."

I nod, not the least bit surprised. Instead of taking advantage of the amnesty I got for him, Yan took over the business—files, shell corporations, team accounts, and all—and has been using the team's contacts to secure new, ever more lucrative gigs. The takeover happened the day after I left for Esguerra's compound, which means Yan had been planning it for a while.

I was right to be wary.

If I hadn't stepped down when I did, one of us would likely be dead.

As expected, Ilya joined his brother in the new venture, but Anton is still deciding.

"I'm already fucking rich, you know," he told me on the phone two weeks ago, when Yan prodded him for an answer again. "I might miss the excitement and all, but I don't need more money—not the way Yan seems to." He paused, then asked carefully, "You're not mad at him, are you?"

"No," I told Anton, and I meant it. I told the guys they can carry on with the business if they want, so what do I care if Yan had been planning to step in my shoes all along? None of us are angels, and deep down, I always knew that Yan wouldn't be content following orders for long.

Even back in Russia, there were hints of that—a red flag I ignored when I offered the Ivanov twins a place on my new team.

In the context of my old world—*our* world—Yan Ivanov had been loyal enough, and since we avoided the ultimate clash, it makes sense to remain on good terms.

You never know when a favor might be needed.

"So what are you going to do here?" Yan asks when I stop to count the chairs in front of the gazebo. "Other than plan weddings?"

"I have a few ideas," I say, finishing the count. We're one chair short—something the venue staff needs to remedy right away. "For now, wedding planning suits me."

"You know you're deluding yourself, right?" Yan's tone lacks all hint of mockery, and when I turn to face him, I see a peculiar seriousness in his cold green eyes. "This is not for you—any more than it would be for me."

Did he and Esguerra read the same script? "Who are you trying to convince of that?" I ask curiously. "Me or yourself?"

He holds my gaze, then nods, as if seeing something I'm missing. "Good luck," he says softly. "I'll be rooting for you."

And turning, he walks back, leaving me to track down the photographer on my own.

CHAPTER 63
SARA

*M*y pulse skips a beat, then roars into overdrive.

This can't be happening.

They can't arrest Peter on the day of our wedding.

"Agent Ryson." I'm proud of the steadiness of my voice. "What are you doing here?"

He gives me a thin smile. "Oh, don't worry, Dr. Cobakis—or is it soon-to-be Dr. Garin? I'm not here in any official capacity."

My frantic heartbeat settles slightly. "Why are you here then?"

"To offer my congratulations, of course." His mouth twists. "You and your Russian lover sure had us all fooled."

I remain silent, because what can I say? I understand how this must look from his perspective—from the perspective of anyone who's been following the story from the beginning, really. I'm marrying George's killer, the man who waterboarded me, invaded my life, and kidnapped me.

The man Ryson spent the past two-plus years hunting.

"Tell me one thing, Dr. Cobakis," the agent continues bitterly. "At what point did you and Sokolov conspire to rid you of your brain-damaged husband? Was it before or during the so-called attack on you?"

I suck in a horrified breath. Is that what he really thinks? "You're mistaken. I never—"

"Never lied to us? Never pretended to need protection from the man you're about to marry?" His gaze is cutting. "Yeah, I thought so."

My neck burns. "It wasn't like that. Not at the beginning."

"Oh, really? How was it then? Did he brainwash you in Japan? Show you a few bedroom tricks to make you forget all the blood on his hands? Maybe you didn't care about the alcoholic you were going to divorce—yes, we know all about that—but your lover killed Cobakis's guards too. Good men, honest men. He blew their brains out—or have you forgotten?"

I swallow the bile rising in my throat. "Of course not."

"No?" Ryson steps toward me. "What about the police officers in the helicopter he shot down when they tried to rescue you from the supposed kidnapping? Or how about all the others he's killed and tortured in the name of whatever twisted justice he's pursuing? Would you like me to give you a list of all his victims, so you can pin it on the wall above your marriage bed?"

I'm shaking now, my stomach in complete revolt. The smell of the warmed-up pasta, so tantalizing a minute ago, is making me want to vomit, and it's all I can do to hold Ryson's gaze instead of curling up into a little ball of shame on the floor.

It's true, all of it.

Peter is a monster, and so am I for loving him.

At my lack of response, the agent snorts derisively. "Nothing to say? Well, let me give you a little warning." He comes closer until I have no choice but to step back. Looming over me, he says softly, "I don't know who pulled the strings, giving the two of you a clean slate, but if I've learned anything over the years, it's that psychopaths like Sokolov don't change. He *will* commit another crime, and when he does, the deal he's made with my higher-ups will be null and void. We'll be waiting—and now, Dr. Cobakis, we also have *your* number."

He steps back and turns, as if to leave, but then he stops and says over his shoulder, "Oh, and congratulations again. You make a beautiful bride. I hope the two of you will be very happy together."

He walks out then, slamming the door behind him, and I just barely make it to the bathroom before my stomach heaves, expelling its contents into the toilet bowl.

CHAPTER 64
PETER

$\mathcal{S}$he's late.

The ceremony is due to start in forty-five minutes, and Sara is still not here.

I give the photographer a scathing look as he pointedly glances at his watch, and he blanches, then looks away and starts fiddling with his cufflinks, as though that's what he was doing all along.

According to the bodyguards watching Sara's apartment, as well as the tracking devices I've planted on her, my bride is still at home with her mother. I've called both of them several times, but only Lorna picked up once. "Sara has an upset stomach," she informed me curtly and hung up—and has been sending my calls to voicemail ever since.

Worried and increasingly irritated, I survey the people milling around the gazebo in small groups, drinking champagne and eating the artfully arranged canapés.

Nearly everyone is here already, seemingly having a good time despite some of the guests—mostly, Sara's friends and former coworkers—eyeing me like I'm Osama bin Laden. Yan is chatting with Sara's new coworkers, while Ilya seems fascinated by what Sara's bandmates are telling him about their performances. Anton is talking to Sara's father about growing up in Russia, and I even see Joe Levinson, the lawyer who likes Sara, knocking back shots of tequila at the bar and staring grimly in my direction.

He's got balls, showing up here. He doesn't know I'm aware of his interest in Sara, but still. If he so much as looks at her the wrong way, he won't live to regret it.

That is, assuming she ever shows up for anyone to look at her in any way at all.

I wait five more minutes, checking my Sara-tracking app every thirty seconds, and then I call Danny, who's part of Sara's bodyguard crew today.

"I need you to go up to the apartment," I say when he picks up. "Hand your phone to Sara and do not leave until she calls me."

"Got it."

He hangs up, and five minutes later, my phone lights up with a call from Danny's number.

"Sara?"

"Peter, I…" She swallows. "I'm so sorry. I just need a little more time."

My worry intensifies. "What's wrong? Did something happen?"

"No, nothing. My stomach is just unsettled."

"Do you need me to send for a doctor? Get you anything?"

"No, it's just…" She stops, then says carefully, "Look, Peter, I know this is awful timing, but—"

"Are you trying to back out?" My voice is soft, betraying nothing of the fury blazing to life inside me. "Is that what this is about?"

"No, not at all. I just need a little more time. Your return, the wedding—it's all happening really fast. I'm not saying we shouldn't do it, but maybe this is too soon, maybe we can just live together for a bit, see if this is even—"

"Even what?" The hard metal of the phone cuts into my palm. "Even possible? Do you really think this is how it's going to go?" The rage is white hot within me, but I keep my tone gentle and my expression pleasant as I step behind a little patch of trees, away from curious eyes and ears.

"Peter, please. I'm just asking for a little extension. We can tell people the truth—that I'm not feeling well—and then—"

"Let me tell you how it's going to go, ptichka," I say in an even softer voice. "You can either go with Danny right now, coming straight here with no delays, or I'm going to come get you. Only we're not going to come back here in that case. In fact, there will be nothing here to come back to, because I intend to leave no witnesses to this unfortunate event." I pause, then ask gently, "Do you understand what I'm saying, my love?"

There's dead silence on the phone. Then she says in a broken whisper, "You wouldn't."

"No? Try me." I wait a couple of beats, then add, "Of course, your parents don't fall into the witness category. I know how much they mean to you, so we'll just take them with us when we leave. How does that sound? They'll enjoy an exotic getaway, don't you think?"

She's silent for so long I'm almost certain she's going to try to call my bluff. Except I'm not bluffing. I don't give a fuck about any of these people, with the exception of Sara's parents. If she pushes me, I will carry out my threat, even if it means giving up the amnesty I've fought so hard to get.

Without Sara, none of that bullshit matters.

If I can't have her, I might as well burn down the whole fucking world.

"You're insane," she whispers finally, and I smile darkly as I hear the capitulation in her voice.

"Yes, I am, ptichka. Don't forget that. I'll see you here soon."

And hanging up, I stroll back to mingle with the guests.

CHAPTER 65
SARA

I'm still shaking as I emerge from my bedroom, clutching Danny's phone in one hand and smoothing the soft lace of the dress with the other.

"I'm ready to go, Mom," I tell her when she rises from the couch, clearly surprised to see me.

"Are you sure? Darling, you look *really* pale."

"No, I'm fine, Mom." I manage a small smile. "The medication is finally kicking in."

My mom returned with the medicine just as I was coming out of the bathroom after being sick, so I immediately took a couple of pills and told her I had to lie down for a few minutes. I thought she'd accepted that explanation, but as her eyebrows pull together, I know I was just fooling myself.

Mom knows me far too well.

"Sara, darling… you know you don't have to go through with it, right?" she says, stopping in front of me. "If you're having second thoughts, you're allowed to change your mind. Everyone would understand. You don't have to marry him if you're not ready."

She's wrong. I'm not allowed to change my mind—not if all our friends are to survive the day. I have no idea if Peter would actually do what he implied, but I can't take that kind of risk.

Not with a man who's capable of such monstrous things.

If the agent's goal was to make me feel lower than a squashed bug, he succeeded admirably. Every word he threw at me felt like a bullet, because all of it was true. The crimes Peter has committed are awful, unforgiveable, and I know it. I've known it all along, yet I let myself fall for him.

I accepted his evil, embraced it to the point that I agreed to marry him of my own free will. Even after Ryson's visit, I wasn't going to reject Peter, though he interpreted it that way. I was just still reeling from Ryson's verbal lashing, and my instinct was to plead for time.

I would've gone through with the wedding—just on another day.

"It's not that, Mom," I say as her eyes skim over my face, looking for any hint of doubt. "I love Peter, and I want to marry him. I was simply not feeling well."

Her gaze drops to the phone I'm holding. "What did he tell you?"

I blink at her. "What?"

"That big driver of yours who came—he gave you that phone. I assume to call Peter, right? So what did your fiancé tell you?"

"Nothing. He just reminded me of the time. And speaking of which"—I pointedly look at the phone's lit-up screen—"we really need to go."

Mom searches my face for a few more moments, then nods. "All right, darling. If that's what you want, let's go. We have a wedding to attend."

CHAPTER 66
SARA

I must zone out on the way because the ride to Silver Lake seems to take just a few seconds. Blinking, I come out of the car to the cheers of some guests, and my gaze falls on a tall, dark figure standing a dozen feet away.

Peter.

My enemy.

My stalker.

My lover.

My husband-to-be.

His eyes are like gray tar, reflecting nothing, but I can sense the volatile emotions within him, feel the coiled violence masked by that predator-like stillness. Still, I can't help but drink him in, running my gaze over the powerful lines of his body. I've never seen him dressed so formally before, but it suits him, the sleek tuxedo emphasizing the

V-shape of his torso and the crisp white shirt making his tan skin glow.

He's magnificent, as striking as any movie star, and despite the continued turmoil within me, a prickle of heat runs over my skin, the reaction as primal and uncontrollable as the accompanying frisson of fear.

I might've saved others by showing up, but I'll pay for that delay.

Peter won't let my moment of weakness slide.

I hold his gaze as I approach, and he extends his hand, his mouth curved in a mocking half-smile. I place my hand in his big palm and feel the warmth of it all the way down to my toes—which I'm only now realizing feel as icy as my fingers.

"Hello, ptichka," he murmurs and bends his head to place a gentle kiss on my lips. Around us, I hear a few "awwws"—probably from my new coworkers, who have no reason to suspect this is anything other than a simple love match. Out of the corner of my eye, I see Marsha staring at us, her face tense and pale, and behind Peter is Joe Levinson, who's wearing the expression of someone attending a funeral... where the casket is filled with explosives.

"Hi," I reply softly, doing my best to ignore all the stares around us. "Is the photographer here?"

"Yes, my love. Let's go."

Placing a possessive hand on the small of my back, he steers me toward a picturesque spot by the lake, where a man with a camera is taking pictures of Phil and Rory.

My dad is already there too, and my mom is on the way as well, walking as briskly as her high-heeled shoes allow.

It warms my heart to see her so strong and healthy; the memory of her in the hospital, bandaged like a mummy, still haunts my nightmares.

When we're halfway to the lake and out of the earshot of the other guests, I glance up at Peter and murmur, "I'm sorry."

His jaw hardens. "We'll discuss this later."

I swallow and look down, focusing on not tripping on the uneven ground in high heels. I didn't lie: I *am* sorry. Now that I'm back in Peter's orbit, I feel the inevitability of it all, the pull of the dark threads that bind us. My earlier doubts seem baseless and naïve, irrational to the point of insanity. What does it matter if our wedding is today, tomorrow, or a year from now? My tormentor is going to be the same man, the same lethal killer I've fallen for.

From the moment I met Peter, I've known there's no escape for me, and what happened today just confirms it.

As we approach the lake, I spot Peter's teammates clustered together, off to the side, and I wave at them. I'm pleased to see that they wave back. It's strange, but I missed them too.

To me, they're like Peter's brothers.

When we reach the lake, the photographer—a chubby, bearded man who resembles a dark-haired Santa Claus—arranges us in a variety of poses, from looking longingly into each other's eyes to sitting together on a bench to Peter holding me in his arms. He takes pictures of the two of us together and then each of us on our own; of the two of us with my parents, and then with all of our friends. The permutations are endless, and after I introduce Peter to everyone, I find myself zoning out, smiling and posing on autopilot.

Would Peter have done as he threatened?

Would he have killed all these people just to punish me for standing him up?

I want to believe that the answer is no, but my instincts tell me yes. He's capable of it, and his obsession with me has always had a tinge of darkness, just like our bedroom play.

Peter loves me, treasures me, would do anything for me.

Including commit mass murder.

It's a terrifying thought—or at least I should find it terrifying. And I do... for the most part. It's only a tiny portion of me that finds something about that level of obsession intoxicating, as thrilling as jumping off a cliff into a stormy sea.

"Ready, my love?" Peter's large hand possessively clasps my elbow, and I look up at him, dazed.

"For the ceremony," he clarifies, and I nod, letting him lead me to the gazebo.

This is it.

Married life, here we go.

CHAPTER 67
PETER

*M*y ptichka is pale and startlingly beautiful as she stands next to me, listening to the judge give his spiel. He talks about love and commitment, about supporting each other through thick and thin, and a dark wave of satisfaction rolls through me as he poses the traditional question to Sara, and she responds quietly, "Yes, I do."

He turns to me then.

"Do you, Peter Garin, take Sara Cobakis to be your legally wedded wife, to have and to hold, in sickness and in health, until death do you part?"

"Yes," I say clearly, making sure my voice carries to our small audience. "I do."

"You may now kiss the bride," the judge says, and I face Sara.

She's looking up at me, eyes wide and soft lips parted, and I bend my head, brushing my lips gently across that tempting mouth. It's very important to be gentle right now. The slightest lapse in control could unleash the rage simmering within me, and I can't have that happen.

Not until we're alone.

There's clapping and hooting, and then a familiar tune starts playing from behind the gazebo.

The band I commissioned—the one Sara seemed so excited about—is here, having set up and gotten ready to play during the ceremony. It cost me a pretty penny to get them here for a couple of hours, but judging by the reaction of the guests, it's worth it.

"Shall we?" I offer my arm to Sara as the majority of the younger guests hurry toward the music, oohing and aahing over the chance to see their idols live.

"Of course." Her slim hand slips into the crook of my elbow as she gives me a cautious smile. "Let's go."

We didn't prepare a dance, but at the urgings of Sara's new coworkers, I take her into my arms and we sway together to a slow, romantic song, one that I recognize as being a classic rather than one of the band's own numbers. Again, I have to be careful, have to keep my touch light and gentle, to maintain the appropriate distance instead of yanking Sara to me and ripping off that elegant white dress to take her right here and now, on this soft green lawn.

Thankfully, the slow song ends before my self-control starts to crumble, and the band launches into one of their most popular numbers. Sara's bandmates and a few other guests join us, laughing and clapping, and we end up dancing in a group before Sara's friend, Marsha, tugs her away to dance with her and two of the other nurses.

I wait until the song is over, and then I signal to the catering staff to start bringing out the appetizers.

Since there are only about two dozen of us, we have three tables: a small round one for me and Sara, and two bigger oval ones for the rest of the guests. I didn't bother with assigned seating, so Sara's parents end up with their friends, and the majority of Sara's friends and coworkers congregate at the other table.

The food is outstanding, as it should be from a Michelin eight-star chef, and as we all start eating, the majority of the guests appear to be having a good time. Sara must think so too, because she says quietly, "Thank you for organizing everything. This is one of the nicest weddings I've been to."

I smile at her calmly, even though all I want is to bend her over the table. "I'm glad, my love. I want you to be happy."

And she will be, once she gets over whatever remaining doubts she has about us. I will make sure of that. I'll do whatever it takes to make her happy.

The only thing I won't do is set her free.

In any case, I don't think she wants that—not deep down, where it truly matters. I don't know what spooked her this afternoon, but I have one suspicion.

Could she have found out about Sonny Pearson's death?

I don't see how, as she hasn't been to the clinic in the last couple of days, but it's the one thing that makes sense. Either way, I'm going to get to the bottom of it.

Tonight.

As soon as we're alone.

After we fill up on food, Sara and I cut the cake—a gorgeous seven-tier creation with sour cream frosting—and then everyone goes back to dancing and picture-taking. The brief introductions Sara performed before the ceremony were clearly not enough for everyone, and I soon find myself surrounded and fielding prying questions from guests whose bravery appears equal to their alcohol consumption.

"How did you two meet again?" Marsha demands, all but swaying on her feet as she downs yet another glass of champagne. "Sara said you've been dating on and off for a while…?"

"Yes, exactly," Joe Levinson chimes in, his jaw set in a pugnacious line. "When and how did you meet? None of us knew Sara was in a relationship."

I remind myself that the knife strapped to my ankle isn't for slicing this man's throat. "We met in a club in Chicago some months ago," I answer calmly and surreptitiously signal Anton. "Since I traveled a lot for work, we decided to keep our relationship low-key until we were certain it was going somewhere."

"And you're from Russia?" Andy, the red-headed nurse, studies me with a confused frown. "As in, the same place as—"

"There you are!" Anton slaps me on the back. "I was looking everywhere for you. The guys need you for a moment."

"Excuse me," I tell the guests politely and follow Anton to the spot by the lake where my teammates camped out with an expensive bottle of vodka.

"Thanks for the rescue," I say when we get out of the earshot of Sara's friends. "I'm not in the mood to deal with their questions today."

"You'll need to eventually," Anton says, and I shrug, though I know he's right.

In order to integrate with these people, I'll have to give them some kind of answers.

"So how does it feel to be a married man again?" Ilya asks, pouring me a shot of vodka.

I knock it back instead of replying, feeling the familiar burn down my throat. I don't drink much—never have—but it's tempting today. I want to forget how it felt when I heard Sara's hesitant voice on the phone, telling me that she needed more time.

"Pour me another one," I say, holding out the empty shot glass, and Ilya obliges.

I down it again, then hand the glass back to Ilya.

"More?" he asks dryly, and I shake my head.

"I'm good, thanks."

This will have to do as far as taking the edge off. My self-control is already on thin ice, and I'm not about to risk hurting Sara when I finally get her alone.

I'm not *that* much of a monster.

"So this is it, huh?" Anton gestures toward the people mingling by the gazebo. "This is what you want?"

"*She* is what I want." I sit down on the grass, watching Sara go from group to group, laughing and chatting, doing a great imitation of a happy bride. "She just comes with all this attached."

"Maybe," Yan says, reaching for the bottle. Unscrewing the top, he takes a swig straight from the opening. "Or maybe not."

I give him a sharp look. "An expert on my wife, are you?"

He shrugs and takes another swig. "She may yet surprise you. You think she's all that different from us? All sweetness and goodness and light? You think any of those people"—he gestures toward the guests with the bottle—"are all sweetness and light?"

I turn my gaze back to Sara instead of answering, and he sighs. "It surprises me that you, of all people, don't see it. She wants you, right? Loves you, even though she knows all about the kind of man you are?"

I don't answer that either, and he continues. "Why do you think she's drawn to you? Because she sees something good in you? Or because she secretly craves the bad?"

Anton snorts. "Oh, please. Not that shit again. Every single time you have vodka—"

"My bet is on the latter," Yan says as though Anton hadn't spoken. "She's more like you than you imagine, and all that shit"—he waves the bottle at the gazebo again—"is what she's been trained to think will make her happy, not what she wants for real."

I get up, brushing a few specks of grass off my pants. "There's more vodka on our table," I tell Ilya, who's enviously watching his brother drain the bottle. "You better go get it if you want it. We're going to be wrapping this up soon."

As fun as it is to listen to Yan's drunken ramblings, I'd much rather take my new wife home to bed.

CHAPTER 68

I feel like Peter and I are in a play, each of us acting out our roles. He's the gracious groom, reserved but exceedingly polite, and I'm the beaming bride, bubbly and excited. Or at least I'm that after three glasses of champagne; they really help with the bubbly-and-excited bit, which in turn helps with avoiding my friends' overly probing questions.

I can always flit away to another group of guests, laughing and encouraging everyone to dance—something they gladly do, given the source of the music.

"How are you feeling, darling?" Mom asks when I join their little circle for a minute. "Any more tummy issues?"

"No, all good, Mom." I give her and Dad my sunniest smile. "How are you guys?"

Mom smiles and reaches over to take Dad's hand. "Having a great time, like everyone else. Your Peter did a wonderful job."

"Thank you, Mom." I beam at them both. My parents' reaction was my biggest worry, and I'm hugely relieved that they seem to have accepted my relationship—at least outwardly. I didn't give them a lot of choice, of course, but it's still nice to know that they're willing to give Peter a chance.

"There you are," a familiar accented voice murmurs as a long arm wraps around my waist.

I look up to meet my husband's silver gaze and grin, forgetting to be wary for the moment. "Hi. Where have you been?"

"Over with the guys," he says, nodding toward the lake shore, and I laugh as I see the three Russians passing around what looks like a vodka bottle.

"So the stereotypes are true?" Dad asks, following my gaze, and Peter nods, smiling.

"For the most part. Personally, I prefer beer, but sometimes you really need to feel the burn." He glances down at me, his lips still curved. "How are you feeling, ptichka?"

My breathing quickens as I notice the dark undertone in that sensuous smile. "Oh, I'm… I'm good."

"Good." He faces me fully and tenderly brushes his knuckles across my jaw. "I was worried."

I swallow as my heart rate jumps another notch. We're approaching the moment of reckoning, I can feel it.

"Why don't you do the bouquet toss, and then we'll say goodbye to the guests?" he suggests, as though reading my mind. "It's been a long day, and you still might not be well."

"Yes, darling," my mom chimes in, happily oblivious to the undercurrents. "Why don't the two of you head out?

It's been a wonderful party, and I'm sure everyone has had enough to eat and drink."

I glance at the sun setting over the lake. "But—"

"Come, my love." Peter's arm tightens warningly around my waist, even as his smile remains in place. "Let's go."

"Okay." I look at my parents. "Bye, guys. We'll see you soon."

"Bye, darling." Mom takes a step toward me, and Peter releases me long enough to let me hug her and then Dad. "Congratulations again."

"Thank you." I give them another bright smile, and Peter leads me away to toss the bouquet and say goodbye to all the other guests.

"So, are we moving?" I ask as we exit the car next to my apartment building. My voice is a little too thin, but all the liquid courage has worn off on the ride here, leaving my heart hammering faster the closer we get to home.

"Do you want to?" Peter looks at me, his gaze veiled as we approach the building. "As I told you, I've found a few nice places, but I didn't want to take the leap without consulting you."

His tone contains no hint of mockery, but I sense it anyway. If today demonstrated anything, it's that he still has all the power—and makes all the rules.

I decide to go along with his pretense. "Yes, I think I'd like to move. This place is too small for the two of us—and it might be nice not to have so many neighbors."

"I agree." His eyes take on a brighter gleam, and his voice deepens as he murmurs, "I want to have you all to myself."

Blushing, I open my mouth to reply, but at that moment, he bends and smoothly picks me up, ignoring my startled gasp.

"Tradition," he tells me, grinning darkly, and walks into the lobby, carrying me with his customary ease.

We pass my young female neighbors on our way to the elevator, and I hide my face against Peter's neck as they squeal and yell out, "Congratulations!"

We definitely need to move somewhere with fewer people.

"You can set me down," I tell Peter once we're inside the elevator, but he just looks at me, his eyes darkening.

"Why?" he murmurs, his arms tightening around me. "I like you like this."

My pulse spikes again as my earlier nervousness returns, and I push at Peter's shoulders. "No, really, set me down, please."

"Why?" His jaw hardens, all playfulness leaving his expression. "So you could run? Hole up somewhere and lie that you're ill?"

"I *was* ill!" I glare up at him, anger displacing my anxiety. "Ask my mom if you don't believe me. I threw up and had to take Pepto-Bismol."

His dark eyebrows snap together. "What?"

"Mom told you that already. On the phone—I heard her tell you." I push at his shoulders again as the elevator doors open and he steps out, carrying me down the hall-way. "My stomach was unsettled."

His frown deepens as he stops in front of my apart-ment door. "Yes, she mentioned that, but I thought…" He carefully lowers me to his feet and reaches into his pocket for the keys.

"You thought it was an excuse? No, it happened." Not because I was ill, though. I bite the inside of my cheek, then decide not to start our married life with a lie—even one by omission.

I wait until we enter the apartment, and then I say in a calmer tone, "Peter… there's something you should know. Agent Ryson came here today, right before I left."

He turns into a statue, then pivots to face me, incred-ulous. "What?"

"Not in any official capacity," I hasten to reassure him. "He just wanted to talk to me."

His big hands clench at his sides. "Why?"

"I think… I think he was frustrated. Over how every-thing turned out. He thinks I lied to him, and that we"—I swallow, my throat burning—"conspired to kill George. That I wanted you to get rid of George because he was brain-damaged and an alcoholic I was already planning to divorce."

Peter swears low under his breath. "That fucking ubly-udok. I should've—" He stops and takes a calming breath. In a softer tone, he asks, "Did he upset you, ptichka?" Stepping toward me, he gently captures my chin, making me look up at him. "Is that why you were going to bail?"

I manage a tiny nod. "I'm sorry about that. I really am. It was already happening so fast, and then he came and…" I squeeze my eyes shut, then open them to meet his storm-gray gaze again. "I'm sorry. I just wasn't thinking straight."

Peter moves his hand across my jawline, the touch soft and tender. "What else did he tell you, my love?"

"Nothing. He was just— Oh, he did say that if you do anything else of criminal nature, the deal would be null and void… and that they now have my number as well."

Peter's gaze hardens again. "I see." He steps back, dropping his hand, and I realize that he's angry—as angry as I've ever seen him.

Suddenly worried, I step forward, catching his hand in both of mine. "You're not going to do anything to him, right? I told you this because I don't want to have any kind of lies between us—not because I want you to punish Ryson."

He doesn't respond, but I glean my answer in the tight set of his jaw and the rigidity of his palm in my hold.

"Peter, don't, please. Listen to me…" I squeeze his hand. "He's a federal agent, and he *wants* you to slip up. In fact, I wouldn't be surprised if that's why he came here today: to provoke you and make sure that you violate the terms of the deal. Don't play his game. It's not worth it."

Peter's expression doesn't change. "Are you worried about him or me?"

I release his hand. "Both, of course. I don't want you to hurt him—and I definitely don't want you to get in trouble because of him."

"Hmm." Peter gently strokes the side of my face again. "I wonder."

I moisten my lips. "Wonder what?"

"Would you be happy if I just went away and let you be? If I got in trouble and had to leave for good?"

I blink at him. "But... you wouldn't do that. You'd take me with you, right? If you had to leave?"

His gaze darkens. "Maybe. Is that what you would want, ptichka?"

My chest tightens, constricting my breath. "Peter... I..."

"You still can't bring yourself to say it, can you?" He captures my chin again, making me meet his gaze. His voice holds a strange note. "You can't admit that this is mutual, that I'm not the only one who's mad."

I swallow thickly and back away, twisting out of his hold. "It's not like that."

"No?" He comes after me, as relentless as a shark. "Tell me why you nearly ran today, then. Tell me what it is about Ryson's visit that got to you like that."

I keep backing away until my back presses against the wall. "I already told you. I told you everything."

"Not everything." He presses his palms on the wall on either side of me, caging me once more. His tone is both cruel and tender as he murmurs, "Not nearly everything, my love."

I stare up at him, my pulse beating in my temples. I don't understand what he's after, what it is that he wants from me. "Peter, please. I'm sorry about today. I really, truly am. I was so upset I wasn't thinking, but that's no excuse. I shouldn't have…" I shake my head.

"No, you really shouldn't have," he agrees, his eyes darkening further, and then, with no warning, he hooks his hand into the bodice of my dress and yanks it down with startling savagery, ripping the handmade lace and sending the pearl buttons skittering on the tile floor.

Gasping, I clutch at the top of the torn dress, but Peter spins me around, pressing my face against the wall. "You really, really shouldn't have," he growls in my ear and yanks the dress all the way down, making it pool around my knees.

I'm left in my white strapless bra and thong underwear—sexy, lacy pieces I wore to match the dress. They don't last more than a moment either, as Peter rips them off me, leaving me completely naked.

Panting, I press my palms against the wall, expecting him to kick my legs apart and fuck me, but instead, his powerful arm slides around my ribcage, lifting me out of the remnants of the dress. My shoes, with their thin straps around the ankles, remain on my feet, even as my legs flail in the air as he ruthlessly carries me to the bedroom.

He throws me on the bed face down, and I scramble to turn over as he steps back to remove his own clothes. I glimpse a flash of metal and hear a heavy thud as he throws aside his jacket—*was he armed at our wedding?*—but then my focus shifts to something far more dangerous.

The expression on his face.

His eyes are narrowed, his nostrils flaring as he undoes his belt, and in the jerkiness of his movements, I see the violent hunger that's always there, the dark, savage need that also pulses in my core.

He's going to hurt me tonight, I can feel it, and my insides clench on a wave of fear and lust. I should run, should protest, but my body acts of its own accord, my legs propelling me off the bed to kneel on the carpet in front of him, my hands reaching for the zipper of his tuxedo pants.

"Yes, that's it, come here," he mutters under his breath, his hands fisting roughly in my hair as I open the zipper and push down his pants, freeing his erection. He's already fully aroused, his cock long and thick, so hard the veins are popping out along the shaft. It's a weapon, that cock, but also a tool of unimaginable pleasure, and my mouth waters as I stare at it, remembering how he choked me with it—and how it made me burn.

He pulls my face closer and slaps his cock across my cheek. Once, twice, a third time. I open my mouth on the fourth slap and catch the tip, sucking it in as I meet his gaze. The familiar musky taste further heats my core, and my left hand snakes between my legs while my right one reaches up to cup his balls.

His face twists with ferocious pleasure as I squeeze him gently, and he thrusts deeper into my mouth, his fists tightening in my hair. "Fuck …" he groans, his voice low and rough. "Keep doing that, just like that."

I obey, letting him fuck my throat as I massage his balls. At the same time, my left hand rubs my clit, my thighs quivering with growing tension as I find the right rhythm. His pupils dilate further, his hips moving ever faster, and

I'm close, so close when he grits out something in Russian and abruptly pushes me away.

Startled, I fall backward onto my palms, and before I can recover my wits, he grabs me and throws me on the bed again.

"You're not getting off that easy," he growls, and I suck in an unsteady breath as he loops his belt around my wrists, securing them to the headboard, and then moves down my body, his strong hands pulling apart my legs.

"What are you doing?" My heartbeat is so fast I can barely speak. "Peter, please, you don't have to—"

"Hush," he breathes against my thigh, and I gasp as his teeth graze across my labia before his tongue pushes between my folds, unerringly finding my throbbing clit.

The ignition is nearly instant. Fire licks through my veins, and I arch, screaming and pulling on the belt as the delayed orgasm crashes over me, making my entire body spasm. But my tormentor is not done. His tongue gentles, softening just enough to let me ride the aftershocks, and then two rough fingers thrust into me, finding my G-spot. I cry out, spiraling again as his tongue resumes its devil's work, and it's not long before I come again.

He's still not done, though, his talented mouth moving up my body, dropping burning kisses on my belly and breasts, sucking on my nipples and the sensitive part of my neck. And all the while his fingers stay in me as his thumb works my clit, bringing me to the edge again.

His lips meet mine just as I start to come, and I moan my release into his mouth, tasting myself on his tongue as he deepens the kiss. My muscles feel like they've liquified inside my skin, my wrists raw from tugging on the belt, and yet he still fucks me with those two rough fingers, all through my climax and beyond.

I'm on the verge of yet another orgasm when he lifts his head and withdraws his fingers, only to move them lower, smearing my wetness all along the way. I squirm, realizing what he's planning, but he's relentless, and I cry out, my eyes squeezing shut as his middle finger finds my back opening, the slickness from my sex acting like lube as the finger pushes into me, past the resistance of clenched muscles.

He's taken me like this before, but it's been over nine months, and his finger feels as enormous as his cock, the edges of his nail abrading tender tissues. My heartbeat spikes, my breath catching in my throat as he withdraws the invading finger slowly, only to have it joined by another.

"Peter..."

"Shhh." He kisses me again, and as the two fingers press on my opening, making me tense in panic, his thumb finds my aching clit. The orgasm that all but receded rockets back, the tension cresting with explosive force, and as I come, moaning helplessly, the two fingers push all the way in.

I tense again, but it's too late, and all I can do is breathe shakily as he stretches my tight passage, making it sting and burn. The fullness is unbearable, invasive, yet underneath the discomfort is a promise of something more, and my body contracts in orgasmic aftershocks, chasing that darker sensation.

"Yes, that's it, ptichka," he breathes against my lips, and I shudder as his thumb finds my clit again. I can't come another time, it's impossible, yet my body doesn't realize that it's spent. The tension gathers in my core, winding it tighter, and I'm on the verge of orgasm, trembling and panting, when the invading fingers pull out of my ass.

I groan in frustration, tugging on the belt and arching my hips, and he laughs softly, the sound low and dark as the mattress to the left of me dips.

Startled, I open my eyes, but he's already back, a small bottle in his hand. "Don't worry, ptichka. We'll get you there," he promises huskily, and I jolt as he tips the bottle, drizzling the cool liquid all over my swollen sex. It trickles lower, to the crevice between my cheeks, and my pulse speeds again as our eyes meet.

In his gaze, I see hunger and something more, a wordless yet fierce demand. Hooking his forearms under my knees, he lifts my legs onto his shoulders and leans forward, stretching my hamstrings as he guides his cock to my ass.

"Is this what you want from me?" His eyes glitter as he presses forward. "Is this what you need?"

He pushes in deeper, and I groan at the stinging pressure, sweat dampening my spine as my sphincter slowly gives in. With my legs draped over his shoulders, I can't control the depth of penetration, and he slides all the way in, filling me until my stomach churns and my breath comes in frantic, shallow gasps.

"I don't..." I drag in a deeper breath, fighting a wave of dizziness. "I don't understand."

"Don't you?" His mouth twists, a cruel gleam lighting his metallic gaze as he withdraws halfway, only to push back in. "Or is it that you just can't say?"

The stinging burn is still there, the fullness as extreme as before, but as his thumb lands on my clit, a tantalizing tension drowns out the pain. His hips move slowly, his massive cock gliding deeper with each merciless stroke, and the orgasm begins to build, the pleasure different from before, stronger and darker, as agonizing as it is exquisite.

It's too much, too intense, and I can hear myself begging and pleading, squirming as much as the restrictive position allows. But the cruel light stays in his eyes, his pace unchanged even as sweat droplets appear on his brow.

"Answer me," he rasps out, leaning in to nearly fold me in half, and I scream as the pain sets off the spark, lighting the fire that consumes me. The ecstasy explodes through my nerve endings, my vision flooding with white light as I shut my eyes. The tingling chills race up and down my spine, the release careening through my body, making every muscle tremble and lock up.

I hear him groan above me and feel a warm throbbing deep inside. He's coming too, I realize dazedly, and peel open my eyelids long enough to see the same agonizing pleasure twist his face.

Breathing heavily, he collapses on top of me, and we stay like that, our breaths synchronizing as we recover. My hamstrings feel like they might tear from the stretch, and my ass burns as his cock softens gradually inside it, but I don't want to move.

I want to stay like this, my body joined with his forever.

"Yes," I say quietly as he slowly lifts his head and pushes himself up to relieve some of the pressure on my legs. Our eyes meet, and a dark triumph kindles in his gaze as I repeat wearily, "Yes, it is."

I understand his question now, and I know the terrifying answer. This *is* what I want from him—and it's definitely what I need. Pain, punishment, force—I require that from him nearly as much as love and tenderness.

I need the total package, as messed up as that may be.

He reaches forward and frees my hands, then carefully withdraws from me and cleans me with a tissue. I close my eyes, too drained to move, and his strong arms slide under me, lifting me off the bed.

He carries me into the shower and washes me there, wiping off the smeared makeup, undoing all the intricate curls and waves in my updo. Then he wraps me in a towel and brings me to the living room, where he sits down on the couch, holding me cuddled on his lap.

I lay my head on his broad shoulder and place my palm over his heart, feeling the steady beat inside his muscled chest as he gently massages my nape, his strong fingers working out knots I didn't even know were there.

"So tell me, derneath my day."

"Be of th s

onfront the ugly facts.

"Because why?" Peter prompts, pausing the massage.

"Because..." A knot forms in my throat as I squeeze my eyes shut, then open them, pulling back to meet his gaze. It's time I stopped pretending and embraced the truth. Taking a breath, I say unsteadily, "Because you were right. Back in Japan, when you said that it's too late for me, you were right." It's getting harder to force the words out, but I make myself continue. "It was too late then, and it's definitely too late now. I don't know when it happened, but somewhere along our jagged path, I fell in love with you. Only I—" I stop, my throat closing up completely.

His gray eyes soften, his hand resuming the light massage. "Only you what?"

"Only I can't take it," I confess, the words like rocks inside my vocal cords. "I need..." I stop, unable to voice it fully, but he understands.

"You need this." He lifts his hand to stroke my cheek. "You need me to make it hurt sometimes, to take control and force you. To take away the other choices, so you can embrace the one you really want."

I nod jerkily, equal parts ashamed and relieved. It's wrong and cowardly of me, but in the context of all the other wrongness, it's the one thing that feels right. Our relationship will never be like that of other people... because tucking a damp strand of hair behind my ear, "you needed that, didn't you, ptichka? You needed to know that walking away wasn't an option... that you had to marry me or else."

I swallow thickly, fighting the temptation to look away. "I think so. Maybe. I—" I stop again, unable to formulate the confusing mix of emotions I'd experienced. His threat had terrified me as intended, but I now realize that I'd also been relieved.

Deep down, I'd been counting on him to do it, to lift away the worst of my shame and guilt.

His warm hand curves around my jaw, his thumb brushing soothingly across my cheek. "It's okay, ptichka. Don't feel bad. It is what it is, and it's okay to admit it."

I stare into his eyes. "You don't think that I'm... an awful person?"

"Because you love me, or because you can't embrace it fully?"

"Either. Both."

His smile is both sensuous and sad. "No, my love. You're a product of your upbringing, as I am one of mine. You were right too, back at the Swiss clinic, when you said that in a different world, a different life, it would've all been different. If I could, I would erase the past, rewrite the history between us, but in lieu of that, I'll give you what you need—what we both need, if we are being honest."

I hold his gaze, my eyes burning. He understands, because he's my dark, terrifying mirror, his cravings both inverse and parallel to mine. He loves me, he's demonstrated that in the most vivid ways, but some part of him also needs to hurt me, to punish me for the pain of the past.

To control me, so I can't leave him.

So he won't lose me, the way he lost Tamila and his son.

"I do love you," I say softly, the words coming easier the second time. "I love you, Peter, with everything I am. And I appreciate what you've done for me... what you have given up."

He chose me over his vengeance.

He chose our love over his desire to deal death.

His smile dims—the reminder about Henderson must still hurt—but then he leans in and presses a gentle kiss to my lips. "I know, ptichka. I know you love me—and one way or another, we're going to make this work. We have to... because I'm not letting you walk away."

I lay my head back on his shoulder, closing my eyes, and feel the heart beating inside that powerful chest.

He's right.

We're going to make this work.

Our love may not be simple and straightforward, but it's no less strong for how it began. This marriage won't be easy, but it's forever.

No matter what happens, we have each other.

For as long as we're both alive.

EPILOGUE
HENDERSON

I stare at my computer screen, clicking from one glossy picture to another, my throat burning and my hand shaking with nauseating rage.

They look beautiful, both young and healthy, dressed in the best wedding finery blood-stained wealth can buy. In one picture, he's lifting her against his chest; in another, they're holding hands and looking into each other's eyes.

I click again and taste the bitterness of bile. They're smiling at each other in this picture, standing next to her family and friends.

Do any of these people know?

Do they realize what he is?

She knows. Of that I have no doubt. I see it in her eyes, her pretty, lying smile.

She knows, and she loves him.

She married him, knowing the monstrous things he's done.

I roll my head from side to side, futilely trying to release the agonizing tension. The steroid shots are no longer helping, and the pain eats at me, keeping me awake at night, adding to my nightmares and insomnia.

Three years of running.

Three years of fearing for my children's lives.

Three years of knowing that everyone I left behind may be killed or tortured… that no one I care about will ever be truly safe.

I click over to a browser window and navigate to my daughter's Facebook page. There's nothing there since three years ago, nothing on my son's social media as well. They, too, have lived in fear all this time.

In fear of the monster smiling at his loving bride.

He thinks he's won.

He thinks it's over.

He's convinced they're going to let his reign of terror slide.

Turning away from the computer, I open the folder on my desk, trying to stay calm as I review the list of names—my own list this time.

Julian Esguerra, CIA's pet monster.

It's time the world saw them for the terrorists they are. One way or another, they'll pay.

Thank you for reading! If you would consider leaving a review, it would be greatly appreciated. Peter & Sara's story continues in *Forever Mine*. If you'd like to be notified when it's out, please sign up for my new release email list at www.annazaires.com.

If you're enjoying this series, you might like the following books:

- *The Twist Me Trilogy* – Julian & Nora's story, where Peter appears as a secondary character and gets his list
- *The Capture Me Trilogy* – Lucas & Yulia's st

Collaborations with my husband, Dima Zales:
- *Mind Machines* – An action-packed technothriller
- *The Mind Dimensions Series* – Urban fantasy
- *The Last Humans Trilogy* – Dystopian/post-apocalyptic science fiction
- *The Sorcery Code* – Epic fantasy

Additionally, if you like audiobooks, please visit my website to check out this series and our other books in audio.

And now please turn the page for a little taste of *Twist Me*, *Capture Me*, and *The Krinar Captive*.

EXCERPT FROM TWIST ME

Author's Note: *Twist Me* is a dark erotic trilogy about Nora and Julian Esguerra. All three books are now available.

Kidnapped. Taken to a private island.

I never thought this could happen to me. I never imagined one chance meeting on the eve of my eighteenth birthday could change my life so completely.

Now I belong to him. To Julian. To a man who is as ruthless as he is beautiful—a man whose touch makes me burn. A man whose tenderness I find more devastating

It's evening now. With every minute that passes, I'm starting to get more and more anxious at the thought of seeing my captor again.

The novel that I've been reading can no longer hold my interest. I put it down and walk in circles around the room.

I am dressed in the clothes Beth had given me earlier. It's not what I would've chosen to wear, but it's better than a bathrobe. A sexy pair of white lacy panties and a matching bra for underwear. A pretty blue sundress that buttons in the front. Everything fits me suspiciously well. Has he been stalking me for a while? Learning everything about me, including my clothing size?

The thought makes me sick.

I am trying not to think about what's to come, but it's impossible. I don't know why I'm so sure he'll come to me tonight. It's possible he has an entire harem of women stashed away on this island, and he visits each one only once a week, like sultans used to do.

Yet somehow I know he'll be here soon. Last night had simply whetted his appetite. I know he's not done with me, not by a long shot.

Finally, the door opens.

He walks in like he owns the place. Which, of course, he does.

I am again struck by his masculine beauty. He could've been a model or a movie star, with a face like his. If there was any fairness in the world, he would've been short or had some other imperfection to offset that face.

But he doesn't. His body is tall and muscular, perfectly proportioned. I remember what it feels like to have him inside me, and I feel an unwelcome jolt of arousal.

He's again wearing jeans and a T-shirt. A gray one this time. He seems to favor simple clothing, and he's smart to do so. His looks don't need any enhancement.

He smiles at me. It's his fallen angel smile—dark and seductive at the same time. "Hello, Nora."

I don't know what to say to him, so I blurt out the first thing that pops into my head. "How long are you going to keep me here?"

He cocks his head slightly to the side. "Here in the room? Or on the island?"

"Both."

"Beth will show you around tomorrow, take you swimming if you'd like," he says, approaching me. "You won't be locked in, unless you do something foolish."

"Such as?" I ask, my heart pounding in my chest as he stops next to me and lifts his hand to stroke my hair.

"Trying to harm Beth or yourself." His voice is soft, his gaze hypnotic as he looks down at me. The way he's touching my hair is oddly relaxing.

I blink, trying to break his spell. "And what about on the island? How long will you keep me here?"

For some reason, I'm not surprised. He wouldn't have bothered bringing me all the way here if he just wanted to fuck me a few times. I'm terrified, but I'm not surprised.

I gather my courage and ask the next logical question. "Why did you kidnap me?"

The smile leaves his face. He doesn't answer, just looks at me with an inscrutable blue gaze.

I begin to shake. "Are you going to kill me?"

"No, Nora, I won't kill you."

His denial reassures me, although he could obviously be lying.

"Are you going to sell me?" I can barely get the words out. "Like to be a prostitute or something?"

"No," he says softly. "Never. You're mine and mine alone."

I feel a tiny bit calmer, but there is one more thing I have to know. "Are you going to hurt me?"

For a moment, he doesn't answer again. Something dark briefly flashes in his eyes. "Probably," he says quietly.

And then he leans down and kisses me, his warm lips soft and gentle on mine.

For a second, I stand there frozen, unresponsive. I believe him. I know he's telling the truth when he says he'll hurt me. There's something in him that scares me—that has scared me from the very beginning.

He's nothing like the boys I've gone on dates with. He's capable of anything.

And I'm completely at his mercy.

I think about trying to fight him again. That would be the normal thing to do in my situation. The brave thing to do.

And yet I don't do it.

I can feel the darkness inside him. There's something wrong with him. His outer beauty hides something monstrous underneath.

I don't want to unleash that darkness. I don't know what will happen if I do.

So I stand still in his embrace and let him kiss me. And when he picks me up again and takes me to bed, I don't try to resist in any way.

Instead, I close my eyes and give in to the sensations.

All three books in the *Twist Me* trilogy are now available. Please visit my website at www.annazaires.com to learn more and to sign up for my new release email list.

EXCERPT FROM CAPTURE ME

Author's Note: *Capture Me* is a dark romance trilogy featuring Lucas & Yulia. It parallels some of the events in the *Twist Me* trilogy. All three books are now available.

She fears him from the first moment she sees him.

Yulia Tzakova is no stranger to dangerous men. She grew up with them. She survived them. But when she meets Lucas Kent, she knows the hard ex-soldier may be the most dangerous of them all.

One night—that's all it should be. A chance to make up for a failed assignment and get information on Kent's arms dealer boss. When his plane goes down, it should be the end.

Instead, it's just the beginning.

He wants her from the first moment he sees her.

Lucas Kent has always liked leggy blondes, and Yulia Tzakova is as beautiful as they come. The Russian interpreter might've tried to seduce his boss, but she ends up in Lucas's bed—and he has every intention of seeing her there again.

Then his plane goes down, and he learns the truth.

She betrayed him.

Now she will pay.

He steps into my apartment as soon as the door swings open. No hesitation, no greeting—he just comes in.

Startled, I step back, the short, narrow hallway suddenly stiflingly small. I'd somehow forgotten how big he is, how broad his shoulders are. I'm tall for a woman—tall enough to fake being a model if an assignment calls for it—but he towers a full head above me. With the heavy down jacket he's wearing, he takes up almost the entire hallway.

Still not saying a word, he closes the door behind him and advances toward me. Instinctively, I back away, feeling like cornered prey.

"Hello, Yulia," he murmurs, stopping when we're out of the hallway. His pale gaze is locked on my face. "I

"No, I can see that." A faint smile appears on his lips, softening the hard line of his mouth. "Yet you let me in. Why?"

"Because I didn't want to continue talking through the door." I take a steadying breath. "Can I offer you some tea?" It's a stupid thing to say, given what he's here for, but I need a few moments to compose myself.

He raises his eyebrows. "Tea? No, thanks."

"Then can I take your jacket?" I can't seem to stop playing the hostess, using politeness to cover my anxiety. "It looks quite warm."

Amusement flickers in his wintry gaze. "Sure." He takes off his down jacket and hands it to me. He's left wearing a black sweater and dark jeans tucked into black winter boots. The jeans hug his legs, revealing muscular thighs and powerful calves, and on his belt, I see a gun sitting in a holster.

Irrationally, my breathing quickens at the sight, and it takes a concerted effort to keep my hands from shaking as I take the jacket and walk over to hang it in my tiny closet. It's not a surprise that he's armed—it would be a shock if he wasn't—but the gun is a stark reminder of who Lucas Kent is.

What he is.

It's no big deal, I tell myself, trying to calm my frayed nerves. I'm used to dangerous men. I was raised among them. This man is not that different. I'll sleep with him, get whatever information I can, and then he'll be out of my life.

Yes, that's it. The sooner I can get it done, the sooner all of this will be over.

Closing the closet door, I paste a practiced smile on my face and turn back to face him, finally ready to resume the role of confident seductress.

Except he's already next to me, having crossed the room without making a sound.

My pulse jumps again, my newfound composure fleeing. He's close enough that I can see the gray striations in his pale blue eyes, close enough that he can touch me.

And a second later, he does touch me.

Lifting his hand, he runs the back of his knuckles over my jaw.

I stare up at him, confused by my body's instant response. My skin warms and my nipples tighten, my breath coming faster. It doesn't make sense for this hard, ruthless stranger to turn me on. His boss is more handsome, more striking, yet it's Kent my body's reacting to. All he's touched thus far is my face. It should be nothing, yet it's intimate somehow.

Intimate and disturbing.

I swallow again. "Mr. Kent—Lucas—are you sure I can't offer you something to drink? Maybe some coffee or—" My words end in a breathless gasp as he reaches for the tie of my robe and tugs on it, as casually as one would unwrap a packa

All three books in the *Capture Me* trilogy are now available. If you'd like to find out more, please visit my website at www.annazaires.com.

EXCERPT FROM THE KRINAR CAPTIVE

Author's Note: *The Krinar Captive* is a full-length, stand-alone scifi romance that takes place approximately five years before *The Krinar Chronicles* trilogy.

Emily Ross never expected to survive her deadly fall in the Costa Rican jungle, and she certainly never thought she'd wake up in a strangely futuristic dwelling, held captive by the most beautiful man she'd ever seen. A man who seems to be more than human…

Letting her go would compromise his mission, but keeping her could destroy him all over again.

———————

I don't want to die. I don't want to die. Please, please, please, I don't want to die.

The words kept repeating in her mind, a hopeless prayer that would never be heard. Her fingers slipped another inch on the rough wooden board, her nails breaking as she tried to maintain her grip.

Emily Ross was hanging by her fingernails—literally—off a broken old bridge. Hundreds of feet below, water rushed over the rocks, the mountain stream full from recent rains.

Those rains were partially responsible for her current predicament. If the wood on the bridge had been dry, she might not have slipped, twisting her foot in the process. And she certainly wouldn't have fallen onto the rail that had broken under her weight.

It was only a last-minute desperate grab that had prevented Emily from plummeting to her death below. As she was falling, her right hand had caught a small protrusion on the side of the bridge, leaving her dangling in the air hundreds of feet above the hard rocks.

I don't want to die. I don't want to die. Please, please, please, I don't want to die.

It wasn't fair. It wasn't supposed to happen this way. This was her vacation, her regain-sanity time. How could she die now? She hadn't even begun living yet.

Images of the last two years slid through Emily's brain, like the PowerPoint presentations she'd spent so many hours making. Every late night, every weekend spent in the office—it had all been for nothing. She'd lost her job during the layoffs, and now she was about to lose her life.

No, no!

Emily's legs flailed, her nails digging deeper into the wood. Her other arm reached up, stretching toward the bridge. This wouldn't happen to her. She wouldn't let it. She had worked too hard to let a stupid jungle bridge defeat her.

Blood ran down her arm as the rough wood tore the skin off her fingers, but she ignored the pain. Her only hope of survival lay in trying to grab onto the side of the bridge with her other hand, so she could pull herself up. There was no one around to rescue her, no one to save her if she didn't save herself.

The possibility that she might die alone in the rainforest had not occurred to Emily when she'd embarked on this trip. She was used to hiking, used to camping. And even after the hell of the past two years, she was still in good shape, strong and fit from running and playing sports all through high school and college. Costa Rica was considered a safe

went to work on Monday, bleary-eyed from working all

weekend, only to leave the office the same day with all her possessions in a small cardboard box.

Before her four-year relationship had fallen apart.

Her first vacation in two years, and she was going to die.

No, don't think that way. It won't happen.

But Emily knew she was lying to herself. She could feel her fingers slipping farther, her right arm and shoulder burning from the strain of supporting the weight of her entire body. Her left hand was inches away from reaching the side of the bridge, but those inches could've easily been miles. She couldn't get a strong enough grip to lift herself up with one arm.

Do it, Emily! Don't think, just do it!

Gathering all her strength, she swung her legs in the air, using the momentum to bring her body higher for a fraction of a second. Her left hand grabbed onto the protruding board, clutched at it... and the fragile piece of wood snapped, startling her into a terrified scream.

Emily's last thought before her body hit the rocks was the hope that her death would be instant.

————————

The smell of jungle vegetation, rich and pungent, teased Zaron's nostrils. He inhaled deeply, letting the humid air fill his lungs. It was clean here, in this tiny corner of Earth, almost as unpolluted as on his home planet.

He needed this now. Needed the fresh air, the isolation. For the past six months, he'd tried to run from his thoughts, to exist only in the moment, but he'd failed. Even blood and sex were not enough for him anymore. He could distract himself while fucking, but the pain always came back afterwards, as strong as ever.

Finally, it had gotten to be too much. The dirt, the crowds, the stink of humanity. When he wasn't lost in a fog of ecstasy, he was disgusted, his senses overwhelmed from spending so much time in human cities. It was better here, where he could breathe without inhaling poison, where he could smell life instead of chemicals. In a few years, everything would be different, and he might try living in a human city again, but not yet.

Not until they were fully settled here.

That was Zaron's job: to oversee the settlements. He had been doing research on Earth fauna and flora for decades, and when the Council requested his assistance with the upcoming colonization, he hadn't hesitated. Anything was better than being home, where memories of Larita's presence were everywhere.

There were no memories here. For all of its similarities to Krina, this planet was strange and exotic. Seven billion *Homo sapiens* on Earth—an unthinkable number—and they were multiplying at a dizzying pace. With their short lifespans and the resulting lack of long-term thinking, they

in some aspects of their thinking. It wasn't particularly

surprising to Zaron; he had always thought this might be the intent of the Elders' grand experiment.

Walking through the Costa Rican forest, he found himself thinking about the task at hand. This part of the planet was promising; it was easy to picture edible plants from Krina thriving here. He had done extensive tests on the soil, and he had some ideas on how to make it even more hospitable to Krinar flora.

All around him, the forest was lush and green, filled with the fragrance of blooming heliconias and the sounds of rustling leaves and native birds. In the distance, he could hear the cry of an *Alouatta palliata*, a howler monkey native to Costa Rica, and something else.

Frowning, Zaron listened closer, but the sound didn't repeat.

Curious, he headed in that direction, his hunting instincts on alert. For a second, the sound had reminded him of a woman's scream.

Moving through the thick jungle vegetation with ease, Zaron put on a burst of speed, leaping over a small creek and the bushes that stood in his way. Out here, away from human eyes, he could move like a Krinar without worrying about exposure. Within a couple of minutes, he was close enough to pick up the scent. Sharp and coppery, it made his mouth water and his cock stir.

It was blood.

Human blood.

Reaching his destination, Zaron stopped, staring at the sight in front of him.

In front of him was a river, a mountain stream swollen from recent rains. And on the large black rocks in the middle, beneath an old wooden bridge spanning the gorge, was a body.

A broken, twisted body of a human girl.

The Krinar Captive is now available. Please visit my website at www.annazaires.com to learn more and to sign up for my new release email list.

ABOUT THE AUTHOR

Anna Zaires is a *New York Times, USA Today,* and #1 international bestselling author of sci-fi romance and contemporary dark erotic romance. She fell in love with books at the age of five, when her grandmother taught her to read. Since then, she has always lived partially in a fantasy world where the only limits were those of her imagination. Currently residing in Florida, Anna is happily married to Dima Zales (a science fiction and fantasy author) and closely collaborates with him on all their works.

To learn more, please visit www.annazaires.com.

Made in the USA
Lexington, KY
05 July 2018